I0736217

PRINT EDITION

IT HURTS EVERY TIME © 2023 by Mirror World Publishing and L.P. Mills
Edited by: Robert Dowsett
Cover Design by: Justine Dowsett

Published by Mirror World Publishing in November 2023.

Mirror World Publishing
Windsor, Ontario
www.mirrorworldpublishing.com
info@mirrorworldpublishing.com

ISBN: 978-1-987976-99-1

IT HURTS EVERY TIME

L.P. MILLS

mirror world
publishing

For me mum and dad

"It was the sudden appearance of the Republic of Wojtek, that strange icy land from another reality, that inspired the mathematician Anton Yemelenov's subsequent discovery of the Wider Probability Matrix. With that our scope was expanded, and with it the breadth of an individual's life became near-infinite."

Alison Yang, *On Potentialities, and Immortalities Therein*

"Death is not the end, sir,

No, sir, not the end of the line,

Just remember what I say to you;

It hurts, baby,

It hurts every time."

Marco Sanskrit, *The Trypper's Elegy*
ProbMat Reality 7406.32

ONE

t is **16:37 in Morrissette**, and Pluto Garcia is bleeding out again.

The afternoon sun glints blindingly off the water, fluttering like TV static as blood pools from the hole in Garcia's back and out onto the pavement. The pain is cold and heavy, resting on his body with the weight of an anaconda, squeezing the air out of his lungs in laboured gasps. Somewhere overhead, a seagull drifts lazily on the thermals that criss-cross the Waterfront district, watching as two cats fight over a discarded sandwich with its keen yellow eye. Pluto Garcia is dying.

It isn't his first time. Now aged fifty-seven, Pluto Garcia has thus far died three times: The first was during the winter of 1969: a jetty he was standing on had been washed away by the surging Pallias river, carrying him screaming along with it. The second time was in 1973 during a scuffle with Khazi's boys up at the Shipyard, back before the Coalition had been established and the districts were more eager to settle things with a short, sharp whack to the base of the skull. And now the third, bleeding out on the Waterfront, having been stabbed in the back by an unknown attacker. He lies there now, cheek kissing the pavement, a cocktail of blood and mucus dribbling from his lips.

With a grunt he tries to force himself up, contorting into a twisted yoga position as his trembling fingers reach for the pillbox in his left pocket. Standard issue: cool, durable aluminium, embossed with a stylish red CMM – the Community Militia of Morrissette. He feels its weight in his rapidly numbing hands, hearing the gentle rattle of the pills inside. Three pills, each the shocking lemon yellow of a paper wasp. Repodimethyltryptamine. Tryp.

He takes one pill between his fingers, rolls onto his side and, ignoring the agony coursing through his body, brings it to his lips. He grits his teeth and bites down on a slowly rising scream, channelling the energy instead into forcing the pill into his mouth and dry swallowing. His arm gives way and he collapses, the obtrusion sliding awkwardly down his throat. As he splays out in a rapidly-expanding pool of his own blood, a thought floats to the surface of his mind and rests there amidst his dying neurons.

Next time: Turn around.

Three.

Two.

One.

There, there we go, streaming from one consciousness to the next across the raging psychic seas of the Wider Probability Matrix – ProbMat – its neon waves crashing into the lingering ego as HERE becomes THERE. Every thought, every synapse fires in conjunction, the dull pinkish-black space behind his eyelids exploding into a vibrant magenta as he vacates his dying body and enters the nearest similar equivalent. The closest available universe is 0.0026% variations away, identical in almost every conceivable manner to his point of origin with one major exception.

It is 16:36 in Morrissette, and Pluto Garcia is about to be stabbed.

The knife flies towards him and he spins just in time, catching the attacker's wrist with the flat of his arm and sending it spiralling away. There is a momentary lag as his motor functions acclimate to their new home, but he has just enough time to see his attacker steady themself and go in for another jab. He leaps back, hands flailing to maintain balance as the knife glances past his chest. He fumbles forward and cracks the assailant across the face with a closed fist, causing them to spin backwards like a Catherine wheel.

He takes the opportunity to dash backwards, putting a couple feet of distance between his body and the blade. Across his back, his nerves scream in agony from a stabbing that technically hasn't happened. He bites down on the pain and closes in, kicking the attacker and sending them tumbling to the floor with a thud. He frantically scans his surroundings for more danger and finds nothing, just sunlight dancing upon the waves and the distant screech of a seagull. The cats, frightened by the commotion, have scattered, leaving the sandwich unmolested.

There is a ringing in his head as sensory input from an unlived life creeps in behind his sinuses. He closes his eyes and swallows hard, counting backwards from ten. The words fall naturally. Affirmations are important when you use Tryp.

Ten. The year is 1994.

Nine. Your name is Pluto Garcia.

The seagulls cackle in the air, cruel yellow eyes surveying the world below.

Eight. You were born in the Marcel Cairo Memorial Hospital, Karnassas.

Water sloshes against the jetty, steady and unfaltering as a pulse.

Seven. You live in the Southern Packing District.

Salt. The air smells like salt, with a tinge of sewage.

Six. You are an administrator for the Community Militia of Morrissette.

A sound. A new sound, not the gulls or the waves, something else. Movement.

Garcia's eyes shoot open to see the attacker staggering to their feet: skinny, dressed in a red bomber jacket and blue jeans, their features hidden beneath a hood. They scuttle away, half-prostrate and clambering on all-fours, barely stopping to cast a furtive glance behind them. The affirmations will have to wait. He reaches down to his right and pulls out his stun gun and, in a voice he only just recognises as his own, he screams.

"CMM, don't move!"

The figure ducks down an alleyway and disappears, the sound of their feet slapping against wet concrete echoing around them as they flee. Garcia dives in after them, hands still tight around the butt of the stun gun, teeth gritted so as to suppress screams of psychosomatic pain. He continues his affirmations, picking up where he left off, muttering under his breath as his eyes examine the shadows.

Five. Your address is Apartment 237, South Seychel Avenue, Block Vingt-Neuf.

He follows the alleyway from the water's edge through to Outer Palissade, where the main road into Central Morrissette bisects the Waterfront district. A Union truck trundles past, its black carriage glinting in the afternoon sun like the shell of an oversized beetle as rickshaws whip around either side of it, their motors whining and kicking out rivets of hot, putrid smoke.

Four. Breathe.

The air rests hot and heavy on the militiaman's chest. He casts his eyes over the busy road, taking in each passing car; each hurried pedestrian; each street vendor selling sticky, sweet-smelling meat from the back of a hand-drawn cart. He looks for a dark shape, moving quickly, knife-in-hand. He looks for the person that killed him.

Three. Feel sick. Keep breathing.

"*Putain de connard*! Out of the damn way!" comes a scream from an oncoming taxi. He spots it in time and dives backwards, feeling it whip past inches from his face. He doubles over, his lungs straining to swallow as much oxygen as possible. In the distance, the driver continues their tirade. "Fucking sharper!"

The world swallows him, all sound and fury enveloping his senses and rattling his brain. The pain from the hypothetical stabbing rips through his back, making each breath haggard and harried. He splutters, bent double and sweating, his adrenal medulla blindly pumping hormones through his central nervous system, his white blood cells rallying to heal a wound that is not there.

Finally, amidst the cacophonous din of his own bodily responses, Pluto Garcia passes out.

Golden orange fades to dim blue as the sun falls beneath the western horizon. Greater Morrissette hums with activity as its citizens leave their jobs – in the Charbon commercial quarter, boutiques and bookshops switch off their neon OPEN signs one by one; to the northeast, dockworkers vacate the bustling docks and ports of the Shipbuilders' Union for the bars and diners of Madame Syndicat; in the beating heart of Morrissette, the grand, impassive bulwark of the Archive cuts a sharp silhouette against the sky, the shadow it casts punctured by streetlamps and headlights; out to the northwest, the imposing skeleton of cast iron that is the Laurent oil rig rests upon heavy concrete legs, its towers lit by a healthy butane glow; and there, over by the Waterfront, where ships bob on the inky black water, their masts swaying like reeds in the wind, Pluto Garcia wakes from a dark sleep.

He sits up, resting on his creaking elbows. His head feels as though it is stuffed with rags soaked in ethanol, waiting for a match. His tongue, paradoxically both dry as old leather and damp as the flesh of a slug, sits awkwardly in his mouth. He looks at his surroundings. Pine wood cladding lines the walls, stopping just short of the corrugated aluminium ceiling. The floor is covered with a dull beige carpet, stained by spilled coffee and the occasional cigarette burn. The filament lights that illuminate the room whine angrily, giving the whole room the feel of a bee's hive on the brink of being invaded by hornets. The Tank. He's in the Tank.

"Eddie?" he calls out, his voice hoarse. His throat stings and he coughs up a thin globule of acidic phlegm. The door opens a second later to reveal a lean man dressed in a black collarless shirt and neat, high-waisted beige slacks, his loose, stretched frame giving him the impression of a person made out of linguini. A thin trail of smoke rises from the cigarette held between his smirking lips. In his hand he holds a grimy tumbler of water.

"Bit of a heavy one, gumshoe?" he asks, his black eyes glinting cheerfully.

"Who brought me in?" Garcia rasps. The man named Eddie Manansala hands the water over, a small cloud of bluish smoke hovering over him like the auspices of God.

"Some rickshaw driver. Saw you shit-can in the street over by Palissade, figured you were a militiaman so he brought you here. You've been out for a couple hours."

"I trypped." Garcia croaks. He licks his parched lips and downs the water; it is tinny and a little warm, like all water distilled from the barrels atop the Tank's roof. Eddie nods, stubbing out the cigarette on his heel and reaching into his back pocket to produce a small notebook and pencil.

"That explains the sweating. Want me to log it?"

"Sure. Put it down as attempted murder. Stabbing. Didn't manage to catch the suspect."

"Where'd it happen?"

"Over at the Promenade de Gloire. About half a street down from the memorial."

Manansala nods, scribbling with pursed lips.

"Hm. I'm gonna need you to file a more detailed report tomorrow morning, but I'll keep an eye out for anything suspicious out that way. You got any Tryp left?"

Garcia reaches into his pocket and pulls out the pillbox. He cracks it with his thumb and counts the remaining pills. Four.

"God damnit," he mutters under his breath.

"What's up?"

"Before I trypped I had three pills. Now I have four."

"That's the Uncertainty Principle for you." Manansala responds with a shrug. "I'll order some more."

"Better safe than sorry, I guess," Garcia replies, pocketing the pillbox. "Who's in today?"

"Just me. Gallardo got the afternoon off to visit his mom over in the Packing district. Marchenko is over at San Madelaine, some meeting or other."

"Meeting?"

"Yeah, some king shit up at the Guild wanted to see her. All very hush hush, real clandestine." He chuckles to himself. "S'a shame we got rid of the secret police. I think we'd be pretty good at it."

"That's what the Bureau are for," Garcia says, softly. He stares at the floor, his head still heavy. The pain in his back has gone, replaced by an eerie numbness, the quiet that falls after a tragic accident. Manansala scans his face.

"You doing okay? Want me to call a doctor?"

"I'm fine, I just need to do my affirmations."

"Trypping is no joke, man. My uncle got brained by a truck out by Liberté. Poor fucker still can't go near the interstate without having a panic attack."

"Eddie, I'm fine."

"Okay, okay," the slender man responds, returning his notebook to his back pocket. "I'll get all that processed. You just shout if you need anything, okay?"

"Sure, thanks, Ed." Garcia puts the glass down on the floor and stares down at his hands. Ten fingers, plump and rough, creased across each knuckle. Delicate whorls and ripples bumping awkwardly into yellowing callouses. A sickle-shaped scar on his left thumb from an injury sustained opening a tin of cat food as a teenager. These are not *his* hands, but they are a *version* of his hands.

He is snapped from his reverie by the smell of coffee drifting in through the open door. He rises to his feet, wobbling unsteadily before catching himself, and heads out into the corridor. He walks slowly, his fingers trailing the treated wood panel walls, feeling the subtle bumps where the lacquer wasn't given time to set properly. A gentle heat hangs in the air as the warmth of the day seeps through the roof and out into the cooling night. This is the Precinct 14 headquarters, informally known as the Tank: a prime example of post-revolutionary architecture in Morrissette. An ostensibly temporary fixture constructed out of shipping containers and the occasional tarpaulin, knocked together by anarchists using materials salvaged from the burnt-out husk of the old regime. In 1962, promises were made by members of the Morrissette Coalition to establish a more permanent base of operations for the CMM in this half of the Waterfront. Thirty-two years later, this arcane tangle of corrugated aluminium and ultramarine plastic stands at the north-eastern edge of the Waterfront district, proud and immovable, an anchor, a set-piece.

Pluto Garcia makes his way down the corridor and into the breakout room, a shabby little corner containing a microwave – a dilapidated relic of clunky white plastic, likely pre-dating the Violet Revolution by some ten years – and a pot of hot, dark coffee. He fishes out an approximately clean mug from the sink, wipes it off on the corner of his shirt, and pours himself a cup. The smell hangs beneath his nose, its familiarity wrapping around his brain like a comfortable cardigan. He breathes deep. Across countless realities, across all uncertainties, coffee remains a constant throughout.

"Feeling better?" says a voice behind him. He turns to see Manansala wearing a sincere smile, a leaflet in his hand.

"This is helping," Garcia says, gesturing to the mug in his hand, the heat soaking into his palms. Manansala offers the leaflet up.

"Look, I know this isn't your first rodeo but I still have to give you this."

Garcia takes the leaflet and lets out a soft groan. A yellow line-diagram of a pill sits atop a blue waving gradient. Above this, the words "TRYP: A POST-MORTEM EXPERIENCE" are sketched out in calming white letters.

"Come on, man," Garcia begins. Manansala puts up a slender palm.

"Policy is policy, Pluto. Without it we'd be nothing more than capitalists."

Garcia cocks an eyebrow before folding the leaflet and slipping it into his back pocket. He leans back against the counter and takes a sip of his coffee.

"I normally bounce back quicker than this."

"No offence meant, gumshoe, but you're not as young as you used to be." Manansala sits up on the counter, his long legs dangling below him like a windchime. "How old were you when you last trypped?"

Garcia does some mental arithmetic, his lips pursing as he works it out.

"Would have been around thirty-six. When I'd just joined the Militia."

"Then you've got twenty-one years of neural plaque and psychic baggage to work through. Every time a person tryps, there's a forty percent chance they leave something behind. Goes up to sixty when it happens more than once."

"I don't need a lecture, Eddie."

"I know, it was an accident and I'm glad you're still alive – in theory, if nothing else. Just," he peers over his glasses, a look of surprising sincerity in his dark eyes, "be careful out there, okay?"

Garcia falters under his gaze for a moment, anchored to the spot, stuck. He attempts a smile – an ill-practised expression on his rough, creased face. The lips curl up at the corners, revealing shadowy wrinkles that frame his eyes. His forehead, similarly, shifts up, carrying with it his receding hairline. The resulting expression seems more a parody of whimsy, or the symptom of some malignant disease.

"I'm always careful, Eddie."

The black-eyed man stares at him, his own expression unchanging. Eventually he breaks, snorting out a quick exhalation of amusement before lowering himself from the counter and returning to his desk.

"Get yourself home, Pluto," he says, softly. "I think you need it."

The road to South Seychel Avenue is a winding one, and one that Garcia's feet are well acquainted with. Curve up the alleyway that runs alongside the Tank, turn left on Rue D'Ecoulement, follow the road for ten minutes into the Southern Packing District, dodging the occasional moped as it whips too close to the curb, before heading right onto Kamote East. Fork out three dollars for a bowl of noodles and a bottle of soda at the food stall on the corner, pocket the change, follow the concrete steps onto Block Vingt-Neuf, and take the third left.

The building looms overhead, its stepped salmon and grey panelling dim against the navy sky. A checkerboard of light shines from the building's face, each window a diorama, a brief glimpse into the yellow-tinged life lived within. Out on the front, a couple kids dressed in the leathers, denim, and scrounged industrial tarp of L'Anormal pass a liquor bottle amongst themselves. One flashes a gap-toothed grin at him as he approaches.

"Ay-yo, sharper," he says, proffering the bottle up. Black Tiger Rum. Eight dollars a bottle, tastes like cat piss and fire. "You want some?"

"Nah, that shit gives me indigestion." Garcia grins. The kid cackles, handing the bottle over to his compatriot, a gaunt youth with tall, hastily-dyed and impeccably coiffed red hair.

"More for us, sharper." He grins. "You look fucked, man – you been raving?"

"You know it." Garcia fires a loose finger gun, which causes the kids to collectively lose their shit. *It's good when they're laughing,* Garcia thinks to himself. *When they're laughing, they don't think of you as a cop.*

"Ay," he says, plucking the key card from his pocket. "You ever seen a guy in a hood over by the Promenade? Wears a bomber jacket?"

"All sorts of creeps out by the Promenade these days," chimes another L'Anormal, a willowy youth clad in a torn dockworker's overalls modified to read "FUCK IS ASS" on the front. "You looking for somebody, sharper?"

"Just got a couple questions for 'em, that's all." Garcia flicks the scratched key card over the reader and the door buzzes open. "Keep an eye out, eh? And say hi to your mothers for me."

"Take it easy, sharper," the kid with the dyed quiff calls out, taking a quick swig of the liquor and coughing. Garcia enters the building, ignoring the busted elevator with its weathered "OUT OF ORDER" sign and heading straight for the stairs. Each step echoes, the sound bouncing up the barren walls and into the darkness overhead. He reaches the first floor and slows down, his pulse racing in his throat as he tackles the second flight. Finally, he reaches apartment 237, panting softly as he unlocks the door.

He flicks a switch and the eco-friendly bulb hums awake, casting the apartment with a dim glow. Humble teal couch pushed against a peach wall, coffee table resting atop a rug the faded red of a manifesto. He locks up and removes his jacket, kicking off his shoes and placing his stun gun on a dresser by the door. He walks slowly into the living room, switching on the cassette player without looking as he passes. The second verse of a song floats on the air — droning with a slight melancholy to it, the kind of song that lingers, clinging to the furniture like cigarette smoke. A pipe organ whines for a moment, changing chords only occasionally, and eventually a high, soft voice, teetering somewhere between masculine and feminine, rises above the music.

"Some days it feels," the voice trills, "like this world is a pale green egg…"

The words are accompanied by deep, melodic piano, one note clunking into the next. Pluto Garcia listens for a moment, eyes closed, probing the noted absence of pain in his back with his mind. The song continues, detailing a cold grey day in Funam Province, the buzzing of mosquitos, the chill of mud. He opens his eyes, inhales deeply, exhales slowly, and prepares a simple dinner of fried pork and rice.

"With the signing of the Morrissette Coalition in 1975, the disparate warring tribes of South Annalise came together to form a city of four major districts, united under a single government: to the south the Waterfront, where the majority of the city's population dwell in community housing projects and commute to the other districts for work; in the north-east, the Scaffolds hold the majority of industry, a vibrant network of factories and company towns centred around the Shipbuilders' Union of Morrissette headquarters at the Shipyard; to the north-west, the pleasures and leisures of Madame Syndicat and the Guild of Earthly Delights; finally, in the centre and governed independently, stands the Bureau of Records Archive, as close to a singular regulatory body as the anarchist nation of Annalise possesses."

Adrienne La Rambla, *A Foreigner's Guide to Morrissette*

"To each man, the will of his brothers. To each heart, the beat of liberty!"

Camille Kamote, *Battle Hymn of Annalise*

TWO

The morning sun begins its steady assault on the city as Pluto Garcia files paperwork.

He sits at his desk, an imposing mahogany thing reclaimed from the old police station over on Trois et Demi, the sharp artificial smell of printer ink wafting up from the wad of official witness forms before him. He writes neatly, carefully, the fleshy blade of his left hand angled up slightly so as not to smudge the page. Once he reaches the end of each paragraph he stops to scan his handwriting, a chickenscratch script of black ink on pale lemon-yellow paper.

"At approximately 16:30 on 16 Février, I, Second Lieutenant Pluto Ramirez Garcia, was attacked on Le Promenade de Gloire, around twenty metres south of the *Fallen Anarchists of the Violet Revolution* memorial. The attacker, who remains at large, was wearing a red bomber jacket and a hood concealing their facial features. They carried a knife, which was used to fatally stab me in the lower back in an adjacent reality. As per the Probability Matrix Statute of 1976 (Amended 1982; 1987), I am logging this attack as evidence in the case despite the fatal wound not being administered in the reality in which this document is being filed."

He sighs and rubs his temples. His morning is spread out in front of him: an incident statement detailing yesterday's crime sits beside a stack of papers containing the logistical data on food deliveries; beneath them, there are enquiry papers regarding the medical supplies yet to arrive at Dubois General Hospital, suspected to have gone missing somewhere between here and the factory they were shipped from in North Annalise; a release from the Precinct 3 admin department explains in clipped terms that due to a printing malfunction several ration booklets for several Waterfront neighbourhoods will be late; beneath all this, lost in the impenetrable sprawl that is his desk, is a wad of wellbeing check-ins he needs to sign off on.

To Pluto Garcia, who has only been awake for two hours and who spent most of the night dreaming about blood loss, the filing of paperwork ranks fairly low on his list of hobbies, often below having his pubic hair pulled with a pair of tweezers. The introduction of Tryp, adjacent realities, and the Yemelenovian Uncertainty Principle lowers that rating to somewhere around having his eyes gouged out with a stick.

He stands and wanders over to the window, looking out over the Waterfront. Light glances off of the undulating waves as the last few fishing vessels head out to sea, navigating effortlessly around the dark, barely-visible ruins of Old Morrissette, swallowed by the churning waters of the Baratte during the flood of 1876. By noon they'll have gathered a sizeable haul of bream, mackerel, and yellowtail scad – awkward piles of cold, glistening skin and wet, inky eyes – and will return to port to drink, smoke, and sing karaoke. Garcia leans against the sill as a soft breeze carries the smell of salt into the office, and his eyes follow the Promenade east towards Place de Moteur.

"Lieutenant Garcia?" a voice comes from the open door behind him.

Of the few things the Community Militia of Morrissette inherited from the old regime, the least meaningful and most called upon is the subject of rank. At the top lies the insurmountable position of major general, currently occupied by one Sara Nguyen over at Precinct 3. Below that is captain, then first lieutenant, second lieutenant, and sergeant. Then, right at the bottom, straining beneath the everyday busy work of answering calls, making coffee, filing paperwork, and responding to the queries of citizens, is the officer cadet. This one, Emmanuel Gallardo, stands at 5'4" and bears a thin, neatly-trimmed moustache on his upper lip, a look of permanent mild exhaustion on his face.

"What's up, Manny?"

"Captain Marchenko just called, says she wants you to meet over at San Madelaine in an hour."

Garcia nods, sniffing sharply.

"She want me to take the car?"

"Yes, sir."

He curses under his breath before letting out a laboured sigh.

"Right you are, Cadet. Thank you for letting me know."

"Not a problem, Lieutenant." The kid nods deeply, lingering in the doorway a moment. Garcia's eyes eventually meet his and, with another put-upon sigh, he speaks.

"What is it, Cadet?"

"Eddie says you trypped yesterday, sir. Stabbed in the back."

"First Lieutenant Manansala is correct."

"How are you doing?"

Garcia's eyes drift over the Waterfront, the concrete bulk of the Promenade, the resplendent statue of Camille Kamote, madame-superior of the Violet Revolution, rifle in her right hand and the flag of the People's Republic of Annalise in her left, a look of triumphant indignation on her bronze features as she squint in the sun. A spot on his lower back begins to itch.

"Pretty good, Cadet."

The Sao-San Valiant is an unparalleled feat of Anarcho-Communist engineering. First produced by the state subsidised Morrisette Motor Company back in 1962 in the style of the ever-popular *Stoykiy* of Wojtek, the Valiant is, to a unit, the worst vehicle ever designed by human hands. With a steel unibody that resembles the elongated face of a borzoi sighthound, clunky panels of durable plastic covering the hood and bonnet, and a miniscule two-stroke engine that smokes like a sailor on shore leave when topping speeds exceeding seventy-seven miles per hour, the Vali is a common sight in the bustling streets of Morrissette – often abandoned at the side of the road in favour of literally any other car.

The Community Militia of Morrissette owns two.

The one that now stands before Pluto Garcia is a sky-blue model, slender and awkward as a teenager mid-growth-spurt, with a chrome plate grinning beneath the grille. Garcia takes out the key and fumbles with the lock, stooping down to climb inside. His knees creak as he adjusts the seat, feeling the lever give suddenly beneath his hand as he jolts back. He checks the fuel gauge, the tachometer, the mileage. All dogshit. The Vali, much like coffee, is a stable presence across all realities.

He cracks open the glovebox and there, sitting between a pair of handcuffs and a spare stun gun, is a cassette. One of Manansala's, *Only the Hits, Pal,* Lupe Celentano's third album and the first released as part of his controversial reconstructionist funk suite. The cover features a black and white Celentano snarling at the camera, eyes obscured by black glass set in a thick Duroplast frame. It's not Marco Sanskrit, but then again *nothing* is Marco Sanskrit. Garcia takes the tape, winds the reels back with the end of a pencil, and slots it into the player. A rolling bassline kicks in, followed by a persistent drum beat and Celentano's heavily accented drawl. Garcia plucks a pair of stashed shades down from the visor and sets the ignition rumbling.

The roads of Morrissette exist in a perpetual state of partial gridlock, a noisy, sweaty sluggishness calefied by exhaust fumes and the ever-present sun. Mopeds and scooters weave between stalled vehicles, cutting through the fetid fug only to get caught behind some other obstacle and be left half-standing in the heat. From the Tank it takes Garcia around forty-five minutes to make his way up Moreau Boulevard and into the narrow streets of the Casa. He is stopped at the checkpoint and displays his papers – Militia-mandated, granting free passage into the neighbouring districts – before being waved along. Contrary to the squat, practical buildings of the Waterfront and the imperious industrial sprawl of the Union District, the architecture of Madame Syndicat is tall, decadent, and grandiose, a hangover from Morrissette's pseudo-imperial heritage and the ostentatious trappings of the old regime. The roads clear as grand Palladian structures of sandstone and ornate wrought iron rise up into the azure sky, their dark windows gazing down onto Garcia as he makes his way towards L'Hôtel San Madelaine.

The hotel stands at the northernmost end of the Old Quarter, fronted by an illustrious plaza lined with beech trees. It is a building of presence, all sharp awnings and lean, tapering pillars, rising statesmanlike from the heart of Madame Syndicat. Garcia emerges from the car and removes his shades, looking up at the headless statues that line the roof. Politicians, deified by the Fascist Party and decapitated during the Violet Revolution. From left to right he can just make out their former likenesses: Gabriel Angara, Prime Minister of Annalise; Jack Sierra, Minister of Propaganda; Hugo LeRoy, Minister of Industry; Rudolph Haushofer, Chancellery.

"Lieutenant Garcia!"

The voice breaks his attention and he looks down to see a young woman at the open mouth of the hotel. She waves at him and he approaches, eyes scanning the plaza. People mill amongst the trees, blissfully occupying some of the only shade in Morrissette at this time of day, drinking soda and chatting happily amongst themselves. At least some of them are tourists, pale skin burnt pink by the sun, their accents increasingly familiar in this part of town. The others, Garcia assumes, are Guild members, escorts and sex workers coyly flirting with Johns, their smiles bright and alluring, their eyes deep and dark. Garcia turns back to the woman.

"Thank you for coming, Lieutenant," she says. Her expression is practised and neutral, but there is an immediacy to her mannerisms that feels much more sincere. She is dressed neatly, white shirt buttoned to just beneath her chin and tucked into a slim black pencil skirt. A logo, the lilting burgundy *SM* of the hotel atop a fleur de lis, is embroidered onto her left breast pocket. Garcia nods sharply.

"Not a problem. The CMM welcomes any opportunity to work alongside the Guild." He points inside. "My captain is already here, I presume?" The concierge nods again, gesturing with a slender hand.

"Yes, sir, right this way."

Garcia is led through the cool interior of the building, the marble floor reflecting the heat of the mid-morning sun back outside. Elegant, well-dressed patrons of enchantingly indeterminate gender sprawl like house cats on cream sofas, sipping cool drinks from tall glasses and curiously watching him as he passes. A militiaman on duty in Madame Syndicat is a rare sight.

The concierge leads him to the elevator and presses the call button. She stands silently, a respectable distance away from Garcia, avoiding his gaze. In the metal of the elevator door he sees a look of warped concern on her face. She speaks in a calm, measured tone.

"Your captain will be waiting for you on the third floor, Lieutenant."

Garcia cocks an eyebrow.

"You won't be joining me?"

"No, sir," she says, still not returning his gaze. "I have work to attend to down here."

Garcia's mind drifts back to the words of Eddie Manansala yesterday. All very hush hush. The doors open and Garcia steps inside, turning back and for one final look at the concierge.

"Thank you for your time," he says as the doors close. There, for a sliver of a second, he thinks he sees her expression change, wobbling into an uncertain mix of relief and dread. He makes a mental note of this as he pushes the button labelled "3", before spinning on his heels to face the large mirror behind him.

He sighs as he inspects himself: short, chubby frame clad in high-waisted slacks, practical shoes, light beige jacket clashing against a thin shirt the colour of cochineal. Two slender eyes set in a tanned, lined face, framed by a dusting of stubble and a mop of salt and pepper hair parted messily to the right. He attempts to contort his face into a characteristic gumshoe smile: wry, professional, knowing. It makes him look a little sickly. Pluto Garcia: world's most conspicuous narc.

There is a soft *ding* as the doors open, and the world shifts on its axis.

The first thing Garcia notices is the smell of blood, tinny and sharp in his nostrils. His hackles immediately raise, a primal response from the most ancient corner of his nervous system. He scans the hallway ahead and sees nothing immediately out of place, just beige carpet and a row of doors the colour of claret. He walks down the hallway, treading carefully, examining his surroundings the way an antelope inspects a watering hole for alligators. At four paces from the elevator he spots a blemish on the carpet, a reddish-brown stain that tapers into a smeared splotch. Another mental note. He eventually comes to an open door – room 312.

"Ah, Lieutenant," a cool, diplomatic voice emerges from the room. "Please come in."

Garcia does as instructed, stepping over the threshold. The metallic scent builds, mingling with putrefaction and an unpleasant chemical odour in the air to form a foul-smelling cocktail, and he has to suppress the coffee and jelly pastry he'd had for breakfast from rising. Looking down, he sees the dead man.

He's tall, maybe around 6'5", with broad shoulders and thick, trunk-like arms. His hair is black to the point of being tinged with blue, and is shaved at the temples with the top scraped close to his skull in the practical cut of a Union man. He lies on his right side as though sleeping, his limp body an insurmountable bulwark of mottled purple flesh emerging from a stagnant pool of thick, black blood. He is dressed only in a pair of white boxer-briefs stained a grisly pink and his expression is one of ever-lasting dumbness: one wide grey eye staring up into the distance, the other swollen shut from the bullet wound currently marring the left side of his head.

"*Madre Kamote...*" Garcia mutters, taking a step back. "What a fucking mess."

"It's a crime scene, Pluto," Marchenko replies, her tone flat and humourless. "They're always a fucking mess."

He looks up to see Captain Cassandra Marchenko. Her short hair is styled back into a neat quiff, and she is dressed in the tidy but practical clothes of a high-ranking Militia member, white t-shirt tucked into black pleated pants that flare out around calf-high boots. A narrow scar runs down her right cheek, the result of a bar fight turned sour enough to put her in Dubois General but not enough to stop her from breaking the assailant's nose.

She is flanked by three others: An elegant, graceful individual dressed in a trim black suit, their nose turned up to the carnage currently occupying the hotel suite carpet; a svelte and proud woman with a pigeon-toed stance favouring the left leg, likely concealing a weapon on the right hip; and a paunchy man in his mid-60s, his dyed hair combed back into a tight ponytail and his face the reddish pink of rosewood. Marchenko steps forward, neatly avoiding the perimeter of the pooling blood.

"Mx. Martinez, Agent Dao, Mr. Chang – this is Second Lieutenant Pluto Garcia. Lieutenant," she gestures a hand out to the assembled coalition agents, "this is Remembrancer Supreme Manon Martinez of the Guild of Earthly Delights, Agent Anne Dao of the Bureau of Records, and Comrade Somsak Chang of the Morrissette Shipbuilders' Union."

"Pleasure to meet you all." Garcia steps back into the room, smiling queasily and offering out a hand. Martinez shakes the hand with a stern, clockwork grace. Agent Dao takes it with a short, firm shake, her palm the eerie cold of a fish's scales. Chang simply looks down at it in disdain. Garcia, used to being icily rejected by Union reps, slides the hand back into his pocket and produces a small teal notebook, pencil dangling limply from a length of string. "What do we have here, Captain?"

"We have," Chang interjects, flashing a venomous glance over at the impassive Agent Dao and the avoidant Martinez, "a travesty."

The statement resonates in the air around them, vibrating every frayed nerve like thunder. After a second or two, Marchenko coughs politely.

"Victim is Krishna Klein, Union Representative for the Electronic Goods Industry in Morrissette and co-chair at Ergot and Klein," she begins, producing a notebook of her own. "Extensive damage to the left temple, likely an exit wound. Extreme lividity along the entire right-hand side of his body, no signs of intravenous drug use or other immediately visible signs of damage, but we won't know for sure until we hear back from forensics."

Garcia squints down at the body.

"Tryp?"

"Unclear. I'll ask Precinct 9 to run toxicology on him."

"Murder weapon?"

"Nothing yet."

"How long's he been dead?"

Another polite cough from Marchenko.

"Seven days, we believe. Bureau was called in not long after the incident." She flashes her own furtive glance at Agent Dao, who observes the scene with the casual interest one might reserve for a game of cricket. "We were alerted last night."

"Uh huh," he says, scribbling down some notes. That explains the meeting. Hush hush. "And who found the body?"

At this, Dao steps forward, her tone clipped and precise.

"One of the hotel's cleaning staff. She has been questioned by Bureau investigators and sent home from work, to cope with the trauma."

An absence hangs in the air, the space left behind by an omitted detail. Garcia glances over at her.

"And when was this?"

Dao pauses, her attention softly floating over to the militiaman.

"That was two days ago."

Ah, Garcia thinks. *So the Guild tried to handle it in-house, realised that the poor fucker is a Union rep, and the crime scene suddenly becomes a diplomatic incident. Martinez calls in the Bureau, who maintain "transparency" by alerting the Union and CMM.*

"I see," he says, simply. He looks back down at the body, all heavy muscle and swollen, puffy skin, lurid veins forming estuaries across the abdomen before merging into a single blotchy seafront of burgundy flesh.

"Am I to assume that I'll be working the case?" Garcia says, not looking up. Martinez, finally, speaks.

"Yes," they speak slowly, each word measured and tactful. "We felt given Comrade Klein's position in the Union, it would be appropriate for the matter to be investigated outside of the Guild."

"Like fuck we did," Chang spits, his face contorting. "I just don't want those damned Bureau spooks poking their noses in any more than they have done already."

"Please manage your tone, Mr. Chang," Dao responds coldly, not looking at him. He spins around, pointing a chubby finger at her.

"I'll mind my tone, Anne, when you people mind your own fucking business! Damn *cào nǐ mā* find a dead Union man in a Guild bordello and spend five days letting him stew in the fucking sun while they clean up after themselves!"

"There has been no clean-up, Mr. Chang," Martinez replies sharply, eyes fixed on the wall some five inches above the Union rep's head. "We simply saw to it that our operatives exhausted every possible lead before consulting with the other Coalition members."

"Please," Marchenko intervenes, fatigue creeping into her voice. "We have gone over this. The case will be handled by the CMM, with assistance from the Guild, Bureau, and Union."

Chang vibrates with barely suppressed fury for just a moment, before eventually bursting with a short, acerbic snarl.

"Fine. But as this crime involves the death of a Union representative, I *insist* that we be represented on the ground. I will speak with Mr. Khazi and see to it that an Auditor joins Lieutenant Garcia in his investigations."

Silence occupies the room once more, heavy as the dead man's flaccid frame. Finally, Marchenko speaks.

"Very well. Lieutenant, are you comfortable with this arrangement?"

The veil drops. There is a hint of longing in her voice, the longing of a woman who has been awake for twenty-plus hours and is seeking a simple, quiet resolution followed by a long, uninterrupted sleep. He nods.

"Yes, ma'am."

"Thank fuck for that."

Back in the lobby, four factions occupy four corners. In the top right, Agent Anne Dao calmly flicks through a manilla case file, eyes flitting from one word to the next, pausing only to chew on a particularly enticing detail. Top left, Comrade Somsak Chang growls down a payphone, slipping effortlessly into the sharp syllables of the Shipyard dialect to punctuate his point. Bottom right, Manon Martinez speaks softly with the hotel manager, a slender hand placed on his arm. Finally, bottom left, Captain Cassandra Marchenko paces back and forth before the seated Second Lieutenant Pluto Ramirez, whose leg bounces up and down on the ball of his foot.

"Captain," he begins, quietly. "Sit down, you look exhausted."

She nods casually but continues to pace, knuckle of her right pointer finger resting against her chin.

"I'll be alright, Lieutenant. If I sit down, I think I'll fall asleep."

Garcia nods, sitting back and casting an eye over the lobby. Most of the patrons have gone, sensing the tension that followed the four Coalition members down from the third floor. He inhales slowly, then exhales.

"Permission to be candid, Captain?"

"Granted."

"This is politics, isn't it?"

Marchenko stops, her back stiff, her pose giving nothing away.

Politics. It is a word despised by every branch of the Militia, every Guild agent, and every Union Auditor. When the Coalition agreement was signed in '75, it was done so as to reduce the need for politics. Each faction would exercise control over their district, interacting when necessary and otherwise leaving one another unmolested. An ideal situation in many ways, leaving the Union to handle the expansive world of labour and commerce, the Guild to the arts of pleasure and recreation, the Bureau to its intricate web of intelligence and taxation, and the Militia to simple matters of everyday policing and community protection. It was only on the rare occasions that felonious activity occurred on the hinterlands between the districts that cooperation was required, and even then it was usually wrapped up quietly and efficiently, with any begrudging collaboration born more out of convenience than mutual respect. Of course, no system is perfect. Sometimes, like the spectre of the grave, politics is inevitable.

"Yes, Pluto." Marchenko sighs. "This is politics."

Garcia takes out his notebook and flicks through the last couple of pages. He speaks quietly, without emotion, his eyes focused on the notes scribbled in pencil before him.

"So just to be clear: a high-ranking Union Representative is found dead in Madame Syndicat. The CMM is called in because the Union doesn't trust the Guild, and the Guild called in the Bureau because they want to wash their hands of the whole thing."

"Correct."

"And the Union is calling in an Auditor because…"

"Because they don't trust us either, yes."

"Good. Good to know."

They both fall silent, leaving only the sound of paper and the quiet chuntering of grumbling of Chang. Garcia closes his notebook and coughs softly.

"Permission to be candid again, ma'am?"

"Go ahead, Pluto."

"I'm not expected to actually solve this, am I?"

Marchenko turns and looks at him. Her eyes are bleary and framed by two dark bags. The corners of her lips dip downwards and her brow furrows for just a second before returning to the practised diplomatic neutrality.

"No, Lieutenant. I don't think you are."

"Very well." Garcia taps the end of his pencil on the front cover of his notebook. Figures. Back in '82, when Garcia had been a sergeant and was working under First Lieutenant François, there had been a similar case. Guildhall property had been ransacked, all signs pointing to a rogue Union Auditor. The CMM were brought in to investigate, mediating between the two factions, but the intent was clear. No evidence was to be found, no suspects interrogated, and once the pageantry had been sufficiently witnessed, everyone was to return to business as normal. Two weeks later the Auditor washed up dead out by Estuary West, skull vacated by a bullet. Nice and tidy. Nice and political. The hair on the back of Garcia's neck stands on end.

"I'm not a fan of this either," Marchenko says, quietly. "It feels too much like the bad old days, before the Revolution. But there is peace to be kept and we are, for our sins, the peacekeepers."

Across the room Chang loudly hangs up the payphone and stomps over to the militiamen. Seeing this, Martinez excuses themself and elegantly floats over, followed shortly by Dao, casefile under her arm.

"I have spoken to Comrade Khazi," Chang begins, hands stuffed in pockets, his tone slightly more measured. "We will be sending through a junior Auditor from our Liberté branch, Esther Dupont, to assist Lieutenant Garcia with his investigations. She'll need a day to familiarise herself with the case, but you can expect to hear from her soon." He turns to Garcia.

"Comrade Klein was a *dear* friend to me," he begins, stressing each syllable carefully. "I would be *extremely grateful* if you could solve this matter *discretely* and with *great care*."

Garcia, sensing the looming threat of politics, nods silently. Marchenko speaks.

"Of course, Mr. Chang. The CMM appreciates your patience." She turns to Dao, absolutely nailing the gumshoe smile. "We would also be thankful for any notes the Bureau may have accumulated on the case so far."

Dao responds with an icy smile of her own.

"Of course," she says, handing over the manilla document to Marchenko.

"In the meantime," Martinez chimes in, "the Guild will ensure that the crime scene continues to be blocked off as best as possible. Are we to assume that the CMM will be performing forensic work?"

Marchenko nods, tucking the notes under her arm.

"We'll call in a team and have them take the body to the Precinct 9 morgue. Lieutenant Garcia and Junior Auditor Dupont will likely need to take a closer look at the crime scene at some point over the next few days."

"Of course," Martinez replies with a shallow bow. "The Guild will be happy to help."

"Good. Now," Marchenko turns to Garcia, still holding her neutral smile. "I need coffee and a fucking cigarette."

"Given that its discovery only occurred in 1953, and that the inconsistencies posed by the Yemelenovian Uncertainty Principle make scientific research across disparate realities near-impossible, the long-term effects of Repodimethyltryptamine are largely unknown at this point. However, the immediate side-effects of Tryp usage are extremely well-documented, and can include nausea, diarrhea, excessive perspiration, audio-visual hallucinations, and a lingering sense of dread or unease as the mind adjusts to having survived a traumatic event."

Artaud Dobb, The Maccinnes Chronicle

THREE

They drive back to the Tank in silence, the car spluttering like a tuberculosis patient the whole way. At points Garcia looks over to find the captain asleep, her chin resting on her chest, her breathing steady and uncompromisingly loud. When they pull up to Precinct 14, Marchenko's eyes shoot open and she sits upright.

"Okay," she begins, unbuckling her seatbelt and continuing as if she had been wide awake the entire drive back. "I'm going to get on the phone to the Icehouse. Send Agent Dao's notes over to this Auditor, give her a fighting chance on this damn case."

"Yes, ma'am," Garcia replies, climbing awkwardly out of the car. He stretches out, feeling his back creak. "Once you've spoken to forensics you really should head home, though. You look like you've been on the clock for, what? Twenty hours?"

"Twenty-two," she says, matter-of-factly. "I can sleep when I'm dead, Lieutenant."

"It'll be sooner than you think at this rate, Captain."

"You'd be so lucky." She smirks, striding towards the Tank. "Now, before I do anything else: where does Eddie stash his cigarettes? I need a smoke."

"They're on the roof, behind the water drum." Garcia says, locking the Vali's doors with a satisfying *clunk*. "I need to chat with Manny for a moment, then I'll come up and join you."

She fires an unenthusiastic finger gun at him and heads inside. Garcia follows, heading over to Gallardo's desk and sliding the keys over to him.

"Anything interesting happen while I was out?"

"No, sir," Gallardo says, taking the keys and secreting them in a draw. "Report of a pretty big pothole over on Rue Kamote, I've got someone from the Roadhouse to go check it out and get it filled. Food delivery got held up over at the Casa but that all seems to be working smoothly now." He squints at a scribbled note on his desk before letting out a sigh.

"Oh, right – we got a report of some private fishing boat being stolen over by Le Lavage. Was planning on looking into that later."

"Le Lavage? And the Guild aren't handling it?"

"No, sir," Gallardo says, scanning his notes. "The boat's owner says they're 'too busy', and that he figured he should talk to some 'real police'."

"Well that's where he's wrong," Garcia says with a grin. "We're not police. Any sign of the guy who stabbed me yesterday?"

"Nothing that's been called in, no."

"Figures." He places the casefile down on the desk and taps it with a finger. "Would you be okay to fax this over to the Liberté Enforcement Corp? We're going to be collaborating with an Auditor on a case."

"Sure thing, Lieutenant." He takes the file and adds it to the ever-present pile of paperwork on his desk, pointing over his shoulder with the end of a cheap ballpoint. "There's a pot of coffee on, if you want to take some up to the captain. Looks like she needs it."

"You're a good person, Manny Gallardo," Garcia says, patting the cadet on the shoulder before heading to the breakout. There, as promised, he finds a pot of coffee – black, thick, warm, the result of a portion of the budget that by all rights should go on maintaining one of the CMM's two Valis, and goes instead on importing ground coffee beans from the island nation of Kumari. Garcia pours two cups and takes them up the rickety wooden stairs leading to the roof.

"Manny put a pot on," he says, handing Marchenko a mug. She takes it and sets it by her feet before bringing the cigarette up to her lips and taking a long, slow drag. A plume of white smoke rises into the air, catching the sweltering midday sun before dispersing in the breeze.

"That man is a saint," she says, casting her eye out over the city. Beneath them, Morrissette goes about its business: gridlocked streets seeping in heat and pollutants; voices calling out, vying for attention over the noise of engines and distant construction; the warm, cloying smell of fish wafts up from the Packing District, hanging in the air like an omen. She takes another drag before turning back to Garcia.

"I left the packet on the drum, if you want one."

Garcia helps himself.

"We're going to have to pay him back for this, you know," he says, lighting it up with the captain's antique kerosene lighter, a relic of her father's from before the Revolution. "He gets these imported from South San Ernesto."

"My uncle grows weed over in the lowlands," Marchenko says with a shrug. "I'll bring him some back next time I get out there."

To the south, fishing vessels crest the undulating waves, silhouettes abstract and mechanical against the blinding light glinting off of the water. Seagulls trail after them, plucking wriggling black fish from the foam and soaring skyward, their hysterical screeches filling the air. Below, scrawled on the whitewashed wall of a smokehouse, the words "WITH MANY EYES I SEE" have been spray-painted in shaky black letters some four feet in height. Garcia squints down at it, arms crossed over his chest, cigarette smouldering between his fingers. He takes it in for a moment, the unsteady hand, the splattered rivets of black where the paint fell astray, the starkness of it against the chipped white. Marchenko turns to Garcia, scanning his face.

"You okay? You look…" She smirks, catching herself. "Well, I was going to say you look tired, but that would make me a hypocrite."

An itch creeps over his lower back, starting at the base of his spine and stopping just short of his kidneys. With it comes a chill, a reminder of his numbing hands and dying neurons, of the dimming light replaced by the magenta burst of a near-death experience.

"I'm fine, Captain," he says, swallowing the discomfort down and attempting that ill-fated smile. She holds his gaze for a moment and he, unnerved, takes a long drag of his cigarette. First Lieutenant François maintained that the most important tool a militiaman has is their stare. With it they seem inquisitive, probing, sympathetic, charismatic, dead-set, certain. *Hold a steady stare,* he had said once before going to interrogate a kid found selling stolen radio sets outside Block Treize, *and let them do the rest.*

"Sure thing, Pluto," she concludes after a moment, finishing the last of her cigarette and stubbing it on her heel before flicking it into the paint can Manansala uses in lieu of an ashtray. "I'll call the Icehouse and get them to pick up Klein's body."

"Yes, ma'am," Garcia says, doing the same. "Manny's faxing those notes over to Liberté. Once he's done I'll go over them, see if I can't work something out."

Marchenko pauses briefly, looking out over the sprawl of Morrissette. She sighs, a lingering weariness in her voice.

"Good luck, Lieutenant."

Pluto Garcia chews the tip of a pencil, the hand-typed notes of Agent Dao sprawled out before him like a deck of cards.

The notes are thorough. Each page contains intimate details of the crime scene: exact positions measured to the millimetre; the location of debris and detritus in the room; the levels of putrefaction updated in a neat handwritten scrawl as day one became day two, day three, day four, day five. Finally, paperclipped to the back of the manilla folder, are two photographs. The first is of the crime scene on day three, on first discovery and without the distracting presence of the Coalition agents. The second is of Krishna Klein, bloated and corpulent, his pale skin criss-crossed with blueish-purple veins and standing sharply against a pool of inky blood. Garcia puts both photographs down and begins with the notes.

Comrade Krishna Klein of the Shipbuilders' Union. Fifty-six years old, 6'7", approximately 220 pounds. Black hair, grey eyes, of mixed Analissian and Laccannesse descent. First seen by staff at the Madelaine fourteen days ago, checking in without luggage whilst presumably under the influence of heavy narcotics. Seen on two occasions between then and his death: First during a grocery-store run, returning with a bottle of cheap raki and a bag of potato chips, second when the cleaning staff caught him – quote – in the "throes of masturbatory passion". Garcia smirks. You can always trust the Bureau for prosaic flair.

Following this incident, a Do Not Disturb sign became a permanent fixture on the door. As far as hotel staff are aware, Klein had no visitors during this time, though visitors in rooms immediately below and above Room 312 issued noise complaints most evenings. Five days after the Do Not Disturb incident the cleaning staff, alarmed by an unpleasant smell coming from the room, reportedly opened the door, saw Klein's body, and screamed. A bullet hole was found to the right of the door, buried in the wall. No gun found at the scene.

He reads over the notes again, trying to visualise the room as he'd left it. Dead man on the floor, his last moments seeping into the carpet. Four additional bodies, and beyond those bodies a room – evidence of a life lived; clothes, used crockery, cigarette butts in the ashtray. This is as far as he's able to visualise before his brain is pulled back to the bickering of the three Coalition members, the stern captain, the blasé agent, the avoidant remembrancer, the smouldering Union man. With a sigh, he looks at the photographs.

First he inspects the room at large, taken from an angle close to what – according to the floorplan he'd managed to dig up from the Tank's decades' worth of files – corresponds to the north-eastern corner of the room. He sees the cream curtains flapping in the breeze, the sunlight cast over the room in thick, wide panes, the dark blood stark and imposing as an inkblot against the otherwise stainless floor. If he squints he can see the bullet hole embedded in the wall on the edge of the room, a thin network of cracks spreading out through the plaster from the initial puncture. He stares closer, trying to picture the bullet as it explodes from the barrel and screams through the temple of Krishna Klein, rending his skull and grey matter little more than a violent spray of jellied goo before burying itself a couple inches deep into plasterboard. He envisages the sound of the gunshot, the crack of splintering bone, the sharp thud of the wall. He winces sharply, feeling the itch crawl up his back as he imagines the final hot-white instant of Klein's death, before turning to the photograph of the body.

As seen before: mottled purple skin, limp body lying on its side. The itching of his back becomes a tingling in his spine, a gnawing of his lizard brain, an adrenal whisper warning of danger. He ignores this and lets his inner eye take him again, picturing the scene: Klein, muscled and half-nude, facing the door. The sun glints off of the water, it is 16:37 and the sun is glinting off of the water.

The trigger is pulled and the bullet streams forth, the blade closing in on the nerve cluster just above his kidneys. It connects, knocking him ninety degrees where he lands on his side, prone on the floor, staring blindly at the bullet that killed him. The blood seeps from the wound and onto the carpet, onto the concrete floor of the Waterfront. Pluto Garcia is bleeding out.

"Lieutenant?"

Garcia jolts upright, eyes snapping to the door, heart racing. Marchenko stands stock-still, eyes cautious and attentive, silhouetted by the dim glow of the fluorescent lighting strip suspended just above her head.

"Everything alright, Pluto?"

"I, ah," he stammers, feeling his pulse strumming in his throat. "Fine, ma'am. Just going over Dao's notes."

She watches him a while longer.

"Well," she says, still eyeing him suspiciously, "I figured you should know: Forensic picked up Klein's body and have taken him to the Icehouse."

"Okay, great." Garcia attempts a queasy smile. Marchenko looks him up and down.

"You trypped, didn't you?" she concludes after a moment.

"Ah. Yes, ma'am." He coughs, forcing his stomach to stop churning. "Stabbed over by the Promenade. Was it that obvious?"

"Yes," Marchenko replies with a shrug. "I saw Eddie's notes from last night, but I'd already worked it out. You're a lousy liar, Garcia. Your face does this thing: it looks like you're trying to smile through a shit."

Garcia's cheeks flush and he bites down the urge to smile. His smiles are rarely convincing.

"I'm fine, ma'am, honest." He drums his fingers on the desk in an attempt at nonchalance. "Just flashes, that's all."

"This is your third time, correct?" Her tone is clear, formal. A moment ago she was Cassandra Marchenko; mentor, confidant. Now she is Captain Marchenko.

"Correct, Captain."

"And you know as well as I do that the Post-Tryp Adrenal Response can take up to a week to fade. Maybe longer, if it isn't the first time."

"I do, Captain."

"Then why in Mère Camille's name are you still here?" she asks, her voice keen and sharp now. He falters a little under her gaze.

"Work helps keep my mind off of things."

"I imagine a lot of people find pictures of corpses extremely relaxing." Marchenko says, dryly. "Go on, Lieutenant. Rest up, see how you feel in the morning. That's an order from your superior officer."

Garcia nods, rising to his feet. He wobbles slightly as the adrenaline washes from his system. Marchenko's eyes follow him up and out of the door. At some point between him sitting down with the notes and now the sun has begun to set, lighting Morrissette in a deep amber glow that creeps in through the windows of the Tank and casts wide rhomboid panels of orange over the floor. Marchenko stops him as he leaves.

"I want you to be more careful out there."

"I am careful, Captain."

"No, Lieutenant," she says sternly, her gaze as unfaltering as a steam train. "No you're not."

Pluto Garcia walks home in the dim golden light of the afternoon, the heat of the day slowly washing out to sea. He passes by revelling fishermen, already half-drunk on rum, grinning sottishly as they ramble through the streets of the Waterfront. Two L'Anormal sit on the dock, their feet swinging over the edge, passing a cigarette between them as FUCK SICK plays from their portable cassette player.

He cuts through the alleyways, narrowly avoiding the Promenade and the spinal tightness that waits there. He heads to the grocery store and picks up a six-pack of beer and some donuts, fried up and served in the San Ernesto style – long, slender, and star-shaped end-to-end, wrapped in thin, greasy paper. He looks down at his lingering paunch, shrugs internally, and hands the money over to the cashier.

The walk home is largely uneventful. Morrissette settles into her nightly throes: folk make their way from Estuary West and the Packing District, snaking through the streets towards the Blocks or the border checkpoints between the Waterfront and its neighbouring sectors; in the distance, the towers of the Laurent cough pillars of black smoke into the sky, striping the heavens like the hide of a tiger; on the edge of Place de Moteur, a busker sits cross-legged outside a food truck, noodling away on a guitar with gnarled, leathery fingers.

Garcia arrives home just after 8PM, kicks his shoes off, and flicks on Radio Promenade. He proceeds to his small kitchen, humming along to a song he's heard a couple times, and produces a plate of raw chicken from the fridge. He slices it thinly and adds it to a bowl of vinegar, peppercorns, salt, paprika, and garlic. He leaves it to steep, cracking a beer open and wandering around the apartment, humming softly to himself. One song moves onto the next, the DJ – John Mark Murphy – intermittently interrupting to give reports on the weather, upcoming sporting events, community news. After half an hour, he takes the chicken and fries it in a splash of oil before serving it with a bowl of rice.

He eats slowly, contentedly, listening to the radio. The Marco Sanskrit classic *Perhaps We Were Kings* comes on and he loudly, tunelessly sings between mouthfuls, foot tapping against the floor to form a percussion with the clinking of cutlery against crockery.

He finishes his meal, runs the plate under the faucet, and sets it aside to dry. He heads to the threadbare couch, propping his feet up and resting a beer on his belly as the radio plays a popular, poppy Revolutionary anthem. He looks over at the stack of crime paperbacks resting on the coffee table and reaches over to pluck one off the top. On the cover, a chisel-jawed man dressed in the style of the Apollo drug runners – pale linen, black tie, and wide-brimmed hat – brandishes a pistol at some unseen threat, while a beautiful dame cowers behind him. He flicks open to a dog-eared page and begins to read, making it through only a couple pages before his eyes drift close, a creeping weightlessness settling over his body.

He stares into the murky greyish-brownish pink of the inside of his eyelids, seeing the residual shards of green and blue light floating over his eyeballs. He sinks deeper, his body replaced piece-by-piece with senselessness, dullness, all save for one spot, that cluster of nerves just beneath his kidneys, a tangle of fairy lights glowing in his lower back. He probes the sensation, this alien scar from a universe where he, Pluto Garcia, is cooling in a mortuary. Then the dull skin on the inside of his eyelids is slowly swallowed up, filled out and replaced by the hot pink emptiness that stretches from one reality to the next. He is falling, careering downwards, the

Wider Probability Matrix threatening to devour him in its gaping fuchsia maw.

The phone rings.

He jolts up, just managing to catch the beer before it tumbles from his stomach, and rises to his feet. He unlocks the door and heads out into the corridor where the communal telephone hangs on the wall, a blocky mass of dull green metal that rattles with each piercing ring.

"Pluto Garcia, Block Vingt-Neuf," he says into the handset.

"Oh good," comes a soft voice on the other end of the line. "I was hoping I'd catch you. This is Junior Auditor Esther Dupont, from the Morrissette Shipbuilders' Union."

"Ah." Garcia sets the beer atop the phone's clunky body and straightens up, trying to pretend that he was not half-asleep moments ago. "I assume you got my number from the precinct?"

"We already had it on record," she replies. Garcia hears the sounds of paper as she speaks again. "Apparently you were involved with an altercation with some of our Community Administrators, back in 1973."

"Something like that," Garcia says, rubbing the spot at the base of his neck where, twenty-one years ago, he'd been brained by a wrench after bad-mouthing a Union rep. "How can I help, Comrade Dupont?"

"I just wanted to establish a rapport before we begin working on Comrade Klein's case together," Dupont says, curtly, "and to inform you that I'll be taking a closer look at the scene tomorrow morning, if you would like to join me."

"Of course," Garcia says, reaching up and plucking the bottle from the top of the phone. "The body is being examined by our mortuary team, so we can take a look at the room without having to worry about the smell."

"Quite." A silence hangs in the air over the line, accompanied by the thin crackly hum of a faulty connection.

"I imagine I'll arrive at L'Hôtel San Madelaine at 0900 hours," she says, eventually. If the CMM inherited its reliance on rank from the police force of the old regime, then the Union's blood is thick with the military language of the Communist Revolutionaries that once made up its ranks.

"Alright, I'll meet you there," Garcia says, swirling the last few dregs of beer in the bottle.

She issues a quick, stoic goodbye and her voice is replaced by the droning buzz of a dead line. Garcia hangs the headset back up and returns to his apartment, where the Petrovic Sisters are harmonising their way through *Once More to Kumari Kandam* on the radio. He drains the last of his beer, lies back on the couch, and closes his eyes.

That night in fitful dreams, Pluto Garcia is probed by the magenta eyes of ProbMat.

"In the years following the Violet Revolution, trips to the Madame Syndicat district have been a rite of passage for tourists. The area, named for the patron saint of lovers and iconoclasts, boasts some of the finest eateries, lounges, speakeasies, and brothels in Annalise. Since the district was taken under the formal control of the Guild of Earthly Delights thirteen years ago, Madame Syndicat has become famed for its safe streets, cheap drinks, and slow pace of living."

Adrienne La Rambla, *A Foreigner's Guide to Morrissette*

FOUR

Junior Auditor Esther Dupont is already waiting beneath the headless gaze of L'Hôtel San Madeleine when Garcia arrives.

She is short, with a narrow frame hidden beneath the faded persimmon jumpsuit that over the years has become the standard uniform for members of the Morrissette Shipbuilders' Union. On the right side of her belt she wears a small multitool, a pair of handcuffs clipped to the rear-left. She's some twenty years younger than him, with a mane of frizzy black hair tied back with a beige cord. Something about her pose, her effortlessly straightened back and upturned chin, gives her the impression of an exquisite carving, an intricate and unwavering hickory icon. Garcia emerges from the Vali and groans as his spine straightens out, feeling each vertebrae slot uneasily back into place. As he approaches she offers out a slender hand.

"Pleasure to meet you in person, comrade," she says, attempting a warm smile.

Must have been practising that in the mirror all night, Garcia thinks as he takes her hand.

"Comrade Dupont, I presume?"

"That's correct. And you must be–"

"Lieutenant Garcia, yes," he cuts her off. "You can call me Pluto, if you prefer."

She scans his face for a moment, looking for a hint of irony or humour in his craggy expression.

"Pluto," she repeats. "A nickname?"

"An eccentric mother," he corrects with a smirk. "Did you have any trouble getting here?"

"I was able to get the subway." She glances back at the Vali with an expression of mild horror. "You…drove here?"

"Ah, yeah." Garcia grimaces, scratching the back of his head. "It's not as bad as it looks. Certainly better than walking."

"I see," she says, returning her attention to Garcia. "Have you gone over Agent Dao's notes?"

"Sure, I've skimmed them," he replies with a smile. It is not reciprocated.

"Well," she says in a prim, clipped voice. "I've read them properly. Our comrades at the Bureau are exceedingly thorough."

"It is their job, I suppose."

"I can't say I've worked extensively with them," she replies. "That being said, despite their thoroughness I'm sure you noticed the incongruity."

"Incongruity?"

She is silent for a beat, her eyes scanning Garcia's features intently. When she has ascertained that he isn't joking, she continues.

"Yes." She waltzes past him and over to the Vali, producing a heavy wad of papers from her bag and spreading them out over the bonnet. She points to a line on the second page, the staccato font of the typewriter underlined and annotated with an exclamation point. "It says here that the victim was only seen twice during his stay at the Madelaine, and that he didn't have any visitors. However, simply going by the photographs of the scene, he clearly wasn't starving. During that time, he presumably had food and drink outside of raki and potato chips."

"Sure," Garcia says, looking over the notes again. "Does the Madelaine have room service?"

"I've just asked around inside and it does, yes," she continues. "And if you look here…" She points at the crime scene photo, to a corner of table that could, with a squint, show a used porcelain plate bearing smudges of soy sauce or marinade. "We see that he likely took advantage of that room service."

"So either staff at the hotel *did* interact with him before his death…" Garcia says, the corners of his mouth beginning to curl up. "Or someone *else* brought this food to him."

"Either way, a fact omitted from Agent Dao's notes." Dupont looks up at Garcia, her eyes twinkling conspiratorially. "What else did she omit, I wonder."

Garcia looks down at the notes in stunned silence, the neat bunches of coiled writing lining the margins of each page. He grins.

"You're a good detective, Comrade Dupont."

"Auditor," she replies curtly, gathering the notes. "We prefer Auditor. 'Detective' is the language of the old regime. We try to reject it, where possible."

"Of course." Garcia nods. "My apologies."

"Not required." She puts her notes back in her bag and straightens up. "I apologise for hitting you with that all at once – I've just been stewing on that one detail since you sent the notes over."

She frowns, leaving a small i-shaped crease between her eyebrows.

"I think that there is more to this case than initial appearances suggest. And you are no doubt aware of the," she pauses for a moment, the word resting on her tongue, "*politics* of the situation?"

There's that word again, the filthy pollutant that seeps into every crack of this case.

"I've been in the Militia for twenty-one years, Comrade Dupont. I've learned to sniff out politics and avoid it like the shits."

She blanches slightly at this, holding his gaze with her own steely stare. Eventually, she cocks an eyebrow, nodding towards the lobby.

"And yet here you are. Shall we go to the crime scene?"

"Beats being outside."

The greeter from the previous day is nowhere to be seen, so they make their way through the cool lobby uninterrupted. There is only one patron this early in the morning, a skinny woman dressed in a billowing linen shirt the colour of lapis lazuli, chain-smoking in the corner of the room. An attendant stops them at the elevator, a skinny man dressed in black.

"What floor?"

"Three, please," Garcia says, fishing out his laminated badge and flashing it at the attendant. "I'm Lieutenant Garcia of the CMM, this is Junior Auditor Dupont of the Liberté Enforcement. We're here about Mr. Klein."

The attendant's eyes widen and he steps out of the way.

"Apologies, officers, please go right ahead."

The elevator lurches slightly as it begins its slow climb upwards. Garcia again finds himself looking into his own reflection, like a canary looking to start a fight. He is significantly taller than Dupont, and significantly wider in frame and build. He is also significantly more slouched than she is, his shoulders hanging low and his hands instinctively reaching for his jacket pockets. She, in turn, stands perpetually upright, her nose turned up slightly, her narrow chin jutting imperceptibly forward.

When the doors open the smell of death and chemicals has dissipated slightly, hanging on the air only as memory. Garcia and Dupont are walking to Room 312 when Garcia stops.

"Ah, this," he says, pointing down to the brown smudge on the carpet. "I remember spotting this yesterday."

"Blood," Dupont nods. "Looks like it could be caused by a footprint."

"Hm." Garcia traces the sloping outline of the smear with a finger. "It does. Heading away from the scene."

"That would certainly imply that Klein wasn't alone. That and the fact that the gun is missing." She looks around the corridor. "Are there any other ways in or out? Any fire escapes?"

"There's a bay window in the room," Garcia says, rising unsteadily to his feet, his knees creaking. "But we're four stories up: if the killer escaped that way, we're looking for someone capable of flight."

They continue to the room to find it in its true state, without the psychic quagmire of a corpse drawing their attention. A beige carpet that extends to a white skirting board. Cream walls covered in reproductions of Revolutionary art, frescoes of red and yellow depicting women standing in knee-high grass, their stance proud in the rising sun. A chair stands against the adjacent wall, piled high with discarded clothes the colour of amaryllis flowers. The window is still open, blowing a warm breeze into the room that gently nudges the curtains. In the centre of the room, stark and threatening as an open wound, is a black stain. Dupont sniffs.

"I can still smell it," she says, finally.

"It seeps into the fabric," Garcia replies, patting his jacket pockets. "You want a handkerchief or something?"

"No," she replies, lips pursed and brow knotted. "I'll be fine."

"Alright," Garcia says, stepping into the room. He stands over the mark in the centre of the room, recreating the crime in his head: a bullet is fired, bursting from the left side of Klein's skull before burying itself in the adjacent wall. He follows the trajectory, stepping over the discoloured patch of carpet and padding to the bullet hole. It's barely an inch in diameter, with a mass of thin cracks radiating out like the legs of a spider. Garcia reaches out.

"Could you hand me your multitool?"

Dupont does so wordlessly, placing it in the centre of his meaty palm. He flicks a small penknife out and tentatively pokes it into the wall, the tip of tongue jutting from between his lips. He works the hole a little before gaining purchase, flicking the spent bullet into his hand. A tiny, brassy pellet, all splayed out like the petals of a flower. He inspects it closely.

"Shit," he eventually mutters, softly.

"What is it?"

"This comes from a Moricco 9mm. Looks standard issue," Garcia says, lifting the bullet up. Dupont squints down at it.

"Well, that narrows it down to around eighty percent of the gun-owners in Annalise."

"Including both the Militia and the Union," Garcia says, pocketing the bullet and handing the multitool back. "I'm going to assume Agent Dao realised this and left it out of her notes. You find anything?"

Dupont raises a bulging leather wallet bearing the Union's logo embossed in a deep walnut brown: a wrench piercing the centre of a laurel wreath.

"Whoever killed him left his wallet, along with around two hundred dollars cash." She nods back over to the pile of clothes on the chair. "His house key, identification papers, and pillbox are also still here."

"So it wasn't a robbery." Garcia nods, rising to his feet. Dupont stays quiet, eyes fixed at a point just shy of Garcia's left leg. She raises a hand and gestures to the casefile she'd left on the hotel table.

"Can you pass me the photo of Klein's body? There's something weird here."

Garcia looks at her wide, dark eyes and does as instructed, retrieving the photograph from the pile. He hands it over and she points to the viscous mush that was once Krishna Klein's head.

"He was shot in his right temple, and a bullet was found over there to the right of the door." She points an index finger at the bullet wound before tracing it over to the hole in the wall. "So why isn't there any blood on the wall?"

Garcia chews his lip, looking down at the photograph.

"Clean up?"

"They wiped up the blood and left the body? Seems a bit careless, doesn't it?"

"He must have weighed around two-ten, maybe two-twenty? Whoever shot him maybe tried to shift him, figured he was too heavy, and gave up."

Dupont nods. "Which means they were probably working alone."

"There's also the trajectory," Garcia begins, pacing over to the other side of the stain. He rises to his tiptoes, close to Klein's height. "Guy was six-foot-five. If he was shot in the head while standing up, the bullet would have landed…there." He points in a straight line to a spot a full foot higher than the bullet hole.

"So he wasn't standing when the shot was fired. Kneeling, then? By the door?"

"Or he was shot from a higher angle…" Garcia squints up and to the right of the door, seeing nothing but white coving separating the cream walls from the ceiling. "Though that would put our gunman at around eleven feet."

"If it were a flying giant," she says, humourlessly, "we would have a much easier job."

"Now you're getting it," Garcia says with a smirk.

"According to Agent Dao's notes, there's also a bedroom and en-suite." Dupont points towards a closed door on the left side of the room. "We should check that out too."

Garcia puts his hands in his pockets and gestures with a nod.

"After you."

The smell of death has thankfully not permeated the bedroom. Instead the air in here is the musty, neutral scent of used linen with a faint hint of lavender and bergamot perfume. The thin curtains are drawn, casting the room in a muggy haze that instantly dissipates when they are pulled open. Garcia glances around – more clothes, mostly the practical red of Union attire, a pair of black size fourteen boots discarded in an uneven heap next to a wicker chair.

"Garcia," Dupont says quietly, unclipping her multitool from her belt and flicking the penknife out. "Look."

She points the blade at another bullet hole, around two feet above the bed. She leans in closer, squinting into the dark pin-prick.

"There's no bullet in this one," she says, almost to herself. "We're not on the other side of the wall next to the door, right?"

"I don't think so," Garcia chews his lip. "Someone has taken the bullet?"

"Looks like it," Dupont says, rising up from the bed. "Bureau?"

"I have no idea." Garcia rubs the bridge of his nose. "I suppose the next thing to do is speak to the hotel staff, see if we can put anyone on this floor at the time of the murder."

"Honestly, just having a more precise timeline altogether would be nice," Dupont replies, taking out her red and gold standard issue Union notebook and quickly scribbling a few lines. "Currently I have it down as taking place at some point within the last ten days, which isn't much to go on."

They collect their notes and head out into the hall, calling the elevator and riding it down to the lobby in silence. It's still mostly empty, just the occasional attendant scurrying from kitchen to breakfast bar and the chain smoker in the corner. Garcia and Dupont head to the reception and ring the bell sitting on the desk. After a moment or so, a willowy man of indeterminate age emerges, his lustrous hair styled into an impeccable side parting. He wears a spotless white shirt with a name badge that reads GABRIEL MORETTI – ASSISTANT MANAGER.

"How may I help?" he says, warmly.

"We're with the CMM and EnCorp," Garcia says, producing his badge. "We have a few questions about the recent occupant of room 312."

"I'm sorry, we aren't permitted to give out any details regarding our guests." The man's smile doesn't falter.

"It would be helping with an investigation sanctioned by the Morrissette Coalition," Dupont says, softly.

"Of course," the assistant manager replies. "But as I'm sure you're aware, L'Hôtel San Madelaine takes its position within the

Guild very seriously. Discretion is an important part of our business."

"We understand," Garcia begins, returning the badge to the folds of his jacket and mirroring his smile. "But we *are* working this investigation in conjunction with Mx. Martinez. If you were to contact them, maybe hear it from their mouth…"

"Absolutely." The assistant manager straightens out the front of his spotless white shirt and gives a deferential bow. "I'll be sure to contact Mx. Martinez as soon as possible. If you could come back another time, perhaps we'll be able to help you further."

Dupont bristles, her jaw clenching.

"But you *haven't* helped us–" she begins before Garcia interrupts.

"Thank you, Gabriel," he says, squinting at the man's name tag whilst tugging on Dupont's arm softly. "We appreciate any help you can give us." The assistant manager, still smiling, watches them as they walk to the other side of the lobby.

"Why did you pull me away?" Dupont snaps, chest puffed forward.

"There's no sense getting pissy with the man," Garcia says, keeping his tone level. "He either doesn't know anything or has been told *not* to tell us. And seeing as we're not his superiors, we can't pull rank."

"But you're Militia and I'm an Auditor. Surely that means *something*."

"It does," Garcia says, watching the serving and cleaning staff moving along the perimeter of the lobby, determined to avoid contact with the two investigators. "It means that, as per Coalition guidelines, we're his equal. We're all equal." He casts a hand out, gesturing wildly. "That's the point."

"Be that as it may," Dupont says, her tone softening, "We should have pressed harder."

"He won't talk to you," a new voice, quiet and husky, chimes in. Garcia and Dupont turn to see the chain-smoker, her billowing shirt hitched around her waist with a tight belt. She is holding a cigarette that has been smoked almost to the filter, and as she speaks she brings it to her lips and finishes the final drag. "Someone told him not to."

Garcia smiles, his cheeks and forward creasing as he does so.

"And you are, ma'am?"

"Nadia," she says, her voice still low. "Call me Nadia."

"Who spoke to the hotel manager, Nadia?" Dupont asks, moving in imperceptibly.

"Not sure who, exactly. There were a couple of them. Grey and black suits, I'm thinking Bureau." She finishes the cigarette and flicks it to the floor, where it smoulders against the white marble. "This is about Maria, isn't it?"

Dupont is about to speak when Garcia interrupts, still holding a friendly tone.

"Is Maria in trouble, Nadia?"

The woman flashes a glance back to the reception desk where Assistant Manager Gabriel still stands, his attention fixed lazily on them. Nadia turns back to Garcia.

"We should talk somewhere else. This is a little too public." She checks her wristwatch and purses her lips. "I have to see a John in an hour. Do you know the Boiler?"

Garcia nods, pulling out his notebook.

"Over by Piston Central, right? Past the checkpoint?"

"That's right," she replies. "I can meet you there at 7PM."

"We'll be there," Garcia says, scribbling a few notes down before pocketing the book. Nadia looks back at Gabriel who, now realising that he too is being watched, is polishing the reception desk with a damp cloth. Her eyes meet Garcia's before she turns and strides away, disappearing into the stairwell and up into the labyrinthine body of L'Hôtel San Madelaine. Silence falls over the lobby for a moment, just the distant squeaking of shoes against marble and the unconvincing chatter of Gabriel to anyone who passes. Eventually Garcia speaks.

"C'mon," he says, nodding a cheerful farewell to the assistant manager as he turns to leave. "I know a coffee place near here."

The sky is the colour of faded denim, speckled with white clouds and the occasional sweeping contrail, and Pluto Garcia sips at a cup of coffee. Esther Dupont nurses a cup of tea, black and imported from Funam, as she watches the patrons of Madame Syndicat pass by the window. In front of her, enclosed in its manilla folder and bearing a discrete stamp from the Bureau of Records, is the casefile. Atop that is her notebook.

"It's nice here," Garcia says, eventually, looking around at the other patrons gently chatting amongst themselves. "Haven't been up this way in years."

"Mmm," Dupont hums in vague agreement.

Silence settles over them, the gentle clink of ceramic and the rich smell of coffee drifting on the air around them. Garcia looks the Auditor over. Her brow is slightly furrowed, and her pointed chin rests on the curled knuckle of her index finger.

"Something bothering you, Dupont?" Garcia asks.

"I'm digesting," she replies, not looking at him.

"I find it's easier when you do it out loud," Garcia says with a smile.

"I don't."

"Humour me." Garcia brings the coffee cup to his lips. "What's on your mind?"

"A man who has apparently not been visited by a single person in over a week shows up dead. Whoever did it took nothing but the murder weapon, tidied up after themselves, but left behind a body. The only people who could reasonably help us have been told not to – possibly by a group we're supposed to be working with."

"That's about the long and short of it, yeah," Garcia says, taking a sip.

"You don't seem overly concerned, Lieutenant." At this she finally looks over at him, her carob-brown eyes meeting his.

"Don't mistake patience for nonchalance, comrade." Garcia places the coffee cup down. "I predominately work domestic cases: housing complaints, immigration aid, that kind of thing. I work with *people*. This Nadia seems like a good lead to me."

"And *I*," she responds, tapping the rim of her cup, "work with materials. Evidence, Garcia: something we don't have a lot of right now."

"Then we find some," Garcia says, simply. "Do you have Klein's address?"

"779 Tekhnoplaza, in the Scaffolds." She rattles it off without looking at her notebook. Garcia looks into the still black surface of his coffee, a few clustered bubbles peeking back up at him.

"We have plenty of time before we need to meet Nadia," he says eventually. "We should make Klein's apartment our next stop. See if we can gather any, ah–" He glances up at her. "Material evidence."

"Fine, I'll see if I can pull a favour from the super, get hold of his keys."

She falls silent again, looking back out of the window, her brow knitted and her lips moving silently. Garcia sighs.

"Something's still bothering you, Comrade Dupont."

"It's that woman, Nadia." Dupont purses her lips and returns to staring out the window. "Why did she approach us?"

"My guess? Her concern for this Maria person proved more pressing than her fear of the Bureau." Garcia rubs his chin. "Though I suppose we won't know for certain until tonight."

"Is there a chance it's a dead-end? Or a trap?"

"Have you ever been to the Boiler, Comrade Dupont?"

"No, I don't believe I have," she says, unflinching.

"It's an industry bar – probably sees between fifty to a hundred heads per night." Garcia takes the cup in his hands again and drains the dregs. "If it's a trap, it's an exceptionally bold one."

"I see," she says, chewing her bottom lip thoughtfully. Garcia sighs.

"I understand why it's a concern: things are a little more intense over on the Union quarter. It pays to be cautious." The patch of skull scrambled by Khazi's boys begins to itch. He rubs it softly before continuing. "Have you been issued any Tryp?"

"Yes." She nods, tapping the breast pocket of her jumpsuit. "Hoping I won't need it."

"I hope so too, but it's good to be prepared. Right?" He moves his head to make eye contact with her and she, begrudgingly, reciprocates.

"Right." She lets out a deflated sigh and rubs the bridge of her nose. "Sorry, I'm just – there's a lot to think about, you know?"

"I do." He sits back in his chair. "Have you worked many cases?"

"A couple," she says quietly. "Recovered a stolen tugboat about a year back. Uncovered a smuggling ring operating out of the Shipyard in May. I was only transferred to Liberté recently: I've spent most of my career dealing with drunks on Laurent."

Ah, Garcia thinks. *She's a rig kid. Probably why she was picked for this job: shows enough promise for her to be the sensible choice, green enough on the mainland for her to not get anywhere.*

"You've got the eye for it," he says eventually. "Detective work, I mean."

"Auditing," she corrects him. "And please, don't patronise me."

"I apologise," Garcia says, raising his hands and attempting a weak smile. Silence falls once more, the calm atmosphere of the coffeehouse bouncing harmlessly off smouldering air surrounding Dupont. Eventually she looks up at Garcia.

"So," she says, her eyes cutting through him, "if I've been assigned this case because I'm a new hat, why are you working it?"

Garcia scoffs.

"I never said anything like that," he begins.

"You didn't have to." She gestures to his face with a loose gesture. "You're an easy read. Go on, why are you working the case?"

Garcia drums his fingers on the table. After a moment, he smirks.

"I'm not really a crimefighter," he admits with a shrug. "Always wanted to be one. Grew up on those shitty San Ernesto crime novels. Truth is, they keep me around because I'm good with people. Sympathetic, y'know? Lucky, too." His smirk breaks out into a grin. "But I can't solve a whodunnit for shit."

She softens slightly, looking down from his lined face into her tea. The ambient sounds and scents of the coffeehouse flood over them again, the chatter of people, the hiss of boiling water. Dupont gives a look of feeble embarrassment.

"Look, I didn't mean to cause offence…"

"Good, because I didn't take any," Garcia replies, sincerely. "The Militia has a lot of jobs in Morrissette, but ostensibly we're there to keep the peace. Stop shit from escalating to the point where the actual crime fighters are needed. It's not as flashy as you folks out in the Scaffolds or that shady business they get up to in the Bureau, but it's good work. Important work."

"Do you think this is important work?" she asks, tapping the casefile. Garcia shrugs.

"Someone clearly thinks it is. That's why they don't want us to solve it."

"Do you think we will?"

Garcia thinks back to the hotel, to the statues lining the roof. He only barely remembers what things used to be like, back when the statues still had their heads, back before the good old boys of the Violet Revolution, armed with hacksaws and ropes, set about decapitating them. Daily life recorded on bulky tapes and pored over for any sign of opposition. Dissenters quietly disappeared in the night, dragged out into the docks and never heard from again. People lined up against the walls of what is now the Morrissette Motor Company, handed a final cigarette, and shot. Purity, always purity.

He feels a lurching sensation, that of sliding backwards. He gives a sickly smile.

"Sure."

"When the Republic of Wojtek mysteriously appeared from an adjacent reality in 1876, it brought with it startling technologies that had not been adequately considered by the people of our Prime Reality. Chief amongst them was the Mechanical Enumerator, capable of calculating and processing information at speeds previously considered impossible."

Merlin Kemp, *Computing Review Magazine*
Issue #176

FIVE

Midday, and the Sao-San Valiant carrying Pluto Garcia and Esther Dupont rumbles towards the Scaffold checkpoint. From the cassette player, Lupe Celentano slurs his way through a cover of the Boogie Nelson hit *Seychel, Disco, and You,* accompanied by whining strings and a pounding organ. The warm glow of the sun washes over them, casting the car in gold as Celentano begins the first verse.

"*You're a renegade, babe, that's why I,*" he begins, growling into the microphone, "*am on the run from you.*"

"Forgive me, Lieutenant," Dupont says, her expression not changing, "but this is piss."

"Agreed," Garcia says with a smirk. "His first album was much better."

"Is this always the kind of music you listen to?"

"Saints, no. No, I'm more of a Marco Sanskrit guy."

"I don't know who that is."

"No-one does," Garcia says sagely, his eyes misty, "but he was a classic. He just… He just *got* it, you know?"

"Hmm," Dupont says. Garcia goes on to describe the nuances between Sanskrit's earlier and later work and Dupont, in turn, looks out at the passing city, the grand and illustrious buildings of

Madame Syndicat slowly replaced by the imperious, pragmatic warehouses and mills that line the fringe of the Scaffolds. A couple of kids play by the road with a skinny dog, whipping a rag into the air and squealing with delight as the hound leaps skyward to catch it. They drive past a bar and she watches a handful of smoking Johns, already in the wobbly throes of drunkenness, negotiate cab fare while elegant Guildmembers smile pleasantly, languid and charming in the bright Annalissian light. Eventually, they reach the checkpoint marking the official border between Guild territory and the industrial expanse of the Union. A stocky, full-bodied man with a bushy moustache and dressed in a white shirt with three black stars on the collar stops them.

"Papers, please," the guard says, offering out a gloved hand. Garcia reaches over, flicks open the glovebox and sends the door crashing into Dupont's lap. He fumbles inside for a moment, feeling around the empty cassette cases, thrift store crime paperbacks, and spare stun gun before coming to his papers.

"CMM business," he says, handing them over. The guard scans over the documents, the Militia stamp, the small passport photograph paperclipped to the top. His eyes go from the papers to Garcia, from Garcia to the papers. He lifts a walkie-talkie and mutters something into the receiver, and a moment later there is a crackling reply.

"One moment, please," the guard says, folding the documents and wandering off to the ramshackle security booth sitting between two barriers. Garcia curses under his breath, sitting back in his seat.

"They were fine with them this morning," he mutters.

"The Union is on high alert," Dupont says, casting her eye over the white guardhouse stained black with soot and pollution. "Klein wasn't popular, but he was still top brass. His death has people scared."

"It's been announced already?"

"The Shipbuilders' Union operates on a policy of total transparency," she says proudly. "If a representative of the people dies, Morrissette should know."

"Kamote would be proud," Garcia says, glancing over as Celentano hits the final squealing note of *Seychel, Disco, and You*. "What do we know about Klein? Might help us figure out if anyone wanted him dead."

"Well he's been in the Union since the Revolution. Fought alongside Kamote, was rumoured to have been on the streets when she died." Dupont sits back in her seat, legs curling up and resting her knees on the dashboard. "He was an engineer, started out tinkering with rickshaw designs and fixing enumerators at his old workshop over by Place de Moteur. Eventually worked his way through the ranks until he was hired as a lead engineer under Martin Ergot, before going on to found Ergot and Klein with Martin's son Dean."

"And from there he got picked up by the Council of Representatives?"

"That's right. Chosen out by Khazi personally, or so the story goes."

"Did you know him?"

"Klein? Not really, no. He visited Laurent a couple years back, just a routine thing to make sure we didn't feel abandoned by the mainland."

"What was he like?"

"Controversial," she says, eventually. "Brilliant. Charismatic, though a little unpredictable. When he first started as Union Representative, people *liked* him. He was *cool.* Kind of like this jerk." She points to the cassette player as the next song kicks in.

"What turned people off him?" Garcia asks, chin resting on his fist as he gazes out into the night.

"No one is entirely sure. He became erratic; dour some days, explosive on others. He started neglecting his duties, spending more and more time in Syndicat." She sighs, looking out of the window and to the towering smoke clouds of the Scaffolds. "Honestly, it was kind of always going to end like this for him."

Garcia nods sourly.

"Did he have any enemies?"

Dupont lets out a short laugh.

"Oh, hundreds. Damn near everyone in the Union thought he was an asshole. Which, hey, maybe he was. Doesn't change the fact that he did right by people sometimes."

"That's why people put up with him?" Garcia asks. "Because he did right by people?"

"I imagine people put up with him because he was smart." Dupont looks out to see a Guildmember cross through the other checkpoint, driving back into Madame Syndicat in a sleek Mazo

Firebrand the colour of a misty sky. The Guildmember, plump and pleasant-looking, flashes her a quick smile as she drives by. Eventually, she speaks.

"Have you ever, you know," she asks, vaguely gesturing at the street, "made use of Guild services?"

"Nah, not really my thing," Garcia says, waving at a passing drunk who, in turn, throws both fists in the air and staggers off.

"The Guild?" Dupont asks, looking over at him. He grins, his craggy face exploding into a roadmap of deep creases.

"The sex," he says, candidly. "I like Madame Syndicat, but more for the music, the dancing. Sex just never particularly appealed to me."

"Huh," Dupont responds after a moment. "I didn't expect such an…honest answer."

"It's because I'm a crummy liar," Garcia chuckles. "How about you? Have you ever used the Guild's services?"

"Once or twice," she says, "When I first came to the mainland a couple Liberté officers insisted I take a look, see what I've been missing. Met a few nice girls, had a nice time."

"There aren't Guildmembers on Laurent?"

"About a dozen, but as discreet as they are it's hard to do anything privately over there." Dupont smiles. "It was nice to just let my hair down."

There is a tap on the window. Garcia winds it down and a gloved hand thrusts the papers back at him.

"You're clear," the moustachioed guard says. "Sorry for the hold-up, Lieutenant."

"Not a problem." Garcia smiles, happy to look at a bridge he has yet to burn. "Have a good day."

"You too, Sir."

The barrier arm shudders upward, and the Vali struggles down the narrow streets of Chemin vers L'Industrie. They continue in silence as Celentano purrs his way through the disco ballad *Wasted on the Young,* the lilting horn and jaunty organ coming in just below his raspy, seductive crooning. All around them, the city hums: the Scaffolds are alive, streets bustling with workers, faces and clothes blackened from work, their shadows long and lurching in the radiant sunshine. They pass by Union trucks piled high with textiles, plastics, and lumber imported down from the mountains. The reeling black shape of the Moricco Factory looms over them, its angles strange and alien against the bare sky. Bit by bit the buildings grow taller, more impressive, more industrial, the concrete and brickwork giving way to skeletal grids of rebar and wiring. Passing by the narrow alleyways of the Charbon Commercial Quarter, Garcia catches the briefest flash of red – a lean shape dressed in blue jeans and a bomber jacket, immobile amidst the bustling crowd. He flashes a hurried glance back to see an empty alley, little more than blue shadows cutting through hazy yellow sunlight.

The Tekhnoplaza Accommodation Block stands in the hurried heart of the Scaffolds, a brutalist wedge shaped like the gnomon of a sundial. Dupont presents her papers to the guard, an old man with the sort of thick, wrinkled skin one might expect to find in a tannery, and they pass into the concrete avenue leading to the building proper. They pull into the concrete car lot, settling the groaning Vali in the white grid and stepping out into the sun. Garcia removes his jacket and leaves it on the driver's seat, two dark sweat stains forming beneath his arms. Dupont gestures with her head and, dutifully, he follows.

In the apartment foyer she excuses herself, dipping off to speak with the Union supervisor in the hushed tones of a practised Auditor. Garcia, in turn, thrusts his hands in his pockets and glances around. Unlike his ramshackle pre-Revolution apartment at South Seychel, Tekhnoplaza is a brand-new building, a testament to the Scaffold's – and by extension, Morrissette's – economic stability in a post-Kamote world. Thick pillars of concrete hold up a white grate ceiling, the dull grey of the walls offset by the chairs that line them manufactured in yellow, red, and blue plastics. On the far wall hangs a framed photograph of Kamote herself, standing on the barricade, cigarette held between her smirking lips. An unusually human visage for a Revolutionary martyr, indeed, but these are unusually human times.

"I got a spare key," Dupont says, jangling the keychain off of her finger as she approaches. "We should head up."

They ride the elevator to floor seven, opening out into a corridor eerily similar to the foyer they just left: concrete walls, grated ceiling, and a tiled floor patterned with large circles set at even intervals. They count down the doors before coming to 779. Dupont enters the key and, with a satisfyingly mechanical *clunk*, the door swings open.

The first thing they notice is the noise. It is constant and permeating, the quiet metallic hiss of several fan blades spinning at once, the low steady hum of dreaming machines. They line the walls, great awkward towers of blinking lights and weaves of multicoloured wire relaying arcane thoughts from one body to the next. The curtains are drawn, letting in only the occasional thin shard of blinding light and casting the room in a sort of grey-blue darkness.

"Incredible," Dupont says, quietly. Garcia looks around, feeling the muggy heat leaking out of the machines and over his damp skin.

"What are they?"

"It looks like he built a supercomputer." She walks around the perimeter, looking through the clear glass casing of each machine and peering at the intricate system of coils and cathodes, the neat gridwork of circuits and breakers, the tight banks of bright-coloured switches in a variety of configurations. She follows a trail of heavy cables to a rumbling engine suspended in a blocky aluminium case, and nudges it with her foot. "Hooked up to a personal generator. Probably so it doesn't drain energy from the whole damn block."

Garcia looks around. The rest of the room is sparse – a coffee table bearing a stack of notebooks all written in the same untidy hand; a couch occupied by several obscure computer manuals, crinkled white paper marked with technical drawings annotated in black ink; a mug filled with coffee crusted over with a thick, furry mould. He turns back to Dupont.

"But *why*?"

"What do you mean?"

"Why go to the trouble of building this?" Garcia gestures with an open hand at the huddled mechanisms praying in hushed tones all around him. "He ran Ergot and Klein, right? They *make* computers. Why have this kind of set-up at home?"

"A hobby?" Dupont replies weakly. "I don't know, this seems pretty consistent with what I know about Klein. Brilliant but erratic engineer, possessed by occasional maddening throes of genius."

"You think this was a passion project?"

"I don't know. Could have been a thought exercise." She flashes a look back at him, eyebrow cocked and sharp. "What are you implying?"

"Nothing in particular." Garcia scratches the base of his neck, looking around. "It just feels like there's something going on here, right? I mean, I like my job but it's not like I take paperwork home with me."

"So what, you think he was building this in secret?"

"Could be," Garcia says, flicking through a legal pad filled cover-to-cover with intricate equations and diagrams. "Look, I'm not an expert in any of this shit. We have one computer at the Tank, and it's easily coming up to its tenth birthday. It just strikes me as weird that a guy working at the biggest computer manufacturer in Annalise would make something of this scale in his apartment."

He stops on one page. At the top, written in black ballpoint ink half-scrawled onto the page, is a single word. ARGUS. He hands it over to Dupont.

"Does this make any sense to you?"

"I can take a look, but I'll be honest: computers aren't my strong suit." She scans her eyes over the page, flipping over to the next and doing the same, before looking up with a shrug. "I have no idea. It looks like plans for a new processor, maybe an upgrade to the Ergoteck Unity he designed back in '86. Beyond that, I don't know."

"Who could we talk to in order to find out more?"

"Best guess would be Dean Ergot."

"Klein's partner, right?"

"In a manner of speaking, yes. Ergot deals more with the business side of things."

"Any chance it was him who killed Klein?"

"It's possible, I suppose. Though he's quite famous – the chances of him getting in and out of the hotel without being noticed are slim to say the least." Dupont purses her lips and furrows her brow. "And based on what I've seen in his files, it seems out of character."

"You have files?" Garcia asks, eyebrow cocked.

"Mmm." Dupont nods, flicking through another notebook. "On loan from the Bureau of Records. I put in a declassification request when you faxed the casefile over. Why? Don't you?"

"Like I said, we deal with domestic affairs. Spy-work isn't really my thing." He picks up a technical manual and finds much of the same; dense scribbles spiralling out from mechanical drawings, impenetrable diagrams detailing recherché machines of unknowable purpose. "Think you can get us an audience with Ergot?"

"Leave it with me," she says, reaching into her jumpsuit and producing a palm-sized pocket camera, a small rectangle of cardboard and plastic striped in Union colours of crimson and violet. "In the meantime, I should probably get some photos of all this. Even if this is all above board, it'll be useful to refer back to."

"Agreed." Garcia nods, looking over to a closed door. "I'll go check out the rest of the apartment. With any luck there'll be a signed confession from the killer stuffed under his mattress or something."

Dupont points the camera at the bank of computers and pushes down on the plunger, sending out a sharp *snap* and a burst of white light. She repeats this a few times with the notebooks and manuals as Garcia pushes through into a dimly-lit bathroom. A thin patina of mould creeps up the adjacent wall, and the white tiles are stained a gentle pink by a film of mildew. Garcia glances around: single bar of soap rests on a stand in the shower, beginning to mulch in the standing water; a three-blade disposable razor covered in miniscule black hairs sits on a hollow by the sink; a trashcan overflowing with discarded dental floss, band aids, tissue paper, and box after box of standard-issue Repodimethyltryptamine.

Next up is the bedroom. The bed hasn't been made, creased plum sheets sit in an ugly heap atop a bare mattress, bedclothes scattered across the floor and draped over the back of a rattan chair. The requisite framed picture of Kamote hangs lopsided on the pale green wall, her smile queasy and seasick. On the bedside table stands an exhibit to a strange life: a short tumbler with less than a millilitre of colourless booze; a cigarette lighter and a half-burnt cone of incense; more impenetrable notes, hastily scribbled on the back of crumpled receipts; a bottle of pain medication, an over-the-counter opioid common in Madame Syndicat; all centred around a book, an ancient, yellow-paged thing with a faded cardboard cover. Garcia picks it up.

The cover is striking: a featureless beige background gives way to a wash of cobalt blue watercolour in the shape of a towering wave. Atop the foaming water, rendered in exquisite blacks and greys, is a young woman, a native Annalissian with ink-black hair flowing in an undulating stream around her narrow head. In her arms she cradles a rabbit, silk-white and wide-eyed, swaddled in a peacock-patterned cloth that flutters up into the air, and in the background a wooden freighter filled with screaming passengers tumbles amidst the crashing surf. Above all this, written in the striking style of the Laccannesse barbarians, are the words "FOLK

TALES OF THE ANNALISSIAN ARCHIPELAGO", and below it all in a small, tight script: "Retold by Yasmin Papoutsis-Coulson, Illustrated by Amelia Lechner."

Garcia opens the book carefully, feeling the well-bent spine crease in his hands as he flicks through page after page of illustrated whimsy: frogs morphing suddenly into pale handsome princes, a milkmaid consulting with a rooster and a basset hound beneath a pale moon, a great and terrible boggart leaping out from behind a gnarled oak tree. He comes to a dog-eared page stopped by a bookmark depicting a sea otter rising out of the still waters of the Baratte, a look of keen-eyed concern on its furry face. In the margin, written in the same unsteady hand as the notes, is the word "PIETNERA" surrounded by floating question marks. He reads for a moment before returning to Dupont.

"Did Klein have any kids?"

"No," Dupont says, winding the counter wheel of her camera with her thumb. "Unmarried, no immediate family. Why?"

"He had this kid's book on his bedside table. Looks pretty well-loved, too." He offers the book out and, pocketing the camera, she takes it, flipping through the pages.

"I think I had the same book back on Laurent. Slightly newer edition, though."

"He'd marked out certain stories, too. There's a bookmark in there on a story about an otter."

"Hmm," she says with a strange smile. "Oszkár the Otter, an old Laccannesse folk tale." She stops at the page bearing the otter's head poking from the water and points to the word written in the margin. "Huh."

"What is it?"

"Pietnera is an island southwest of Morrissette. Tiny place, I don't even think anybody lives there." He flashes a puzzled look at her and she shrugs irately, passing the book back. "I learned to sail when I was at college. Spent a lot of time in the archipelago."

"You're a woman of many talents," Garcia says, turning the book in his hands. Dupont, unamused, nods curtly. She gestures to the room.

"Anything else in there?"

"Nah, just a messy bed and some more programming notes. Couple of empty boxes of Tryp in his bathroom. Do we have everything we need?"

"Sure." She stuffs her hands into her pockets and looks around. "Might as well submit the storybook and some of these notes for evidence. Not a lot to go on, but I guess we've killed some time."

"Speaking of," Garcia says, glancing at his wristwatch, "with traffic it'll be about an hour to get to Piston from here, and I wouldn't mind grabbing something to eat. Got any preference?"

"I'm not hungry."

"Very well," Garcia says with a grin. "Junk food it is."

"Wipe that blow from your nose,
Dry your eyes, strike a pose,
You're dancing now, dancing now,
Plus rapide, plus rapide."

Lupe Celentano, *Plus Rapide, Plus Rapide*

"There are few things worth importing from the noble lands of Karnassas. Its music is dismal, its literature overly verbose and terribly dreary. Its politics are several hundred years out of date, as is its language. But its beer? Why, its beer is some of the best in the known world."

An ill-fated advertisement campaign for Kosmos *brand lager.*

SIX

The sun has dipped below the horizon, and the hazy blue of twilight is pierced by the occasional passing headlight. Heat radiates up from the soft asphalt, baking the underside of the car and leaving the air feeling sticky and damp. With weary eyes and a belly full of kebab meat, Pluto Garcia drives Esther Dupont through the winding streets of the Scaffolds.

Eventually they come to the intersection between Chemin vers L'Industrie and Piston Central, a crowded crossroad of noise and light teeming with honking cars and red-clad Union members, flanked by huge, commanding spires and luminous electronic billboards. The Boiler sits on the eastern edge of the intersection, an inconspicuous abandoned factory of red brick, bearing only a single buzzing neon sign marking its presence. Garcia pulls the Vali up to the curb and the two step out, looking up at the building. Along the western edge, a faded mural reads "TO EACH MAN, THE SPOILS." Above this, two square-jawed, dark-haired men rendered in red, yellow, and black paint stare proudly off into the distance, their strong arms around one another's shoulders. Dupont nods up at it.

"There's a similar one on the Laurent," she says. "Always found the language a bit exclusive."

"I get you." Garcia scratches the back of his head, squinting up at the two figures. "Especially given that the Revolution was started by a woman."

"Exactly," Dupont exclaims. "Camille Kamote would spit if she saw this."

"Spit? She'd burn the fucking place down." Garcia grins. "What time is it?"

"19:07," Dupont responds, looking down at her watch. "We're late."

"It'll be fine, no-one shows up on time at the Boiler." Garcia thrusts his hands in his pockets and walks towards the entrance. Dupont glances back quickly.

"Are we okay to leave the Vali here?"

"Eh, more than likely," Garcia says with a shrug. "They might be notoriously easy to hijack, but nobody ever wants to hijack them. C'mon, I'll buy you a beer."

The interior is a loud, throbbing mess of steel and concrete, filled with muscular labourers and the occasional impeccably dressed Guildmember. A bar has been set up on the mezzanine, and Garcia and Dupont push through the throng to reach it.

"Two Kosmos, please." Garcia places five dollars down on the bar and smiles as the bartender, a squat man with a shaved head and dusting of stubble, winks and heads over to the fridge. Garcia turns back to Dupont as her eyes scan the crowd. He watches her reach into the left breast pocket of her jumpsuit and pull out a slim red pillbox, cracking it open and taking an acid yellow pill in her hand. She surreptitiously pops it into her mouth and dry swallows before looking over at Garcia.

"Feeling paranoid, Auditor Dupont?"

"Just in case," she says as the pill makes its way down her throat.

Garcia nods, looking out over the bar patrons, tapping his fingers on the bar in time with the music. "Any sign of Nadia?"

"Over there," she says, standing on her tiptoes and pointing into the bar below. "On the left, by the dance floor."

Garcia looks out and sees her, sitting alone at a table, nursing a beer. He squints before turning back to the bartender.

"Sorry, can you make that three Kosmos?" He gives an apologetic shrug and the bartender, muttering under his breath, procures a third bottle. He sets them down, slick with condensation, as Garcia slides another two-fifty over the bar. He collects all three bottles and the two set off down the cast iron stairs towards the dance floor.

"You're late," Nadia says as they approach.

"That's Scaffolds traffic for you." Garcia sets the drinks down on the table, removing his rumpled suit jacket and running a hand through his messy hair. "Bought you a drink to apologise."

She stares at the beer bottle before bringing her gaze slowly up to Garcia. Her eyes are wide and smoke grey, and her dark hair falls straight down over her narrow shoulders. She has changed from the billowing blue shirt into a black blouse buttoned up to her throat, tucked into a pair of denim bell-bottoms. She reaches out a slim hand and takes the beer.

"Forgiven. For now," she says, no hint of a smile on her face.

"So." Dupont takes a seat beside Garcia and leans forward slightly. "Maria."

"Maria," Nadia says with a dry, humourless chuckle. She reaches into her pocket and produces a gas lighter and a packet of cigarettes – a red and white cardboard cube bearing the word "VANGUARD" in gold leaf, an import from the United Republic of Wojtek. "Do either of you mind if I smoke?"

"Not at all." Garcia waves a hand. She lights a cigarette and brings it to her lips, breathing deeply.

"You're sharpers, aren't you? Detectives?"

"In a manner of speaking." Garcia gestures between himself and Dupont. "I'm Lieutenant Pluto Garcia of the CMM, my colleague here is Junior Auditor Esther Dupont of EnCorp. Does that change things?"

"Not particularly. I'm just glad you're not Bureau." She exhales a cloud of smoke and sits back in her chair.

"You said they spoke to the hotel staff?" Dupont asks, swilling the beer bottle slightly.

"I think so." Nadia nods. "Came in not long after you arrived this morning. Spoke to Gabriel, the assistant manager, all stern-like. I just stay at the hotel, so they left me out of it."

"What do you think they were talking about?"

"You," she says, flatly. "Though to be honest, I've been seeing them sniffing around the hotel for just over a week now. Figured it was something to do with," she says, gesturing vaguely, "you know."

"Maria?" Dupont says again.

"Maria."

"Who is Maria, exactly?" Garcia asks, his tone casual and reserved.

"She's a Guildmember. We've worked together at San Madelaine for about three years now."

"May we ask about her role within the Guild?"

"Sure, we're not bashful." She smirks, taking another long drag and letting the smoke leak from her nostrils. "She was a sex worker. Escort, more often than not, but would occasionally have specific clients she had sex with."

"And you think she's involved with…" Garcia mimics her vague gesture.

"Maybe." Nadia shrugs. "All I know is that one day she was at the hotel acting cagey, then the next she'd disappeared and the shit had hit the fan."

"What was she cagey about?" Dupont asks. Nadia goes quiet for a second, looking down at the beer bottle before her. She purses her lips.

"I wish I knew." She sighs eventually. "She'd mentioned that things were getting intense with one of her regulars, some Union guy, but she didn't go into details."

Dupont leans forward, her eyes narrowing slightly.

"Did she tell you his name?"

"We work for the Guild, Comrade." Nadia flashes a practised smile. "We don't give out our clients' names."

"Of course," Garcia interjects, diplomatically. "And we would never pry–"

He is cut off by Dupont.

"Klein," she says. "His name was Krishna Klein, wasn't it?"

Nadia's eyes widen and she sits back, going silent. Garcia takes a sip of his beer and inhales slowly, breathing in the smell of stale booze and cigarette smoke. Dupont continues.

"I understand your discretion, Nadia. It's an important part of your job." She sets her beer down. "But Krishna Klein is dead. Murdered, we think, and it's our job to find out who did it and why."

Nadia stares at Dupont in silence, shaking her head softly. Her mouth opens slightly, cigarette clenched between two trembling fingers. Garcia also leans forward, his forehead wrinkling.

"It doesn't look good, does it?" he says, his voice now soft and sympathetic. "Some hot shit at the Union shows up dead around the same time Maria goes missing. The Bureau get involved, and that gets *us* involved…"

"Maria didn't do anything," Nadia objects, weakly.

"Maria fled a crime scene," Dupont replies.

"Maria didn't do anything," she repeats, more firmly this time. "She isn't that kind of person. She's smart, too smart to get herself caught up in something like this."

"Be that as it may," Garcia says, raising a hand, "we still have to talk to her. Maybe you're right, maybe she doesn't have anything to do with this. But if one of her regular Johns shows up dead, it's important that we hear her side of the story."

Nadia falls silent, the thrumming bass of a disco track pulsing through the air around her. The cigarette between her fingers has burnt down to the filter, a smouldering white tip that she flicks into the ashtray.

"I don't know where she is," she says, eventually. "I promise you that. She's not at home, she's not been to the hotel, or any of the bars she works out of. I've asked around the Guild and no-one has seen her."

"Do you know where Maria lives?" Dupont asks. Nadia eyes her suspiciously.

"You going to ransack her place?"

"Not if we can help it," Garcia says, soothingly. "We simply want to ask around, chat with her neighbours."

Silence again. Nadia chews her lip, looking between Garcia and Dupont with her wide grey eyes. Beyond her, a steady stream of Scaffold labourers have taken to the dance floor, awkwardly swaying and nodding their heads in time with the music. Garcia attempts a sympathetic smile.

"Please, Nadia."

Finally, she assents.

"She lives at 673, Gatineau North. Near the Jardin Communautaire."

Garcia nods, taking out his notebook and jotting the address down in pencil.

"I think I know it," he says, pocketing the notebook as Dupont drains the last of her drink. He leans forward in his seat, speaking softly. "Look, if Maria is caught up in something… We'll help her get out of it. However we can."

"And the Bureau?" Nadia's voice is sharp now, intense.

"Like I said: I'm with the CMM and Comrade Dupont is with the Union. Until they directly involve themselves, this has nothing to do with the Bureau."

"Okay," she says, finally, eyeing them as she reaches into her pocket and produces another cigarette. "Is that everything?"

"It is for now, yes," Dupont says. "But we may still have further questions. What's the best way to contact you?"

"I come here most evenings," she says, a thin filament of smoke trailing from the corner of her mouth as she speaks. "And I can give you the number for my apartment, if you need it."

Garcia nods and slides his notebook over to her. She scribbles the number down and hands it back, her expression somewhere between stoic and exhausted.

"If that's all you need from me," she says, exhaling a plume of blue-grey smoke that drifts up to the ceiling, "I'd like to be left alone."

Garcia drives the Vali through the winding streets of the Scaffolds as Dupont checks her notes in the passenger seat. All around them the factories lie silent, their floodlights illuminating the cadaverous silhouettes of cranes, static as sleeping giants.

"Want to know what I think?" Dupont says to no one in particular.

"What's that?"

"I think Nadia's hiding something from us."

"Oh?" Garcia says, eyes fixed on the asphalt ribbon stretching in front of him, pock-marked with oil stains and chewing gum smuggled over the Madame Syndicat border.

"Think about it," Dupont continues, tapping a pen against her teeth, her body coiled up between the seat and the dashboard. "She knows that the Bureau is involved, and she's smart enough to know that the Bureau has agents in the other Coalition groups. She wants to keep Maria safe, and so far she doesn't know if we can be trusted."

"As far as she's concerned, we *can't* be trusted," Garcia says with a shrug. "The Guild prefers to deal with these things in-house, so the fact we've been brought in at all is a red flag."

"Mmm," Dupont murmurs in agreement. "And then there's the fact that we're different agencies."

Garcia glances over at her.

"What do you mean?"

"We-ell," Dupont speaks slowly, "how well do we actually know each other? For all I know, you *could* be a Bureau agent. Same goes for me with you. Between you, me, and Nadia, we just end up with three people, none of whom is capable of trusting the other."

Garcia's brow furrows as he stares at the road. After a while, he speaks.

"You know, this is what ended up toppling the old regime." Wave after amber wave of light shines over them from passing streetlamps. The cassette player is switched off, Celentano having run to the very end of his spools, leaving only the inconsistent rumbling of the Vali's engine. "The secret police got to the point where they couldn't trust anyone, not even themselves. They spent so much time crossing and double-crossing one another, by the time the Revolutionaries came they had no way of fending them off. No solidarity."

He smiles to himself, his voice growing soft.

"Trust is a practical thing, you know. It has a purpose, a function. In an ideal world, each part of the Coalition would place trust in one another, and in turn Morrissette would place its trust in us."

Dupont looks over at him.

"What are you saying?"

"I'm saying," he says, carefully, "that I trust you. And that if we're going to work on this case, I'd like it if you could trust me too. Once we have that, Nadia and the people like her will have more reason to trust us." He chuckles softly. "The secret police are gone now, sure, but scars like that take a while to heal."

He keeps driving, turning off from Rue d'Arbitage to the coastal road leading up to Mechanograd, where atop the black water the oil rig looms. He drives a little further, turning onto the pragmatic grid of Union-sponsored housing that is the Warrens. He pulls into a wide, concrete courtyard lit by gangling iron streetlamps painted a dull, faded red. Dupont steps out of the car and leans through the open window, wearing a soft, strange expression.

"Thanks for the lift, Pluto," she says.

"Don't mention it." He flashes a grin back at her. "I'm planning on going to the Icehouse to check on Klein's toxicology report in the morning. I'll fax anything over to Liberté when I get the chance."

"I can come with," she says. "I handed over all my other cases so I can concentrate on this one."

"Well alright then," Garcia says, rubbing his eyes with the heel of his hand. "Meet you there at 9?"

"Sure." She slaps the roof of the car and smiles. "You get home safe, okay?"

"I intend to. It's been a long day."

She nods a quiet goodbye and heads into the concrete sprawl of the Warrens. Garcia ejects the tape, coils it back with the end of a pencil, and drives back to South Seychel while *Plus Rapide, Plus Rapide* plays.

"Once ingested, Repodimethyltryptamine remains within the patient's system for a total of twenty-four hours. Should their vital signs cease at any point during these twenty-four hours, the patient's conscious mind will vacate the body and travel across the Probability Matrix to the nearest reality in which a still-functioning similar brain resides. The assimilation process – that of two minds melding into a singular entity – is invariably considered a traumatic experience, and as such death under the influence of Tryp should be avoided if possible.

The Voidt-Hart Foundation, *Tryp: A Post-Mortem Experience*

SEVEN

Morning comes to the Republic of Annalise, bringing with it the unforgiving glow of the sun.

Pluto Garcia stands in his boxer-briefs, inspecting his wardrobe: three pairs of near-identical high-waisted slacks in varying shades of brown, eight short-sleeved shirts, plus one white shirt with a slight yellowing on the collar for formal occasions. Hung up on the door, a single beige suit jacket, his summer jacket. Somewhere at the back, neatly folded and forgotten, is his official CMM jacket: navy blue with two red stripes on the right arm, the insignia of the Revolutionaries emblazoned over the left breast pocket.

In the end he opts for a floral shirt two sizes too big tucked into his pants and, anticipating the coming heatwave, forgoes the crumpled suit jacket. He pockets his key card, a couple dollars in change, and the ID badge he'd left on the arm of his couch. Ready, he slips his shoes on and heads downstairs, the smell of fried breakfast and laundry detergent mingling in the air around him. He reaches the front door, already having worked up a mild sweat, when he spots the kid with the dyed, coiffed hair. The kid flicks the Vs up at him and he, in turn, grins.

"How's the indigestion, sharper?"

"Pretty good, I got these pills for it. You're up early."

"Doing laundry for my ma," he says, pointing back to the washroom. "I asked around after that creep up at the Prom, by the way. Apparently my man Suda saw some *hayop gago* hanging around the dock, acting shifty-like. Says his name is Nanti Bukowski."

"Huh," Garcia says, rubbing his chin. "Red bomber jacket?"

"Yeah, Suda figured he was just *tulak-droga* selling speed or some shit. You say you wanna ask him some questions?"

"Yeah, we figure he's involved in some shit is all," Garcia says, shrugging and scratching the back of his head. "Thanks, I appreciate you asking around. I'm Garcia – you ever need something, I'm up at 237."

"Scud, 241" the kid replies, offering out a hand. Garcia awkwardly shakes it, feeling its slight clamminess against his palm.

"241? Your mom is Marcie, right? Marcie Bautista?"

"That's right," Scud replies, bringing his hand back to rest clumsily in his pocket. "How'd you know?"

"I worked her immigration case a couple years back. Didn't realise she had a kid, is all."

"Eh, I only just got here." He gives a disaffected teenage shrug. "Lived with my dad back in Funam Province, finally saved up enough to move here."

"You got your papers sorted?"

"Almost." He sniffs. "Just waiting on the CMM."

"Yeah, we're a little understaffed in the admin department." Garcia winces, heading back out into the foyer. "Leave it with me, I'll chase up some of the guys at the office. You tell Marcie I said hi, okay?"

"See you round, sharper," Scud calls after him over the distant rumble of the washing machine.

Garcia cuts through the Waterfront district, winding his way towards Estuary West. Along the way he grabs a donut from a street vendor and eats it as he walks, each step trailed by a swarm of squawking, amber-eyed gulls. He tosses the crumbs of pastry and sugar out behind him, watching them descend into a screeching sphere of feathers and violence, grinning to himself as he deposits the greasy paper into a trashcan. On the water, fishmongers sell fresh produce from their creaking wooden boats, stalls glistening with vibrant striped mullet and fat, heavy yellowfin, scallops still lining their shells and sitting plump and pretty in the sun. The smell of salt floats upwards, washing in with each pulsing wave as the water crashes against the concrete foundations and sends sea spray rising into the air.

Garcia crosses a thin, rickety jetty from one side of the estuary to the other, dipping off to one side to let the occasional fisherman squeeze past in their canvas salopettes. By the time he reaches the Icehouse it is just shy of 8:45, and the sun glinting off of the water has pulled a thin patina of sweat from his forehead. He looks up at the building for Precinct 9: a hunched structure of brown brick, whitewash, and plate glass, a sun-bleached CMM stencilled above the door in yellow paint, the northern face lined with blocky air conditioning units. He heads into the Icehouse, where he is greeted by a broad woman with a shaved head and bright eyes. She thrusts out a hand and Garcia happily shakes it.

"Good to see you again, Lieutenant Garcia."

"Right back at you, Sergeant Navarro. How's the wife?"

"Unfailingly patient," she says with an impish grin. "You still living over at Block Vingt-Neuf?"

"I am. It gets great sunlight in the mornings, really wakes you up." He follows her through the precinct, feeling a slight chill wash over him as his skin acclimates to the air conditioning. "You've been looking after our mutual friend, I assume?"

"As best we can, though he was in pretty bad shape when we picked him up," she says, leading him through to a breakout room. There are a handful of militiamen scattered around, playing cards and smoking, poring over paperwork. In the corner a fax machine buzzes, printing out details sent in from the third precinct, lists of disturbances that need addressing and the like. A coffee machine softly gurgles to itself like an unattended infant. "Can I get you anything?"

"Just a coffee," Garcia says. "I've arranged to meet a Union Auditor, Comrade Esther Dupont – any sign of her?"

"She's already in there with Doc Vincent." Navarro chuckles. "Pretty uptight, isn't she?"

"That's the Union for you." Garcia grins. They head over to the machine and pour two cups of thick, black coffee. Garcia blows before taking a long, grateful sip. "God damn, that's good shit."

"San Ernesto," she says proudly. "Captain Freigeld paid for it out of pocket."

"I need to get Marchenko on this," Garcia says, holding the cup in both hands, letting the warmth soak into his palms. "You been busy?"

"Ay, you know it." Navarro leans in, eyebrow cocked. "Some horse cock over in La Lavage got his boat stolen and won't stop riding our ass about it."

"Ah, Gallardo mentioned that – he called the Tank too."

"You're kidding?" she exclaims, shaking her head. "It was just a shitty fishing boat! He could get another from Place de Moteur just by trawling the scrapyard!"

"Sentimental value," Garcia flashes a wry smile. "I hate our Vali with a passion, but if that old fucker ever got stolen it would be like losing an uncle."

"That old thing still works?"

"Barely." Garcia finishes the coffee and pours himself a second, listening to the machine hiss and sputter as the cup fills. "It broke down on Eddie a couple weeks back – completely shit-canned, right on Rue D'Ecoulement, ended up having to call in a favour just to get it towed out to the shop."

"Ay, we need to get new vehicles." She shakes her head. "Our old skiff is on her last legs, and apparently the Vali up at the Docket is little more than a spark plug with wheels these days."

"Ah, I dunno: I quite like walking. Keeps me close to Morrissette, and it's better than taking a streetcar." He gestures towards the morgue. "I'm gonna go check on Dupont, make sure she's not bothering the doctor."

"Have fun, gumshoe," Navarro says with a grin.

Unlike the ramshackle shipping containers of Precinct 13, the Icehouse is a sturdy, stalwart structure, an old storage warehouse ceded to the Militia from the Packing District for the purpose of storing bodies ahead of an autopsy. Garcia works his way down the winding corridors, padding the familiar beige carpet pocked with cigarette burns, before eventually coming to the chrome double doors marking the entrance to the morgue. He pushes through and sees his breath hanging in the air before him.

In the centre of the room, laying flat on a stainless-steel table, is Krishna Klein. In this sterile environment he looks all the more lurid, his vibrant purple skin glaring against the spotless white and shining metal of the morgue. On one side he sees Dupont, jumpsuit collar pulled up around her neck to keep the cold out, her hair tied in a kinky bun atop her head. On the other side he sees the proud, narrow features of Doc Vincent, a tall woman with deeply tanned skin and ink-dark hair.

"Morning, Lieutenant," she says, cheerfully. "I've just been going over my initial findings with Comrade Dupont."

"Alright." Garcia approaches the body, the warmth of the coffee in his hands the only thing stopping him from bursting into a fit of shivers. "What've you found, Doc?"

"It's difficult to say." Vincent chews her lip, looking down at the body. "Lividity was already pretty bad when he arrived, so I can't say for certain that he hadn't sustained bruising before he died. That said, he doesn't have any signs of cuts or abrasions, so a struggle seems unlikely."

She traces a finger over the left side of his head.

"This is, predictably, what killed him. Bullet entered the right temple, exited the left. There's some slight charring reminiscent of a muzzle burn, but again: it's difficult to say for certain given how badly degraded the corpse is. The bullet itself seems to have passed clean through."

"That makes sense," Dupont says, looking over at Garcia. "We found a Moricco 9mm casing at the scene."

"Seems pretty consistent with this mess," Vincent says, nodding down to the corpse. "Beyond that, no other signs of major wear and tear. He seemed to be in fairly poor shape for his age, but nothing especially noteworthy. Liver damage, that kind of thing."

"Toxicology?" Garcia asks. Vincent takes out a clipboard and scans her eyes over it.

"He was practically a one-man pharmacy," she says grimly. "Alcohol, amphetamines, antacid, benzodiazepine, a couple different types of painkiller, some residual cocaine."

"Any Repodimethyltryptamine?"

She pauses, going over the list again.

"Huh," she says finally. She looks up at Garcia. "No. No Tryp at all in his system."

Garcia falls silent. He chews his lip, his brow furrowed. Somewhere in the infinite stream of realities, countless Krishna Kleins continue to live their lives; all of them bar this one. He turns to Dupont.

"You said he had his pillbox when you searched his things, right? Were there any pills left?"

"Three, by my count. And you said there were some empty boxes in his apartment," she says. "So he *had* Tryp, he just didn't use it."

"Meaning he wasn't expecting to die." Garcia takes a sip of his coffee, his mind turning a single thought over and over, working at it the way a dog works at a gristly piece of meat. He looks up at Vincent. "Thank you, Doc, you've been incredibly helpful."

"Don't mention it." She turns to Dupont. "We're happy to keep hold of the body for now, but I imagine the Union will be wanting to work out funerary arrangements fairly soon."

"I'll speak to Comrade Chang at the first opportunity," Dupont replies, business-like. "Thank you again, Doctor."

The two leave in silence, Dupont lowering her collar, Garcia cupping his coffee in both hands. Eventually she turns to him.

"You first."

"So," Garcia says, pacing down the corridor, "he was high. Dressed in underwear and nothing else. Someone comes in, puts a gun to his right temple, and pulls the trigger. Given that he wasn't wearing clothes, we can assume he either wasn't expecting company or was expecting company that wouldn't mind seeing his johnson."

"You're thinking Maria."

"I never said that," Garcia says sternly. "But yes, it crossed my mind."

"And he didn't have any Tryp in his system." Dupont scratches her neck absently, looking down at the floor. "So he either wasn't expecting this visitor, or he didn't think they would kill him."

"Looks that way." Garcia lets out a long, deflated sigh. "We should try and track down Maria."

"Should we go to her apartment?"

"Seems as good an idea as any. Maybe there'll be a clue as to where she's gone." They come to the breakout and Garcia places the mug in the sink. He runs the faucet and lets the water sluice over it before turning it up and swilling a little. "Any luck getting us an audience with Ergot?"

"Afraid not. Like I said, he's a busy man. Not the kind of person you can pull rank on."

"Figures." Garcia purses his lips as he sets the mug back in the drying rack. "Well, we might as well check Maria's apartment in the meantime and hope that his schedule clears."

"Agreed." Dupont nods. "Did you bring the Vali?"

Garcia winces and gives an apologetic shrug.

"Sorry – it's back at Precinct 14."

"No problem," Dupont says, shivering slightly. "A walk might help to warm me up."

It takes them just over half an hour to walk to the Tank from Estuary West. Panting and sweat drenched even in the early heat of the morning, they push through the heavy reinforced oak doors to find it mercifully air-conditioned. At his desk, Manny Gallardo pores over delivery receipts.

"You here for the car?" he asks, not looking up.

"Yes indeed, Cadet."

Manny reaches into a drawer and fumbles for the keys, eventually snatching them up and tossing them to Garcia, who catches them limply.

"Thanks, Manny." He spins on his heels before catching himself and turning a full one-eighty. "Actually, could you do me a favour? I need details on a guy called Nanti Bukowski."

"This the guy from Promenade de Gloire?"

"Possibly, yes."

"I'll add it to the pile, Lieutenant," he says, scribbling a note down on a scrap of paper.

"Thank you, Manny. I'll split my next beer import with you."

Gallardo raises a single thumb, head still buried in paperwork. Garcia grins and turns to leave, unlocking the car with a disconcerting *clunk* and beginning the drive into Madame Syndicat.

"What was all that about?" Dupont asks as they pass the Casa checkpoint. "Back at the Tank?"

Garcia feels a tightness coil around his lower back and his body clenches imperceptibly.

"Ah, yeah. There was an attack over on Promenade de Gloire the other night. Some guy with a knife – we're just keeping an eye out for him, that's all."

"Seems a little out of your wheelhouse, Lieutenant. I thought you worked domestic cases."

"I do. When an attack like this happens, it's usually part of a mental health crisis or an ongoing addiction. If that's the case, the CMM likes to check it out, make sure everyone involved is safe. If not: referral to Dubois General."

"I see." She scans his face closely. "And that's everything?"

"Everything that's important, sure."

"All right, then."

She falls silent as they pass into Jardin Communautaire. Densely packed apartments and hotels give way to long, open streets lined with elm, plane, and sycamore trees that droop in the midday sun. Beyond them the rolling hills of Morrissette drift upwards, bearing a patchwork quilt of community gardens that stretch out to the distant city limits. Garcia drives with the window down, breathing in the closest thing Morrissette has to clean air. In the allotments, sinewy labourers sow seeds and harvest vegetables where bombs once fell, their skin tanned varying shades of brown, pink, and red. Bushels of wildflowers grow in roadside fringes; small, hardy things the colour of fine silk and honey.

"No cassette today?" Dupont muses, looking out at the greenery. Garcia chuckles.

"I felt you could do with a break," he says. "Why, do you miss it?"

"Not in the slightest." Dupont turns her nose up, a slight smirk on her lips. "Do you have any Marco Sanskrit?"

"Me? Sure, I have a whole five-cassette collection back at my apartment. You looking to get into the classics?"

"I just figured he'd make a nice change from Celentano."

"Agreed," Garcia says with a wide grin. "I'll bring a cassette tomorrow."

Dupont stares lazily out of the window, her breathing slow and rhythmic. Garcia glances over.

"Everything okay? You seem quiet."

"Mmm," she says with a small smile. "I didn't sleep so great last night. Crazy dreams."

"That'll be the Tryp," Garcia says, checking his wristwatch. "Got a good nine hours left before it leaves your system, too. You going to be alright?"

"Sure, fine." She rubs her eyes, pausing for a moment before continuing. "Have you ever trypped before?"

"Three times." He nods solemnly. "It's awful."

"It's incredible," Dupont says, softly. "A drug that lets you cheat death, and we all agree that it's a terrible thing."

"It doesn't let you cheat death," Garcia replies. "You get back up again, sure, but you still die." He wags a finger in the air. "*That's* the part that sucks."

"Change is always difficult," Dupont says, vacantly. "Why shouldn't changing bodies be any different?"

Garcia smirks over at her.

"You get philosophical when you're sleep-deprived. What did you dream about?"

"You don't want to hear that." She chuckles. "Talking about your dreams is the least interesting thing a person can do outside of talking about politics."

"Not at all!" Garcia exclaims. "Both dreams and politics make excellent talking points. Doubly so when they overlap."

"Alright, alright." She grins, rolling her eyes. Her gaze softens as she looks over the passing flowers. "I don't exactly *know* what it was about. I just… I got this feeling like I was being watched. No, like I was being *seen,* like something was devoting its attention to me. As if I was being scanned, understood, assessed by these huge magenta eyes."

She falls quiet as they drive through the meandering streets of Jardin Communautaire, the distant sound of chittering birds in the trees only just audible above the Valiant's snarling engine. Dupont looks over to Garcia in the driving seat.

"Told you it's boring," she says, smiling. Garcia shakes his head.

"Not even slightly. It's strange, is all."

"Dreams tend to be, don't they?"

"True," Garcia says with a small shrug. He glances up at the sun, feeling the strange tightness of his retinas closing as he looks into the light. When he closes his eyes, he sees a vast magenta cigarette burn imprinted on the inside of his eyelids.

Gatineau North sits on the eastern fringe of Jardin Communautaire, a bank of lean sandstone buildings with dark windows and ornate frontage draped in ivy. It is beautiful, evidence of a different world and the lives lived within it, a world in which people free of labour grow blissfully still and bask like cats in the sun. A world of leisure, open to all. Garcia grabs his ID as he and Dupont step out of the car.

"673, right?" Dupont asks. Garcia checks his notebook.

"Yes, Ma'am," he says, squinting up at the building. "Let's hope the elevator works."

They enter the building lobby and find, to their chagrin, that it doesn't. They head to the stairs and pace up them, Garcia beginning to pant with exertion around the second floor and Dupont joining him around the fourth. By the time they reach the sixth, both are covered in a thin coat of sweat. They pause for breath, Garcia almost bent double as he hungrily swallows oxygen. Dupont places her hands on her lower back and inhales deeply, her eyes scanning the stairwell walls. She nods to a piece of graffiti, scrawled in shaky black spray-paint.

"'With many eyes I see', huh?"

"What was that?" Garcia pants, looking up. He spots it, secreted about half a floor up and a couple feet out from the stairwell. "Well I'll be damned."

"What?" Dupont asks, glancing back at him.

"I saw the same graffiti out by the Tank a couple days back."

Dupont cranes her neck to peer out into the stairwell, scanning the graffiti.

"Huh. Think it's important?"

"I'm not sure," Garcia says, leaning on the guardrail to get a better look. "Gives me the creeps, though."

"What?"

"I dunno," he says, absently. "Feels like it's following me, is all."

Dupont turns to look at him, an expression of blank bemusement on her face.

"Garcia," she says simply, "it's graffiti. It's not following you. Probably just some new L'Anormal thing, like when they started writing "SHIT PIG'S GOT LEGS" on old government buildings."

"Could be," Garcia says, finally looking away. "I'll ask Scud the next time I see him. C'mon, let's go check out this apartment."

Dupont gives the graffiti one final look before continuing down the hall after Garcia, passing wooden doors painted a royal blue, eventually coming to apartment 673. Garcia tries the doorknob.

"Locked," he says, turning to Dupont. She purses her lips, looking at the doorframe before reaching for the multitool clipped to her belt. Garcia watches on as she effortlessly taps the hinges loose, sliding them out and setting them neatly to one side. She then hoists the door up and slides it clear of the lock, resting the door up against the wall. She returns the multitool back to her packet and looks over at Garcia.

"Would you like to go first?"

Garcia looks through the open portal in bemusement.

"Are you going to put the door back when we're done?"

She shrugs.

"I'll certainly try."

Garcia grins and reaches down for the stun gun resting on his right hip. He steps softly into the apartment.

"Maria?" he calls out. "This is the CMM, are you in here? We just want to talk."

Silence. He looks around – a deep crimson rug, woven in the Sarinetti style, covers aged pine floorboards stained with the occasional fleck of white paint. The hallway opens up into a tidy sitting room, forest green walls decorated with ornate mirrors, picture frames, and plants dangling from macramé cradles. In the centre of the room a coffee table of mahogany and smoked glass – an antique – holds up an incense holder in the shape of Madame Syndicat herself, her eyes turned skyward in beatification. Around this, an old armchair with tattered upholstery and a tired-looking couch are positioned. He tries again.

"Maria?"

Nothing. Dupont follows, hand on the Moricco 9mm resting in its holster. She looks around.

"She's not here," she says eventually, kneeling down to inspect the coffee table. She traces a finger around the incense holder, catching a smear of sweet-smelling ash on her finger. "Left in a hurry, I'd say."

Garcia proceeds from one room to the next, peering around. A dining room table set with a single placemat; an empty liquor bottle being used as a candlestick holder, crusted with drippings of wax; a print of Camille Kamote, mass-produced and set in a gilded frame above the radio. In the bedroom he sees a bed, hastily made up in mustard sheets, a seldom-used mosquito net suspended from the ceiling above it by a bamboo frame. In the bathroom a variety of shampoos, perfumes, tinctures, and lotions line a bathtub the colour of oxygenated copper. A faucet drips periodically, the water splashing into a sink. Garcia opens the medicine cabinet to find two boxes: one of high-strength painkillers, half full; the other of Repodimethyltryptamine, both blister packets missing. He picks up the box and inspects it – retail pack, sold at quite the expense by only the most boutique drug pushers. Without the subsidised deals guaranteed by the Militia or Union, a single eight-pill pack of Tryp can easily come to three hundred dollars. He places the box back and returns to the sitting room.

"Find anything?"

"Only this." Dupont lifts up a laminated card. "Guild ID. Turns out her full name is Maria Melnyk. Born March 2nd, 1972."

Garcia looks over the card. There, amidst the tidy black writing and above a looping signature, is a photograph: a slender, pale face dashed with faint freckles, a proud jawline that slopes into a narrow chin. Huge, hazel eyes set beneath heavy lashes and a wash of straight, mousy-brown hair, her lips twitched ever so slightly upwards into a comfortable smile.

"She won't get far without it." Garcia sniffs. "She'd get stopped at the first checkpoint."

"Which means she's presumably still in Madame Syndicat." Dupont takes out her notebook and slots the ID card between the first two pages before returning it to her pocket. "Did you find anything?"

"She has Tryp," Garcia says. "Over the counter stuff. Left the box behind, along with some painkillers."

"How did she get Tryp?"

"Who knows? All sorts of shit passes through Madame Syndicat. The question is, why does she think she needs it? Sex workers have been pretty safe since the Guild took over."

"True." Dupont purses her lips. "I mean, she must have known that there'd be an investigation? That's why she left town in the first place, right?"

"Sure, but the Militia hasn't killed anyone in over twenty years, Dupont. Same goes for the Union, to the best of my knowledge."

"You think she's worried about someone else?"

Garcia chews his lip before giving a weak shrug.

"I have no idea."

"Come on." Dupont sighs, glancing around the room. "Let's see if we can find any indication as to where she—"

There is a moment, a fleeting cosmic ache, and for less than a second Dupont's world goes purple. Her back straightens, her eyes shoot wide open, her heart pounds. Throughout her vascular system capillaries squeeze shut, rerouting blood from her face to the sinewy network of muscles in her arms and legs. She screams.

"Down!"

Her arm shoots out and she drags Garcia to the ground as the world immediately above her head explodes. A thunderous shockwave rings out as the bullet crashes into a nearby mirror, sending shards of sparkling glass flying across the room. Dupont crawls on her elbows and knees to the armchair and Garcia, ignoring the tightness in his lower back, follows. She props herself up against the legs of the armchair and reaches for her pistol, feeling its weight in her hands. Her jaw is clenched tight, the muscle visibly twitching through the skin.

"We're with the Liberté Enforcement Corp!" she calls out, her voice breaking ever so slightly. "Drop your weapon or we will be forced to return fire!"

Through her ringing ears she hears the sound of footsteps followed by a short, sharp scream coming from down the hall. Garcia rises to his feet, helping her up. He may have said something but she cannot hear it, not clearly. He gestures and she follows, gun held tightly in both hands. She glances quickly into the hall and sees a shivering man, a skinny thing of maybe twenty years, pointing to the door leading out into the stairwell.

"They're getting away!" she yells over the fading ringing of her ears. She sprints down the hall, Garcia following closely behind her. She looks into the downward lattice of stone stairs, eyes frantically scanning for movement. Footsteps echo up from below and, her mind racing, she follows the sound down the stairs and out into the street just in time to watch Precinct 14's Sao-San Valiant drive away. She curses, running a single hand through her hair as she watches it spin around a corner and into the twisting heart of Madame Syndicat.

She feels her periphery closing, her line of sight narrowing into a pinprick haloed by darkness. Her body lurches as a sickening headache, the sensation of her brain being shattered by shards of cranial bone, reels over her. She hears Garcia, distant and muffled, through the sound of her own head exploding.

"Dupont, are you alright?"

Before she can respond, Esther Dupont blacks out.

EIGHT

Somewhere, in an adjacent world.

"Come on." Dupont sighs, glancing around the room. "Let's see if we can find any indication as to where she–"

A burst. A violent, hellish burst, ripping through the drywall and soaring through Maria Melnyk's sitting room, all sound and fury, hot as the wrath of God. Miniscule shavings of metal sail alongside it like the rings of some alien world, burnt coils of shrapnel invisible to the naked eye. She looks up just in time to see it. The bullet.

It makes contact in her left cheekbone, knocking her sideways in a spray of plaster dust, and blood. She goes to scream but can't, the pain ripping through her like a lightning bolt, disconnecting the foreground of her mind and replacing it with sheer hot, animal agony. As her functions slow and her neurons begin to shut off, the Repodimethyltryptamine still lingering in her system begins to activate. Synapses fire on a quantum state, feelers reaching out over the breadth of possibility, seeking connection, seeking warmth. Her senses begin to dilate into a single string of experience, smell and texture and sound and sight become one prolonged input. Carpet. Pain. Screaming. Pain. Drywall. Pain. Blood. Pain.

Magenta.

Somewhere, in an adjacent world, Esther Dupont dies.

"Our stakes are forever lowered, and yet we play the game all the more."

Nibiru Atreides, *Camille Kamote: An Unofficial Biography*

NINE

White.

That's the first thing she sees as her eyes struggle open. A white expanse, featureless and plain. Winter, 1978, her eighteenth birthday. She'd driven north, out of Morrissette to the footlands of Montetrieste, where the stark black shape of the Rampart mountains rise up into a crowded grey sky. The snow was uncut, marked only by dark, bare tree trunks that wavered in the wind.

It takes her a moment to realise she is looking at the ceiling of Maria Melnyk's apartment.

"Welcome back, comrade," a voice says softly. She looks up to see Garcia sitting on a wicker chair, one leg crossed over the other, a pair of half-moon spectacles perched on the end of his nose and a pulpy crime novel scrounged from one of Melnyk's bookshelves in his lap.

"I," she begins, her throat hoarse. There is an acrid smell in the air undercut by the smoky scent of sandalwood. "I didn't know you wore glasses..."

"I'm an old man," he says, taking them off and secreting them in a soft case that he returns to his breast pocket. He waves the book cheerfully. "How are you feeling?"

"Dreadful," she says, propping herself up on her elbows. She looks down at the bed – crumpled yellow sheets and a stained oak frame, a few loose springs poking into her back. Her head throbs. "What happened?"

"You trypped," Garcia says, placing the book down. "Someone shot at us. You managed to duck just in time, though I figure another version of you wasn't so lucky."

"What's that smell?" she croaks, her throat stinging. Garcia winces.

"Ah. You threw up. Don't worry – you didn't get much on yourself." He gestures at the thin smoke hovering in the air. "There are spare clothes at the Tank, and in the meantime I cracked a window and burned some of Melnyk's incense."

"Mmm," she says, lying back. "Water?"

"There's a glass on the bedside table. Take your time with it, you're still adjusting to your new motor functions."

She scans over her new hands, noting the subtle differences from the pair she'd left behind. A freckle on the knuckle of her left pointer finger that had previously gone unnoticed is now hyper-conspicuous in its absence.

She shudders, sitting up and reaching for the tumbler to her left. She brings it slowly to her lips and feels the cool, slightly tinny water wash down her throat. She drinks half in one gulp before pausing for air, then returns to finish it off in slower, more reserved sips. She sets the glass down and lies back on the bed, groaning softly.

"Better?"

"Not especially," she says, bringing a hand to her head. She winces as her palm touches her damp forehead, half-remembering the sensation of her neurons being severed in an instant by a bullet. She feels her stomach lurch at the memory and manages to lean over the side of the bed before throwing up into a waste paper bin.

"It's called a ProbMat Hangover," Garcia says. "The residual memory of dying, translated across the Wider Probability Matrix and into your new limbic system."

Dupont pushes herself up and wipes her mouth on her sleeve.

"It's fucking awful."

"It is. Would you like some of Melnyk's painkillers? It's the least she can do, seeing as you got killed in her apartment."

Dupont nods weakly and Garcia rises to his feet. He walks through the sitting room, pausing briefly to assess the carnage. A fist-sized hole in the wall peers out into the hallway, enclosed by a web of fractured plasterboard. The floor is littered with dust and shards of glass that erupted from the gilded mirror, and the impact caused by the bullet has knocked the neatly-arranged cluster of paintings askew. He sucks his teeth and continues through to the bathroom, grabbing the painkillers from the medicine cabinet and returning to find Dupont sitting upright, hand on her head. He hands the box over and she pops a couple pills out of the blister pack.

"Thank you," she says, choking them down with the last dregs of water. She blinks and rubs her eyes before looking up at Garcia.

"There was a man," she says, distractedly. "In the hallway."

"I spoke to him while you were out. He heard the gunshot and came out to see what was going on. Saw the shooter run past; didn't get a good look at their face but he saw the gun."

"Don't suppose it was a Moricco 9mm?"

"He didn't say. I'm planning on checking out the bullet hole before we leave, see if it matches the one left at the hotel." Garcia cocks his head to one side and examines her face closely. "You alright?"

She stares down at her boots, her headache subsiding from a violent drumming to a low, aching pulse. Her breathing is slow, as if each inhalation and exhalation requires her immediate concentration.

"Does it get easier?"

Garcia looks down at the floor, looking at the whorls and blemishes in the wood, the scratches and pockmarks where dropped items have chipped the varnish.

"First time I died," he says, "I was sent to a therapist. I was living by the Pallias river, back in Karnassas. Took a shitty job unloading cargo to get through the winter, working for a shady type who'd gotten his hands on some knockoff Tryp. There was a flash flood and I drowned. Came to with just enough time to get away from the riverbank, but I was shot to shit: I kept missing time, having nightmares, convincing myself that my lungs were filled with water. Hell, I forgot my damn birthday.

"Figured that the worst of it was caused by the shitty Tryp I'd been taking, but trauma rewrites your brain pretty bad, so I ended up going to therapy. My doctor was this old-school Yemelenovian academic type – lot of tweed, Wojtecci accent, big old eyebrows like a pair of caterpillars – and he taught me about affirmations. Reminding myself who I am, where I was born, that kind of thing. Then the *next* time I died… Well, it still wasn't easy. But that helped to ground me a little."

Dupont continues to stare down at her boots, her hands trembling slightly in her lap. Garcia continues.

"Start small. What year is it?"

"1994."

"Good. What's your name?"

"Esther Dupont."

"Excellent. Where were you born?"

"Dubois General Hospital."

"Great, you're doing great. Where do you live?"

"Mechanograd, in the Scaffolds."

"What do you do?"

"I am a Junior Auditor with the Liberté Enforcement Corp."

"Good work. Try focusing on just that for now."

"The year is 1994," she says, quietly. "My name is Esther Dupont. I was born in Dubois General Hospital, December 4th, 1960. I live in Mechanograd. I work for the Liberté Enforcement Corp. The year is 1994…"

She continues for a moment, quieter with each repetition until only her lips move. Her headache dulls into a low, buzzing static, the white noise of a radio between stations. When she raises her eyes from her boots, there are tears in them.

"Thanks, Pluto."

"Don't mention it," Garcia says with a smile. "How are you feeling?"

"Okay," she says, wiping her eyes off on her sleeve. She sniffs sharply before throwing her feet over the side of the bed. "I ought to stand, my back is starting to cramp. Melnyk favours aesthetic over comfort, I think."

"How do you mean?"

"This bed feels like it has a couple springs loose or something." She pushes down, feeling the obtrusive shape beneath her palm. Garcia scratches the back of his head.

"Ah, sorry. Should've made sure the bed was comfortable before putting you on it."

"No, no, it's fine, I appreciate it." She pushes down a little more, inspecting the mattress with her fingertips through the bedsheets. "There's…something…"

She falls silent, brow furrowed as she pulls back the sheets to investigate the bed closer. She stands, wobbling slightly before steadying herself and peeling the mattress protector back to reveal a long, ugly scar cut into the fabric of the mattress and haphazardly sewn back up. Garcia watches on as she fumbles for the multitool on her belt, flicking out a small penknife extension and wordlessly dissecting the seam until two flaps remain. She pulls them back and the smell of stale blood fills the air. She reels back and Garcia, hand over his nose, grimaces.

"Dear God! What is that?"

They peer into the entrails of the mattress like seers seeking augury, finding a scrap of cloth amidst the grid of rusted springs and stuffing. Garcia reaches in and plucks it out, holding it between his finger and thumb and letting it dangle in front of them. A nightdress, flimsy and translucent, little more than a trail of white silk stained with brown dried blood.

Garcia rifles through the draws under Maria Melnyk's sink before exclaiming loudly.

"Ah!" he cries, pulling out a thick, green plastic bag. "It's not perfect, but it will do for now."

He returns to the bedroom and deposits the dress into the bag, squeezing the air out and tying the top shut.

"This is what we would do in the old days, when the Militia had only just started up and we didn't have the budget for evidence bags." He offers the bag up proudly to Dupont, who sits in the wicker chair with a bashful look on her face.

"I'm sorry about the Vali," she says, nails idly scratching at a strand of rattan.

"Eh, couldn't be helped," Garcia says with a shrug. "All you need to hijack a Valiant is a thin piece of metal and about eight seconds."

"But it had your evidence bags, your spare stun gun…"

"Not to mention Eddie's Celentano cassettes… He's going to be pissed."

She looks up at him incredulously. A piercing stare, effortless and penetrating. A gumshoe stare. Garcia buckles.

"Alright, yes. It's not ideal. I'm probably going to be in the shit when I get back to the Tank. But you had just trypped into a new body and I'm not exactly known for my sprint." He leans against the wall, shoulders slumped, one hand fiddling with the key card in his pocket. "Frankly, losing the car is nothing compared to getting shot at."

Dupont rises to her feet.

"I suppose so." She nods down at the bag. "Is that everything?"

"Just got to check the bullet hole and then we can head back to the Tank."

"I've got my papers on me, so we should be able to cross the checkpoint." She pats her breast pocket. "Do you have money for a taxi?"

"Got a couple dollars for a rickshaw," Garcia says, checking his wallet. Dupont nods and they head into the sitting room, Garcia awkwardly tucking the plastic bag into his back pocket. As her eyes meet the ugly puncture in the adjacent wall, Dupont's pulse begins to pick up. She spins on her heels and looks out into the hallway.

"Could," she begins, stifling the urge to throw up again. "Could you handle this?"

"Of course, you go wait outside if you need to."

She nods hurriedly and rushes out, the sounds of her footsteps quieting as she races down the hall. Garcia stands eye-level with the bullet, taking out his penknife and, just as he'd done in room 312, slowly levers it out. The plaster cracks and crumbles, and it takes him a few attempts before it pops out with a soft *twing* into his palm. He raises it up to the sun and inspects it closer, turning it back and forth in the light. A small, tarnished flower, thick fleshy petals of brass extending forth from a cylindrical stem. He looks back at the hole in the wall where the gun had been fired through, holding the bullet up against it. After a moment, he pockets it and heads out to the stairwell to find Dupont.

"Well?" she asks.

"Looks like a .44 Magnum. You can't fire a round this big out of a 9mm, so we're probably looking for a hunting pistol of some kind, something with stopping power. Fuck knows how they got hold of it."

"Wait," Dupont says, looking up. "It's a different weapon than the one that killed Klein?"

"Sure looks like it," Garcia says grimly. "Which means that if Melnyk fired *that* bullet, someone else probably fired this one."

Dupont stares down into the stairwell, chewing her lip as she thinks.

"That'll be why she has Tryp on her," she eventually says, looking back to Garcia. "Someone is chasing her."

"Someone with access to an old hunting pistol, no less."

"Who, though? I thought all the old Magnum weapons were melted down after the Revolution."

"Most were," Garcia says with a shrug, leaning back against the guardrail. "A couple were kept as heirlooms, souvenirs, that kind of thing."

Dupont goes quiet, looking down into the stairwell again. After a second or so of silence she points towards the door.

"Come on, we should go. We have a lot to do."

The rickshaw ride back through Madame Syndicat towards the Waterfront is about as quiet as such a ride can be. From the relative tranquillity of Jardin Communautaire to the bustling leisure district of the Old Quarter, through the narrow streets of the Casa and past the checkpoint into the salt-bleached sprawl of the northern packing district, neither Garcia nor Dupont say more than a few words each. By the time the rickshaw pulls up to the Tank, the sun has begun its slow crest downwards to the horizon. Garcia hands the driver the fare, waves him off, and looks up at the blue and black metal exterior of the Tank.

"Ready?" Dupont asks.

"No," he replies.

They head inside, finding Manansala at the desk. He peers over his glasses at them both.

"Ah, gumshoe! And this must be Comrade Dupont. First Lieutenant Eddie Manansala, it's a real pleasure to meet you."

"Not for long it isn't," she says softly under her breath. Before Manansala can respond, Garcia bursts.

"I lost your tapes."

Eddie stays perfectly still, his eyes fixed on Garcia. His face, usually contorted into a wry smile, is neutral. He lets the silence linger in the air, the unsettling quiet of an impending castigation.

"You lost my tapes," he says, simply. Not a question. An assertion of fact.

"Yes."

"My Lupe Celentano tapes."

"I'm sorry, man."

"The ones I had imported from Lacan."

"I can buy you new ones."

"Is this about Sanskrit? Are you making a point?"

"Hey, come on, let's not do that again–"

Manansala slams a hand on the desk, his voice raised ever so slightly.

"Lupe Celentano is the single greatest pop musician of all time, and you lost my god-damned tapes!"

"We lost the Vali too."

"You lost the Vali?!" He throws his hands up in the air. "Ay, Pluto, what the hell man?!"

"It was hijacked," Garcia says, limply. "We were in Syndicat, investigating this Union case. Someone shot at us, Comrade Dupont trypped here from another reality, and by the time we caught up with the shooter they were driving off in the car."

Eddie falls silent, his eyes staring up at the ceiling. He removes his spectacles and rubs the bridge of his nose.

"Well. Looks like we're walking from now on." He sighs and turns to Dupont. "How are you feeling, Comrade?"

"Better. Lieutenant Garcia was very helpful in keeping me calm."

"That makes a change," he says, looking back at Garcia. "Does the Guild know about the shoot-out?"

"Not yet, I'm planning on calling them now."

"And does the captain know about the car?"

"No."

"Ay, well, she's got the day off so you can tell her yourself tomorrow." He pulls out his notebook and flicks through the pages of blue chicken scratch before stopping on a half-filled page. "Oh, call came in for you earlier. Agent Anne Dao from the Bureau of Records, she asked if you could call her back."

"I'll get right on it. Is there anything else?"

"Manny thinks he's tracked down that Nanti guy you were looking for. Real name Jonah Bukowski, lives over at 187 Centre de Paix, Place de Moteur." He roots around his desk, shifting his spectacles up his nose as he pulls the files together. "Turns out we picked him up a couple months back for unlicensed graffiti."

Garcia takes the file and looks it over. Pinned to the top right corner there's a small square photograph of a young man, defined jaw and mop of unruly black hair falling over his slim, dark eyes. A thin, ratty moustache lines his top lip, and a single glinting stud hangs from his left earlobe. His expression is a queasy one, not quite a smile, not quite a sneer, cheeks and forehead shiny with sweat. Garcia feels that tell-tale grip around his tailbone and shudders.

"Do we know where he works?" he asks. Manansala shrugs.

"Contractor, I believe. Takes odd jobs around the Scaffolds, unskilled labour gigs mostly. Moricco, Ergot and Klein, Kusunoki Inc., that kind of thing."

"Great, thank you Eddie." Garcia jots the name down and underlines it. "I'll head over to Place de Moteur at some point, see if I can find this guy."

"Exercise some caution, please. At some point you have to consider that your luck is fine, and that you're just a dumbass."

"I'll be careful, Eddie."

Eddie Manansala looks over the second lieutenant, his creased shirt tucked into beige pants, his crop of shaggy salt and pepper hair falling over blatantly tired eyes. He looks over Dupont: drooping, fidgety, the faint smell of almond soap not quite covering the lingering scent of sick. He sits back in his seat.

"You two should probably head home. It sounds like you've had a day of it."

"Not yet, Sir," Garcia says, reaching into his back pocket and producing the plastic bag. "I have to call Dao and we still have evidence to log."

Manansala's eyes pass over the bag and he gives another exasperated sigh.

"Fine. I'm going to be here another couple hours – come get me when you're done, you both look like you could use a cigarette."

Dupont raises a hand in objection.

"I, ah–" she says. "I don't smoke."

Eddie's face returns to its usual resting smirk.

"When my uncle trypped he woke up able to speak a new language. Who knows? Maybe the new you has a smoking habit." He gestures towards the twisting corridors of the Tank with a flick of his head. "Now get going. I have paperwork to sort through."

"Is it the boat guy?"

"It's the boat guy, yes."

Garcia chuckles, patting Eddie on the shoulder as he passes.

"I got shot at today and you're still having a shittier evening than me."

"Eat shit, Lieutenant."

Garcia stands before Precinct 14's phone, directory open on the desk before him. He dials the number for the Bureau of Records and navigates through the automated call-in system, pushing buttons to forward himself through its robotic gauntlet. Eventually, a human voice asks for a name and Citizen Identification Number, which he dutifully rattles off. The voice then asks for the nature of his call and, upon hearing Agent Dao's name, the line goes dead with a sudden click, replaced by a low, electric whisper. He hangs up with an exasperated sigh, only to leap backwards when the phone rings.

"CMM Precinct 14, Lieutenant Garcia speaking."

"Thank you for calling, Lieutenant," the clipped tone of Agent Anne Dao purrs.

"I got your message. What did you want to speak to me about?"

"One of our operators mentioned that you and Auditor Dupont have been hoping to speak with Comrade Ergot, over at Ergot and Klein."

"That's correct," Garcia says, shuddering at how this information came to rest in the capable hands of the Bureau.

"You'll be pleased to know that the Bureau of Records has gotten in touch with Comrade Ergot and, how do you say..." She pauses for just a moment. "Pulled some strings."

"Oh?"

"Yes. If you'd still like to speak with Ergot, he will be free tomorrow morning, 9AM onwards."

"Very gracious of you, Agent Dao. Has the Bureau spoken with him already?"

"No. As per the Coalition's directive, the Bureau is leaving this investigation to the Union and CMM. I'm sure you understand."

The spectre of politics buzzes down the line and Garcia shudders again.

"Of course. The CMM thanks you for your cooperation, Agent Dao – we'll speak with Comrade Ergot at the earliest convenience."

"You are most welcome, Lieutenant." She pauses and, for just a second, there is a faint smile in her voice. "Goodbye."

And with that, the line goes dead again. Grimacing, Garcia sets the receiver down and closes the directory, padding through the narrow corridors of the Tank towards the locker.

The Precinct 14 evidence locker is a small, cramped room lined with filing cabinets, drawers, and safes loaned from the Bureau of Records. Dupont sits hunched over the one desk in the room, meticulously filing the dress. Spread out in front of her is the evidence logged so far from the case: the crumpled 9mm Moricco bullet; the wallet owned by Krishna Klein, embossed with the Shipbuilders' Union logo and complete with his Ergot and Klein ID card; the two crime scene photographs collected by the Bureau, stark carnage in black and white; more photographs, developed the previous evening and displaying bank after bank of impassive, murmuring computers; a storybook of Annalissian fairy tales, the word PIETNERA written in its margins. To this she has added the .45 Magnum bullet, Maria Melnyk's ID card, and the dress, transferred into an official CMM evidence bag, striped white and red like a Laccannesse barbershop pole.

Dupont does not look up from the assembled evidence as he enters.

"What did the spook want?"

"We have an audience with Dean Ergot. Tomorrow morning, 9AM."

Her eyes dart up towards his.

"Seriously?"

"Looks that way."

"Well, that's good. Right?"

"Esther, I wouldn't trust the Bureau of Records to set up a food stand, let alone assist in an investigation like this." He gives a pained shrug. "However, we *could* use the help."

Dupont looks back down at the table, eyes flashing over each item, each jagged jigsaw piece, her brow knitted as she moves her lips silently. Garcia sits by her side.

"What're you thinking?"

"I don't know," she says, finally. "This is a mess."

Garcia props his chin up on his laced fingers.

"Let's go over the facts first. Krishna Klein was shot and killed in a hotel room in Madame Syndicat. Now that we have the dress from Melnyk's apartment, we can reasonably assume she was there when this happened."

"Right," Dupont continues. "The fact that Klein didn't have Tryp in his system suggests he wasn't expecting to die. Given that we've found an empty box of Tryp in Melnyk's apartment, we know that she was."

"And finally, whoever killed Klein used a different bullet than the one fired at us, implying that it's either two shooters or one shooter with two guns."

Dupont stares at the collected evidence in silence. Garcia cocks an eyebrow.

"Okay," he begins carefully. "*Now* what are you thinking?"

"This is guess work, but..." She points down at the photographs of Klein in the hotel room. "Krishna Klein had been soliciting Maria Melnyk for some time – maybe from the beginning of this bender, maybe preceding that. Things grow increasingly intense, and Maria expresses her concerns to her friend Nadia. One night that intensity becomes too much too handle. Melnyk shoots Klein in the head using a service pistol – possibly Klein's – and flees the scene, leaving the bloody footprint we found in the corridor.

"She gets back to her apartment in Gatineau North and prepares to leave Morrissette. She sews her bloody dress into her mattress – suggesting she had both the foresight to hide any evidence of her direct involvement with the crime *and* the time to do so – grabs whatever Tryp she had left in her apartment, and bolts, leaving behind her ID." She stops, looking up at Garcia. "How does that sound?"

"It all makes sense." Garcia nods, lips pursed. "But if she left her ID behind she won't be able to get past any checkpoints, meaning there are two possibilities: she was either smuggled out, or is still in Morrissette."

"Then there's also the matter of the second shooter." Dupont points to the .45 bullet, its tip blossoming outward like a kernel of popped corn. "Do we think that was someone covering Melnyk's tracks for her?"

"Could be." Garcia nods. "Or they could have thought we were Melnyk, and *she* was the actual target."

"You think so?"

"Maybe." His lower lip curls back behind his incisors for a moment as he thinks. "I mean, the shooter fled when you announced we were with the Union. Maybe they weren't expecting us to figure out Melnyk's involvement so quickly. Heard someone moving around in her apartment, took that as their opportunity to strike."

"Which is why she's got the Tryp!" Dupont exclaims, slapping her hand on the desk and causing the bullets to rattle in their sealed see-through bags. "The only question is, who in Kamote's name is trying to kill her?"

"Shit, man. Could be Union or L'Anormal, trying to get revenge for Klein's death. Could be someone in the Guild trying to tidy up loose ends. Hell, the Bureau *did* try to interfere with our investigation over at L'Hôtel San Madelaine. We can't rule out their involvement."

Dupont rests her forehead on her closed fist.

"So what now?"

"Now," Garcia says as he picks up the pen and taps it against his teeth, looking up at the ceiling, "now I guess we take a deeper look into Klein. Find out who he was, what he was up to. Should help us narrow down potential motives for Melnyk. Might even help us figure out who the second shooter is."

"Well I guess we ought to start with Ergot," Dupont says. "He works at the Ergot and Klein factory, past Place de Moteur. That'll likely be where we need to meet him."

"That's quite the drive." Garcia grimaces, rubbing the back of his neck. Dupont shrugs.

"I'll see if I can call in a favour, get hold of a Union vehicle."

"I'd appreciate it – it's getting hotter and I'm not as young as I once was."

Dupont flashes a smile that borders on impish.

"I've got your back, old-timer."

Garcia grins back at her, collecting the evidence up and putting it in an open filing cabinet drawer.

"Come on, I'm going to take Eddie up on that cigarette."

"There is something deeply inexplicable that exists in a Post-ProbMat world. It is as though, beneath those lingering purple eyes that seem to watch us all, that our actions are not our own."

Vega Braun, *Daemonic Numbers: Yemelenovian Probability and Free Will*

TEN

The walk home is uneventful. A navy sky hangs overhead as Pluto Garcia makes his way through the Waterfront, the occasional passing streetcar bathing him in canary yellow light. He forgoes his usual order of beef noodles and picks up a greasy hamburger from a food truck on West Rue D'Ecoulement, feeling a thin dribble of warm fat run down his wrist as he takes a bite. He finishes it just before arriving at South Seychel, crumpling the paper and tossing it into a trash can before burping the worst of the indigestion away.

"Ay, sharper," Scud says, flicking a hand up in greeting as Garcia comes to the steps of Block Vingt-Neuf. He is propped up on the wall, feet dangling below him, the kid with the FUCK IS ASS jacket sitting off to one side. Garcia gives a limp wave.

"Hey, Scud."

"You alright, man? You look fucked."

"It's been a long day, that's all." Garcia rubs his eyes and leans up against the wall. The kid with the jacket proffers up a bottle of Black Tiger and Garcia shakes his head. "How's your mom?"

"She's good. Working the night shift at DuBois, won't be back for a couple hours." He gestures back to the apartment block. "Got her a stew cooking for when she gets home."

"You're a good kid, Scud," Garcia says, straightening himself up. "You guys have a good night, okay?"

"You too, sharper," the kid with the jacket replies as Garcia turns to head inside.

A heavy, pale moon shines through a gap in the curtain of Pluto Garcia's apartment, gilding his threadbare furniture in filaments of silvers. He kicks his shoes off, grabs himself a beer, and parks his ass on the couch with a heavy *thud*.

A wave of tiredness washes over him, crashing into him like the waters of the Baratte, seeping into every aching bone and muscle in his body. He inhales sharply and forces his eyes open, determined not to sleep cat-like and coiled on the couch. He glances around the room for something to do within arms' reach: His radio-cassette combo is by the door, its remote control hidden in some dark and secret corner of the apartment; his television, a seldom-used Ergot and Klein Model S, gathers dust on a nearby dresser. With an irate sigh, he resolves himself to lie in silence, digesting the day along with the grease-laden burger that now sits heavily in his gut.

He thinks about Scud, and the look on the kid's face. It's true that he won't be deported, but Garcia remembers those first few years in Morrissette, back when his place as a citizen was uncertain, back when he couldn't find work in the Coalition and instead relied on government food parcels and whatever back-breaking dock work he could find.

He thinks about Dupont, the look on her face as the realisation that she'd been shot crashed into her. He thinks about the Repodimethyltryptamine coursing through her system, about the magenta maw of ProbMat swallowing her and spitting her out into a new body, about the countless other realities where his friend lies dead. To him, their relationship had thus far been one uninterrupted stream — to her, it was a series of tidal pools, each one brimming with strange and alien life.

He thinks about Krishna Klein, a great bulwark of cooling meat, a brilliant mind reduced to about one-point-three kilograms of grey mush smeared across a hotel wall.

He thinks about Maria Melnyk, wherever the hell she is.

He lets out a slow, soft sigh, and feels another wave of tiredness crest over him and, putting up no resistance, he washes away in the surf.

Moonlight, and a phone is ringing.

Grunting with exertion, Garcia rises to his feet and staggers through the blue-lit confines of his apartment, keenly catching his shin on the coffee table as he passes. He unlatches the door and steps out into the hallway where the phone rattles on the wall like a great, plexiglass cicada. He takes up the handset.

"Pluto Garcia, Block Vingt-Neuf," he grunts, rubbing his unfocused eyes. His hands and feet are leaden and stiff, replaced with heavy bags of sand barely capable of the fine motor skills required to manipulate the phone. There is a pause, the sound of breathing quietened as if on the other side of a still lake.

"I have a message," comes a strange, hoarse voice tinged with a Laccannesse drawl. "A warning, I guess."

The sounds of a sleeping Morrissette waft up through the window at the edge of the hall, carried upon the moonlight.

"Dean Ergot is not innocent," the voice continues, dreamily, "but he did not kill Krishna Klein."

Garcia rubs his eyes, trying to place the voice.

"Who is this?"

"He will try to escape," the voice goes on, seemingly ignoring the question entirely. "He will be desperate, and he will do desperate things."

Stiff-limbed and drained, Garcia sighs in the eerie blue light.

"I'll ask again," he says. "Who is this?"

"I... I haven't been thinking so clearly." Silence. Blue light. The moon bulges eye-like from a bruised sky. "Goodbye, Mr. Garcia."

There is a sudden click, followed by the dull robotic hum of a disconnect tone. Garcia looks blankly at the handset before returning it to the hook. He stands there in the hall in his bare feet, his arms hanging heavy by his sides. He looks over to the window and, without thinking, staggers towards it. He looks out into the Morrissette skyline, the dark buildings black against the grey-blue sky, a twinkling constellation of streetlights and apartment windows spread out before him.

There, in the street, a figure stands by a payphone.

Garcia squints, trying to inspect their features, but they are too far away. The only thing he can make out is the crude outline of a bomber jacket. The figure turns and, silently, walks into the dark streets beyond Block Vingt-Neuf.

A chill runs through Pluto Garcia's body as he returns to his apartment, locking the door and double-checking before retiring to bed, soon succumbing to a fit of restless dreams.

"At some point in the early 1950s, Camille Kamote discovered the writings of Anton Yemelenov. While the broader implications of the Wider Probability Matrix were well-known by this point, Kamote was equally interested and disturbed by the following thought experiment: if one considers the infinite potential of neighbouring realities, then it stands to reason that there is an infinite capacity for the existence of Capitalism and – by extension – an infinite need for it to be dismantled. This – what Kamote referred to as 'the quantum necessity for Communism' – is thought to have lit the fires that would eventually lead to the roaring engine of the Violet Revolution."

Nibiru Atreides, *Camille Kamote: An Unofficial Biography*

ELEVEN

Early morning, and Esther Dupont makes herself known with a short, sharp honk.

Garcia peers out of the Tank's back window and sees her sitting in a Union Sudumobil, its red paint glinting dully in the sun. It is a sleek machine, low to the ground and stretched out, a modification of the classic Vali design put together in a way that is somewhat passable. He can hear the engine's rolling purr from here and as he waves to her, she swiftly waves back.

He grabs his files, tucks them under his arm, and pads down the corridor past Captain Marchenko's office. She coughs conspicuously, and he turns her head to see her, still smouldering. He gives a small, apologetic shrug, his expression one of sphincter-tightening shame.

"Comrade Dupont is here, so…" he begins, pointing to the door. "I'm going to head out."

"Sure," she says, holding his gaze. He withers, nodding hurriedly and dashing off into the muggy Morrissette morning. Dupont grins as he sits in the passenger seat.

"Rough morning?"

"Just drive."

She grins, pushing down on the acceleration and rumbling the car into life. They turn the corner up Promenade de Gloire and out of the Packing district, curving northeast along the coastline towards the Union checkpoint. A squat man in Bureau colours checks their papers, scanning his eyes suspiciously over them both. Garcia gives a wan smile and the guard retreats to his booth, returning a couple minutes later.

"You're good to go," he grumbles, waving them through as they drive. After a moment of silence, the delicate chirring of the engine and constant clinking, beeping, buzzing, and yelling of the Scaffolds their only soundtrack, Garcia animates.

"Oh!" he says, reaching into his breast pocket. He produces a cassette tape – chunky, translucent plastic case with a faded paper interior bearing a slender, snake-hipped nymph with a halo of luxurious blond hair leaning up against a wooden door frame. Beneath this, written in a blocky font reminiscent of the old Wojtek propaganda posters, is the words "MARCO SANSKRIT – PAGAN".

"As promised." Garcia beams as he sets it down on the dash. "I figured this would be a good starting place – it's not as weird as his second album, nor as mainstream as his fourth. Nice middle ground listening, you know?"

"Oh, great," Dupont replies, tapping the cassette player. "Put it in, let's hear it."

Garcia cracks the case and takes the cassette in his fingers, slotting it into the square orifice and pushing the play button. First the sound of tuning and synching – a bass thrums a few notes, inching up and down the fretboard, followed by a strum of jangly guitar and a couple soft, experimental blows on a Laccannesse horn. The guitar enters a steady rhythm, the melody punctuated by a soft, flattened horn. A wobbling theremin follows suit a half-pitch above the horn, layering into a cosmic orchestral timbre that floods the interior of the car. This carries on for four bars before Sanskrit himself joins in, his reedy voice singing descending with the instrumentation.

"The dead don't die like they used to," he begins, voice wavering with each word. "Maybe they were living all along…"

Garcia sits back in his seat, eyes closed, finger tapping his upper thigh in time with the music. A timpani rattles in and he begins to tap his foot along with the beat, a faint smile on his face. The tall, rickety buildings of the Scaffolds roll past, unlit billboards bearing Union slogans of unity and utility and the value of the Communist ethic, and Dupont weaves the car from one street to the next. They pass close to the coastline again and she looks up to see the tripodal alien form of Laurent rising from the sea, the familiar trail of smoke rising up from one of its many towers. She smiles at the sight of home. By the time the song has ended, it has sunk back out of view, a great thalassic monster returning to the depths.

"What did you think?" Garcia asks, eyes open now and focused on her.

"It was… Good."

"Good?" he repeats, hopefully.

"Sure, good." She gives a loose shrug. "Look, I've never been that into music, you know?"

"What, they didn't have music on the rig?"

"They did, it just… It was never my *thing*." She turns to him, a rueful smile on her lips. "I enjoyed it, though! I can see why you're so into him."

"He's a poet," he says, quietly deflating in the passenger seat. "One of the best."

"That's probably it," Dupont replies, flicking an indicator and turning left onto Route Vers Nulle Part. "I've always had a hard time with poets, even at school."

"You don't like poetry?"

"I don't like *poets*. Poetry is fine, I just get frustrated with it." She tightens her grip on the wheel slightly. "I just feel you should say what you mean, you know? Don't hide behind metaphor, just be *honest*."

"Poetry *is* honest," Garcia mewls, throwing his hands up. "Poetry is the most honest thing in the world!"

"No, see, there you go again! It *isn't* the most honest thing in the world. It's meaningful, sure, and important. Hell, the Violet Revolution probably wouldn't have happened were it not for poets and artists. But it's important to be candid sometimes too, right?"

"I suppose." Garcia winces as the words leave his mouth. "But even Kamote relied on poetry to get her ideas across."

"She did, sure, but she also used rhetoric. Concrete ideas expressed openly. For every slogan about the innate dignity of the worker there were ten whole speeches about the express evils of society. Capital, empire, dogma. She *used* those words, she didn't just talk about swimming pools or whatever."

She is animated now, a flash in her eyes as she continues.

"Besides, it's not just poets. We all do it – we fall back on vagaries because being honest about our situation is difficult. We joke, we shrug, we laugh it off, because if we all were to be honest things would have to change, and change *hurts*."

Garcia sulkily stares out of the window, still tapping his foot in time with Sanskrit's piping voice. Dupont taps the steering wheel awkwardly with her thumbs, looking straight ahead. Sanskrit enters the third verse of *Bang It Goes* and she turns back to Garcia.

"I'm sorry, I do appreciate you sharing this with me. I've just… I've had a lot to think about since yesterday, you know?"

"I know," Garcia says, eventually looking her way. "How are you feeling?"

"Honestly?" She bats the steering wheel a little. "I feel good. Alive, I guess."

"I can tell."

"Look, Sanskrit isn't that bad, he's just not for me. Besides," she says, giving a sparkling smile, "he's better than Celentano."

"Don't let Eddie hear you say that," Garcia says, an impudent grin crawling to his lips. "He'll kick your ass."

The heat goes from gentle to choking as they drive deeper into the Scaffolds, the sky growing hazy as they close into the apocalyptic ramble of factories that is Place de Moteur. Here all manner of life is hewn from dead material, metals and plastics beaten and moulded into machines that think, amble, digest, and create. The sounds of whirring pistons and pulleys leak from open factory windows, the sounds of workers cursing and laughing over the mechanical din. Union presence is strong here, persimmon jumpsuits smeared with grime and oil, a reminder that the Scaffolds is a district of rough hands and strong arms. They pass a mural to Camille Kamote, her cheeks blackened with coal dust as she thrusts a wrench into the sky, and Dupont gives a curt nod as she drives on. Eventually, the twin industrial spires of Ergot and Klein rise up out of the sprawl, dark against the blue sky.

They park and head inside, Dupont taking the lead as Garcia falls behind, hands stuffed into his pockets. They are greeted by a short woman with dark hair pulled back into a neat ponytail. The factory, contrary to the admittedly grubby district it is situated in the centre of, is immaculate, and she exemplifies this in her prim demeanour and faint aura of almond soap. Dupont smiles and produces her papers.

"Salut, Comrade. I'm Junior Auditor Esther Dupont, this is my colleague Lieutenant Pluto Garcia from the CMM. We're here about Comrade Klein."

The woman's expression wavers ever so slightly and she gestures towards two black chairs set against a spotless white wall.

"Of course," she says, her voice low and demure. "If you'd kindly take a seat, I'll send a message up to Comrade Ergot."

Dupont and Garcia do as instructed, making themselves as comfortable as they can on the narrow plastic seats. Through a large window on the opposite end of the foyer they are able to see the factory floor: countless workers in orange jumpsuits sit about stationary conveyor belts, poring over the intricate knots of circuit boards and coloured wiring with strange, arcane devices; gangplanks lined with guardrails crisscross the open air above their heads, and people scurry along them with documents under their arms or clipboards in their hands; robotic reels paint solder paste onto flat vinyl boards and shunt them forward to be studded with the esoteric geometry of resistors and capacitors that turns a polymer sheet into a brain.

They hear a soft ding and look up to see a slight man with blond hair shaved close to the temples stepping out of the elevator, his narrow face and dimpled cheeks giving him a fey pleasantness. He is dressed in the traditional Union jumpsuit, though he has unzipped it to the waist and tied the arms around his waist, revealing a svelte frame in a tight-fitting black t-shirt, a tin of breath mints sticking out of the left breast pocket. He offers a hand out.

"Thank you so much for coming, Comrade Dupont, Lieutenant Garcia." He smiles. "I'm Comrade Dean Ergot. You're welcome to call me Dean, should you wish."

"Thank you for agreeing to speak with us, Dean," Dupont says warmly, shaking his hand.

"Not at all. When Comrade Chang alerted me to Krishna's passing." He pauses for a moment, gathering himself. "Well, needless to say I resigned myself to doing everything in my power to help track down those responsible."

"We appreciate your cooperation, Comrade," Garcia says with a slight nod. "Do you have somewhere more private we can go to talk?"

"Of course," he says, pointing back to the elevator. "Let's head up to my office."

The elevator lurches smoothly upwards, climbing through the building, its glass front looking out over the factory floor. They pass through an intestinal coil of pipes and rise above it, now out in the open and ascending up the side of the southernmost tower overlooking the Scaffolds. Further up they go, rising over the factories and rooftops and the gridded blocks of the Mechanograd apartment complex and into the featureless sky. Garcia looks down at the traffic stalled on Rue D'Ecoulement, the glinting bronze statue of Camille Kamote on the Promenade, the distant labyrinthine mess of the Tank, the imposing shadow of the Bureau of Records. His stomach tumbles and he looks away, turning back to Dupont and Ergot.

"This is, ah," he says, his face a pale green. "This is a remarkable building, Comrade Ergot."

"It is," Ergot says humbly. "Designed by a Funam architect back when my father still ran the company. Total height of three hundred metres, ninety-five floors, twelve-thousand-five-hundred tonnes of steel, glass, and concrete, all owned by the workers. They only completed construction seven years ago."

"Incredible," Garcia mumbles, suppressing the urge to throw up.

"Have you always worked for the company, Comrade?" Dupont asks, her tone formal and present.

"Since I left college, yes." He gives a sorry shrug. "I'll admit, I inherited my position. Nepotism is an ugly thing, but you must remember: my father was an old-fashioned man, a child of fascists who survived only through his Communist leanings."

Leapt to that a little too quickly, Garcia thinks in the back of his dizzied mind. *Defence against an allegation not yet levelled – or one levelled frequently.* Ergot turns to Dupont.

"What about you, Comrade Dupont? Auditors are no rare sight in the factory, given Klein's position on the Council, but I don't believe I've ever seen you before."

"I'm with the Liberté Corp. Transferred over from Laurent a few years ago."

"Oh," Ergot says, a hint of curiosity in his voice. "This is a far cry from the usual cargo control work you're used to, I imagine."

"All in a day's work, Comrade," she replies, curtly. Ergot smiles, reaching up and plucking the tin of breath mints from his pocket. ICEBURG, a Sao-San brand. He flicks the lid open and empties it straight into his mouth, clicking it shut. Garcia, stomach churning, raises a wavering hand.

"Mind if I have one of those?"

Ergot gives an apologetic simper.

"Sorry, Lieutenant, that was my last one."

The elevator door pings and opens out into a large, clean office space. There are two desks, one situated on either side of the room, and on the far wall are three framed portraits: on one side there is Ergot, young and regal, his blond fringe swept back and his expression one of bright-eyed confidence; on the other side is Klein, a broad indomitable figure, a head of full bluish-black hair and two dark eyes set in a proud, defined face; in the middle is Camille Kamote, the People's Revolutionary, her kinky black hair bursting like a halo around her head, her pose one of defiant, beatific grace.

"Good, aren't they?" Ergot says, ushering them into the office. "Found a charming painter in Madame Syndicat willing to whip them up for us. Mine and Krishna's were done from life – of course, the same cannot be said for Lady Revolutionär."

He approaches the desk on the left, taking a seat and gesturing to the chairs before him. Dupont and Garcia sit down, Dupont crossing her legs and producing her notebook, Garcia grateful to be on something solid. Ergot leans forward.

"So, how can I help you both?"

"We were just hoping you could tell us more about Comrade Klein," Dupont says, her pen poised over her notebook.

"You've come to the right place: he was my friend and mentor for over thirty years. What would you like to know?"

"Let's start by working out a timeline," Dupont says, pen poised over the page. "Where were you on the night Comrade Klein died?"

"I would have been here, at the office. With Krishna out I like to put in a couple extra hours. Keep things ticking over in his absence, you know."

"You were here alone?"

"Yes." He taps his forehead suddenly, an absent smile on his lips. "Ah, no – one of our maintenance staff was in here fixing Krishna's chair."

"How did it get broken?"

"An... Outburst. Krishna was prone to expressing himself physically and, well," he says as he nods to the painting, to Klein's huge bulwark frame, "you've seen how big he was. It didn't take much for him to break stuff."

"Can you remember what the outburst was about?" Garcia asks, his face finally returning to its usual sandy shade.

"Not really, no. Some frustration or other, no doubt."

"Could we speak to your maintenance personnel? Just to corroborate, of course."

"Absolutely." Ergot gestures a hand vaguely. "Have a word with my receptionist on your way out, she'll be able to give you his details."

"What was he like?" Garcia leans forward, smiling sympathetically. "Krishna, I mean."

"He was a genius," Ergot says, simply. "Unparalleled. He could take an enumerator apart, work out exactly what was wrong with it, and put it back together working twice as fast in under an hour and with only a handful of spare parts. The kind of brilliance born of necessity."

"How so?" Dupont asks.

"Well, you know he was born on the Waterfront, during the old regime. He was a punk, poor as dirt. It's not often I subscribe to the Capitalist ethic, but he really *did* work his way up. He was brilliant because he *had* to be brilliant, and he used that brilliance to improve the lives of others."

"That's how he came to work with your father."

"Correct. To each man his ability, right?"

Dupont taps her pen on the notebook softly.

"He was responsible for the Ergoteck Unity, correct?"

"He lead the team, yes." Ergot's hands splay out on the desk. "A processor capable of computation speeds previously unheard of. The sort of invention that changes the way we think about technology; the purview of science fiction."

He pauses for a moment, a queer smile on his lips. He lets out a short, sharp exhale, the ghost of a laugh, and shakes his head.

"When someone passes away it is tempting to sing their praises. Please know that is not what I'm doing when I say he was a genius."

There's something there, Garcia muses. *Something about the way he keeps falling back to that point. Brilliant. Genius.* He thinks back to the unmade bed, the mouldy coffee cups, the stacks of scribbled notes, the worn and beaten children's book by his bed. Brilliant perhaps, but messy, disordered.

"We don't doubt that for a second," he eventually says. "His reputation certainly... Preceded him."

"Yes, well, he made a name for himself."

"Tell me." Garcia leans in, a genial smile on his lips. "What do you know about Pietnera?"

"The island? Only that it's basically uninhabitable." Ergot looks puzzled for a moment, hands splayed out on the desk. Eventually, this expression gives way to one of wry understanding. "Oh, wait – is this about those stories? 'Folk Tales of the Annalissian Archipelago', or some such?"

"Klein mentioned it, then?"

"Yes. To me and to just about everyone else." He shakes his head and a warm, nostalgic smile lights up his cherubic features. "Sometimes a person's mind will be so brilliant it will piece together disparate information and come up with the most astonishing conclusions."

"How do you mean?"

"It's funny, really: he had, somehow, worked out exactly which islands had been used as a reference for the illustrations in his copy of that blasted book. Told damn near everybody he spoke to, a little bit of trivia to show off about."

Garcia rides the warmth of Ergot's tone like a predatory bird cresting a thermal.

"Was he popular?"

"He was adored by the workers. He represented them at their best, their most noble. I'd go as far as to say he was friends with a lot of them, especially some of our contract workers."

"And amongst other board members?"

There. A slight crack, a drop in the façade.

"He was occasionally... contentious," Ergot stammers, shrugging vaguely. "Not unliked, so much as... Unamenable."

"He didn't respond well to others?"

"Not as such. He knew he was brilliant, had since he was a child. When the Revolution came he joined up with the hope of bringing about a new world, one led by brilliant people. And, well," Ergot says as he gives that same limp shrug, an admission, "people seldom meet our expectations."

"He was arrogant, then." Garcia asks, stone-faced.

"No, no! He simply had an idea for what the world should be, and was angered when his standards weren't met."

"What ideas were those, Comrade Ergot?" Dupont asks, her brow knitted.

"About the end-point of technology. The things we could do with it." He brings a long-fingered hand up to rub the bridge of his nose. "You must understand: Klein was, to his core, a visionary. He saw futures that few else could see, and exposing others to those futures was his main goal."

There, again. High praises and speaking in metaphor. He's talking his way around something. A big something, a great churning engine of something, a something that began as an idea and ended in a bullet to the head. Page after page rise in Garcia's mind, detailing in blue and black the intricacies of a new system, a new mind rendered in scrawled ink. He leans forward and takes his shot.

"He was working on a new product," he states, simply. Ergot does not respond for a moment, attempting a stony, stoic expression that just comes across as a touch bewildered. He assents with a small smile.

"Is it that obvious, Lieutenant?"

"Only if you know what to look for," Garcia replies. "What was Klein working on?"

"It is, I'm afraid, strictly confidential."

"That," Dupont interjects with the sternness of a schoolteacher, "is the language of the old regime, Comrade. Yours is a company owned by the people of Annalise, and *nothing* is confidential in Annalise."

"Tell that to the Bureau," Ergot says, wrinkling his nose. Garcia pushes on, intuition guiding his motions.

"Comrade Ergot," he begins, the words rising to his lips before he's even had a chance to think them, "what is ARGUS?"

Ergot sighs and drums his fingers on the desk. The sound, rhythmic and mechanical, hangs in the air, mingling with the faint hum of the air conditioning to form a lilting corporate soundscape. The stiff-backed, upright form of Krishna Klein hangs over them, a dark-eyed spectre looming from the next realm. Ergot, once more, assents.

"What do you know about ProbMat?"

"It is not hyperbole to say that the discovery of ProbMat made men into gods."

Washington Turi, *Extra-Potentiality and the
Ascent of Humanity*

TWELVE

The ride down from Ergot's office is slow and darkening, like the descent into a restless sleep. Garcia turns his face away from the sickening heights of Morrissette for much of it, fiddling with the hem of his shirt. Ergot remains silent, hands tucked into the pockets of his overalls, his calm gaze fixed on the horizon. The elevator door opens to a narrow corridor with a security gate at the far end, and Ergot turns to face Garcia and Dupont.

"Please wait here," he says, flashing them a strange smile. "I just need to check in with our researchers, explain to them what's going on."

"Go right ahead," Dupont replies curtly. Ergot spins and briskly walks to the security gate, disappearing into the bowels of the building. Dupont turns to Garcia.

"Did you see his desk?" she asks.

"What about it?"

"There was a box of Repodimethyltryptamine next to his computer."

"Union-issued?" Garcia asks, colour returning to his cheeks.

"No, private import I think."

"Weird that a Union man like Ergot would feel the need to keep Tryp on him though, right?" Garcia scratches his chin, lowering his voice. "Do you think he was worried that whatever killed Klein is coming for him next?"

"Maybe," Dupont replies. "I don't know, it could be something else."

"Such as?"

"It could be a safety net," she says. "You see it in the Enforcement Corp sometimes. Tryp gives you a free pass on doing reckless shit."

Garcia goes quiet, feeling the tin box in his pocket pressing against his leg.

"You think he'd spend that much money on a precaution?"

Before Dupont can reply, the security gate buzzes and Ergot pokes his head through.

"Alright," he says. "Follow me."

The Ergot and Klein laboratory is a sterile jungle of blinking lights and matted wires, through which quiet scientists with tired eyes and pale lab coats scurry like mice across the forest floor. Ergot ushers them through the beating heart of the building, offering curt, professional smiles to passing researchers, clasping shoulders and asking after family. It is only once they have passed through the main laboratories and into the underbelly of the Ergot and Klein facility that his managerial streak drops and he descends once more into sullen silence.

"I really would appreciate your discretion regarding what I am about to show you," he says, coming to a locked door and swiping a small alabaster key fob over a scanner plate embedded into the wall. The door lets out a soft buzz and he pulls it open, escorting them further into the building. "While Ergot and Klein *is* a company of the workers, I believe what we are working on right now has a potential that goes beyond the interests of the proletariat."

They are led through corridor after spotless corridor, white walls and laminated flooring illuminated by humming fluorescents in plexiglass frames. Eventually, they come to a door with two scanners, Ergot running the fob and a laminated ID card over both. The door slides back and he gestures through. Beyond it, lights.

Row after row of lights, red and white and green eyes blinking in the gloom and seated in great monolithic faces of aluminium and plastic. Wires bunch in baffling tangles, intertwining between breaker boards and input ports. The room itself is warm, uterine and still save for the flickering electronic stars that line its outer perimeter. In the centre of the room there is a great, recondite mass of off-white Bakelite in the approximate shape of a human head, connected to a mounted terminal via a thick, umbilical cable suspended by an esoteric network of mechanical arms over a plush, faux-leather chair.

"This," Ergot says, quietly, "is the Alternate Reality Guided Usership Sensor." He gestures at the machines that line the walls, at the bulky headset that hangs in the centre of the room. "This is ARGUS."

"A supercomputer," Dupont muses, looking around the room. "Like the one Klein was building at his apartment."

"That was a prototype. This is in beta testing now."

Dupont turns to him, her face lit by the eerie constellation of blinking LEDs.

"What does it do?"

"It does… A lot." He sighs, his face looking pale and drawn in the low light. "Simply put, it gathers data from the seventeen-thousand-four-hundred-and-ninety-two alternate realities we have already observed across ProbMat, compiles the differences between them, and extrapolates that data into predicted outcomes accessed by that terminal." He points to the plastic contraption in the centre of the room. Dupont's brows knit as she processes this.

"It can predict the future."

"It can predict *certain* futures, yes," Ergot says, his shoulders slumped and his eyes turned upwards. "If there are an infinite number of realities across ProbMat, then there are an infinite number of potential futures. ARGUS calculates the likelihood of any specific action leading to a specific outcome."

"And Klein invented this?" Garcia asks, padding across the tile floor towards the terminal.

"He designed it, yes. The code was put together by a team of Yemelenovian Physicists in our Quentin Facility. Between them and our engineering staff here, there were only around twelve people involved in its construction, all told. Including testers that figure rises to about twenty."

"Why is this project so secretive?"

"Lots of reasons. We have oversea competitors who would kill for a piece of technology this robust. If we can establish an international patent first, it would mean securing hundreds of billions of dollars for Annalise."

Garcia gives a queasy smile, the wrinkles on his face deepened into dark gashes by the sickly light.

"But that's not the only reason, is it? This machine would change the way we think about free will and determinism forever. You're looking at the kind of invention that draws people's focus." He glances up at Ergot, scanning his narrow face. "And I'm sure the Bureau of Records have already caught wind of it, right?"

Ergot deflates as he exhales.

"We believe so." He paces the perimeter of the room, eyes passing over the blinking consoles. "Pre-empting criminal behaviour has always been a pipe-dream of the Bureau. If they were to intercept ARGUS, it would certainly make their jobs easier."

"Do you think they have any involvement in Klein's death?" Dupont asks.

"It's possible. They have agents in the Union, CMM, and the Guild." He pauses, his brow furrowed. "And, well... We do suspect sabotage."

"How do you mean?" Garcia leans forward.

"ARGUS isn't running at full capacity. There's a component, a storage disc, that's gone missing. I thought Krishna had taken it during the start of his bender, but now with him dead I'm not so sure."

"What's on this disc?"

"Around two-point-eight-eight megabytes of data. It's one of around six hundred discs, but even a small amount of missing data radically affects the accuracy of our predictions. Had it been working at full operational capacity, we could have probably used it to work out who killed Krishna."

"Why haven't you alerted the Enforcement Corp?" Dupont asks.

"With the best will in the world, Comrade Dupont, we have no way of knowing if your colleagues are Bureau agents."

"And you believe that we're not?" Garcia asks, flatly.

Ergot shrugs; a helpless little gesture, one of a man so far out of his depth that no amount of paddling can save him.

"Frankly, I'm past the point of caring," he says, softly.

"You said that around twelve people have worked on ARGUS," Dupont says. "How many work here in Morrissette?"

"Including Krishna, I think five in total. I'm unsure of how many testers live locally, however."

"Is there any chance we could speak with any of them?"

"I imagine there will be an engineer or two on the factory floor you could speak to. As for the testers, they were all on private contracts. They won't be in the facility, but I can track down their details for you."

"You hired people from outside of Ergot and Klein?" Garcia pads around the perimeter of the room, hands in his pockets. "Risky move, considering you're concerned with industrial espionage."

"I agree, but it was one necessary to make."

"Why?"

"Well, ah." Even in the dull red light of the room, Ergot's face grows visibly dark. "There were certain concerns that had to be accounted for. For reasons we can't quite work out, ARGUS doesn't allow for automatic testing: in order for it to process information from adjacent realities, a human tester has to be present."

"So why hire from outside the company?"

"The safety of our employees is of utmost importance, Lieutenant."

"And the safety of drifters and contractors is less important," Garcia concludes. "Good to know."

"You don't understand."

"Then enlighten me." He removes a hand from his pocket and gestures vaguely at the room. "I'm fairly ignorant to all this computer stuff."

"ARGUS is a unique machine. As such there are unique user-interface issues."

"You're avoiding the question," Dupont adds. "What '*issues*' were too dangerous for your employees but just fine for external contractors?"

The heat in the room grows, a pulsing warmth that washes over the three occupants. Ergot withers, a look of anguish across his keen features.

"We're not sure how deep it goes," he wails, hands crossed over his chest. "Audio-visual hallucinations, depressive episodes, muscular spasms, migraines, delusional behaviour. ARGUS is still in early development; side effects are to be expected."

"And let me guess," Garcia's voice pitches a little, his jaw clenching at the hinges as he speaks, "you didn't report these side effects to a hospital."

"Dubois General has absolutely been infiltrated by the Bureau of Records," Ergot whines. "If people working for Ergot and Klein show up, all with identical symptoms, that will attract attention we simply cannot afford right now."

"You took an unknown number of Morrissette citizens, filled their heads with neuroses and psychotic delusions, and turned them out onto the street at their most vulnerable?" Dupont hisses. "Comrade Ergot, this is *monstrous*."

"I know. It doesn't sit well with me, either," he says softly. He chuckles sadly to himself, shaking his head. "It was inevitable, really: Krishna would often make these big, terrible decisions and then disappear, leaving me to clean up after him."

"The testing was Klein's idea?"

"The entire project was his idea. I think he'd been working on it for years." Ergot brings his hand up to his eyes and rubs the bridge of his nose forlornly. "It never felt right, doing this. But Klein insisted it was necessary."

"You could have stopped him," Dupont says. "Alerted the Auditors."

"And lose the single greatest invention in human history," he replies, bluntly. "Yes, I suppose I could have."

"We'll contact the Enforcement Corp and schedule a full investigation," Dupont says, her eyes steely and cold. "We may be able to avoid Bureau involvement, but at this rate you'll be lucky if you are subject to immediate exile from Annalise."

"In the meantime," Garcia adds, "we will need you to provide us with the details of these testers. Investigation notwithstanding, *someone* needs to check in on them, make sure they're not at risk of harming themselves or others."

"Of course," Ergot gestures sadly. "Their details will be on my computer."

"You head up with him," Dupont says to Garcia. "I saw a payphone in the lobby. I'll use that to get in touch with Liberté."

Garcia nods to her and the three return to the elevator, walking slowly and quietly. The sounds of the slumbering ARGUS fade as they step squinting into the bright fluorescents of the factory at large. Garcia scans his eyes over Ergot; features that looked youthful only a few hours ago seem worn and plastic now, the pale artificiality of a doll's face spoiled by time and experience. He walks with his arms crossed over his chest, picking at the skin on his thumb with his forefinger, his brow furrowed and his full lips pursed. They cut through the lab, Ergot's managerial charisma weighed down beneath sullen shame, and arrive at the elevator. Dupont pushes the button for the reception lobby and Ergot pushes the button for his office. The elevator begins its steady climb up through the body of Ergot and Klein, its three inhabitants still and stonily silent. The doors open noiselessly and Dupont nods back to Garcia, who smiles in turn. She steps out, and they close behind her.

"Exile," Ergot announces, softly.

"Mmm." Garcia nods in vague agreement.

"I don't know what I'll do." He thrusts his hands in his pockets, his face cast a sickly yellow beneath the strip light. "Where will I go?"

"Wojtek accepts exiles, I believe. Karnassas too, but as someone who grew up there you'd likely be better off taking your chances in Morrissette."

He does not respond to the joke, his cold eyes fixed firmly on the floor.

"I know what you're thinking," Ergot says, a gloomy expression on his youthful face as the elevator pushes through the factory roof and out into the open sky. Garcia, facing away from the window, remains silent.

"Like father like son, eh?" Ergot continues. "Fascist hold-out calls himself a Communist and expects everyone to believe him. Of course *he* would do something like this." Garcia casts a furtive glance over the city, the summer sun high in the sky above the whirling activity of Morrissette. Dizzied even by such a swift glance, he turns back to face the smouldering Ergot.

"It's not the case," Ergot spits, hands bunched in the pockets of his overalls, a knot of muscles around his temples visibly clenching as he speaks. "Everything I have done, I have done for this city. I have built an empire for Morrissette, given its people steady jobs and funded their leisure, even worked with that... Reckless *idiot*. I'm not a fascist, Lieutenant Garcia. My family let go of that life."

"Hmm," Garcia hums, immobile. He looks once more out onto the sprawl of Morrissette, out into Estuary West where the waters of the Baratte split the land, to the rising spires of Old Morrissette just off the coast, out onto the dark spire of the Archive.

"If you don't mind me saying, Lieutenant," Ergot says. "You're being awfully quiet."

Garcia's face crumples into genial wrinkles and he removes his hands from his pockets, showing the roughened palms to the businessman.

"I simply don't have anything to say."

The elevator door slides open, revealing the spectres of Camille Kamote and Krishna Klein. Ergot's concentration breaks and he gestures with a nod.

"This way."

He heads to his computer, his fingers moving rapidly across the keyboard as he enters a long, veiled password. The tower whines into alertness, electricity flooding into the bulky CRT monitor and striping the black background with phosphorous lines of green text. A command is entered, bringing up a page of names, addresses, birth dates. Another command and the machine narrows the wall of text down to a short list. It rattles through them – nine in total, most unfamiliar, but one seems to glow just a little brighter on the screen.

"Jonah Bukowski," he says quietly to himself. He thinks back to the picture of the kid with the not-quite-smile, to the figure in the red bomber jacket, to the knife in his back. It is only when he hears the soft sound of heavy plastic scraped across wood that he looks up, spotting Ergot's hand secreted in a desk drawer, resting timidly on a Moricco 9mm handgun.

"I'm sorry," he says quietly. "Morrissette is my home."

"I understand," Garcia replies, unmoving. "I would be heartbroken if I were ever exiled."

"You *don't* understand." He faces away from Garcia, his hand trembling over the grip. "I have given up so much to this city. To this regime."

"Sure. We all have. That's the point, comrade."

Ergot's fingers tighten around the gun and he pulls it from the drawer, spinning around to point it at Garcia's chest.

"Did you shoot Krishna, too?" Garcia cocks an eyebrow and fixes his brown-black eyes on Ergot's faded blue.

"Don't be stupid," Ergot hisses.

"Nothing stupid about it. He was your friend, your mentor, a brilliant man... But also a difficult man. Infuriating. Prone to *outbursts*. Whereas you: you've worked so hard for this company, for this *city*,"

"Shut up."

"And yet here you are, having to face the consequences of *his* actions." Garcia flashes a sympathetic look. "This isn't how you thought all this would go, is it?"

Ergot pulls the hammer back with a steady, resonant click.

"I said shut up."

"Go ahead," Garcia says simply, not lowering his notebook. "I took Tryp before we came out here. I'll have a couple shitty hours, but my consciousness will survive and head someplace else. You, however, will remain in this universe. With an extremely angry Esther Dupont who – like yourself – is armed with a Moricco 9mm and is a much better shot."

Garcia tries to hold his expression. Neutral, stoic, unflinching. He *tries* to hold the expression, but there is some small thing, some faint twitch in the lines of his left cheek, some small wrinkling of the eye. Ergot's aim is unwavering, the barrel of his pistol hovering a meagre twelve inches from Garcia's solar plexus. In the bright fluorescents of the office his angelic features have contorted into a clownish expression of rage. Tears form in his eyes as his fingers tighten around the trigger.

In countless worlds across the churning sea of ProbMat, Pluto Garcia dies. In each of these worlds, he is as shitty a liar as he is in this one; in each of these worlds, Ergot is quick to call his bluff. He is shot, point-blank, the bullet exploding in his ribcage and splintering the bones into the torn canvas that were previously his lungs. Blood explodes and he is knocked back, hitting the wall with a short, wet thump. In some of these worlds the bullet punctures his heart, killing him instantly. In others the death is slow, protracted, bleeding out onto the carpet of Dean Ergot's office, living just long enough to see the businessman sprint to the elevator door and escape into the arcane guts of Ergot and Klein. In all of these worlds, he dies under the smiling eyes of Camille Kamote, Our Lady of Revolution.

However.

However, in this world, he does not die. In this world, in the same instant the trigger is pulled, a door opens. The elevator slides noiselessly on invisible rollers and Esther Dupont steps into the office, hand on her service weapon. In the same instant the bullet leaves the barrel, Dean Ergot has already begun to turn to face her, his face blanching as she points her pistol at him. In the same instant the bullet begins its fated trajectory, it has already been thrown off-target by the momentum of Ergot's spin and, instead of landing in Garcia's chest, it careers left and clips his right bicep.

He spins back, an inch of flesh torn away by the bullet and splattering across the wall behind him. He lets out an agonised scream, hitting the floor and clutching his arm. Dupont rushes into the office, gun trained firmly on Ergot, who stares with the blank eyes of a rabbit moments before the hawk's talons descend.

"Comrade Dean Ergot, you are under arrest and are to be held by the Shipbuilders' Union of Morrissette," Dupont says sharply, clearly. "You have the right to remain silent. Anything you say can and will be used against you before an assemblage of the Morrissette Coalition. You have the right to an attorney, as provided by the Community Militia of Morrissette or a neutral party of your choosing."

Ergot's eyes flit between her face and her gun. A shudder runs through the room, electric, heart-stopping. Without a word, Dean Ergot brings the pistol to his temple and pulls the trigger.

His head bursts into a Catherine wheel of gore, a firework of visceral pink and grey, a fingerpainting rendered in hideous technicolour. Dupont screams and darts forward, but it is too late. In that single instant, Ergot falls to the floor, his angel-blue eyes staring blindly up at the ceiling, the tin of breath mints in his pocket clattering open and spilling half a dozen acid yellow pills onto the carpet.

"Fuck!" She kicks the desk and spins away, suppressing the urge to vomit. Garcia, quickly but gingerly lifts himself into a chair. His nostrils gush with snot, and his eyes are wet and unfocused as he looks down at the corpse.

"Shit, shit, shit," he hisses through gritted teeth, his heart crashing into his ribcage and sending a new pulse of pain through his body with each beat. Dupont steels herself and turns to Garcia.

"Are you okay?"

"Yeah, yeah I'm fine. He pulled a gun on me. Tried to de-escalate, told him I took Tryp." He sucks in air through his teeth, having to forcibly look away from the crumpled mess that was formerly Dean Ergot.

"Damnit, Pluto," she says sharply, approaching the corpse. She stands over the body for a moment, her face a mask of horror and pity, before crouching down and picking up one of the spilled pills.

"Fuck," she says, raising it to the light. "It's Tryp."

The dull thrum of air conditioning and the distant sound of approaching EnCorp sirens breaks the heavy silence. Garcia whimpers softly in his seat, cradling his arm, the pain a hot, fleshy fire spreading down to his wrist. He looks up, past the black computer monitor and its furrows of glinting green text; past the crumpled form of Dean Ergot, his blood-spattered cheek pressed against the carpet; up into the smiling, implacable face of Camille Kamote.

Outside the facility, the body of Dean Ergot is hoisted up into the back of a black Union van by a burly Auditor dressed in the customary deep red of the Enforcement Corp. Dupont speaks quietly with a colleague, notebook in her hand as she relays the cabbalistic interior of Ergot and Klein, and the electronic prophet that slumbers within. Garcia watches through the door in the lobby, wincing as the last few metal shavings are removed from his arm and placed in a small ceramic plate from the canteen. The medic, a small, fleshy man whose body looks like one large, poorly-formed lump of clay fashioned into a crude homunculus, daubs at the wound with a yellow antiseptic liquid, causing Garcia's features to crumple into a mass of agonised lines. He snarls, clenching his fist as the dressing is applied and the tourniquet removed. The medic rises stiffly to his feet.

"It's clean," the medic says in a thick Laccannesse accent, removing his gloves and placing them in a rubbery heap on the plate. "You got off lucky, compared to the other guy."

"It's a small comfort, but thank you," Garcia replies through clenched teeth as the antiseptic burns away any pathogens. The medic gives a wide grin, rattling a small pill bottle.

"I'd take tomorrow off, just to give yourself time to process what happened today. Take these for the pain. One pill every four hours until it's manageable. You might feel a little drowsy, so I wouldn't drive if I were you."

"No harm there, my car was stolen." Garcia reaches up with his left hand, taking the pill bottle. "Thanks, comrade."

"Don't mention it. Make sure Esther drives carefully, eh? You hit a speed bump too hard and that's going to pop open like a purse."

"I'll have a word with her." Garcia gives a wan grin, rising to his feet. His face is pale and drenched with sweat, and as he palms a painkiller and slams it into his mouth, the chalky texture makes him grimace. The medic packs up his kit into a small crimson doctor's pack and secretes the contents of the plate into a transparent bag, tying it off and dropping it in a nearby trash can. Garcia gives him a grateful farewell and steps out into the midday light, a pale sky hanging overhead into which towering spires intrude. Dupont wraps up her conversation and approaches.

"How are you feeling?"

"Like I got shot." He gestures to the Union van as it drives off. "What'll happen to him?"

"Union autopsy, I imagine. Just to confirm that he definitely had Tryp in his system. It's not particularly relevant to the case, but it should be mentioned in our reports." She rubs the back of her head, looking up at the building as it rises into a striped Morrissette sky. "Now with both chairmen dead, Ergot and Klein will officially be reclaimed by Coalition and its assets distributed fairly amongst members."

"He didn't do it," Garcia says after a moment, watching the van turn a corner into the shadowed streets of Place de Moteur. "Klein's murder, I mean."

"What makes you say that?"

"Hunch, mostly." Garcia inhales sharply, holding his arm at a crooked angle. "He didn't seem especially comfortable holding that gun, and from what we saw of the bullet's trajectory Klein was shot execution style. Professional." He shrugs. "Besides, he may still have an alibi."

"Pluto," she says. "He shot himself in the head. That looks pretty guilty."

Garcia thinks back to a night drenched in moonlight, a sonorous voice on the phone.

"Oh, he was definitely guilty alright. Just not of the murder."

"All the same, EnCorp will investigate his involvement." She looks back to him. "Did you get the names of the ARGUS test subjects?"

"I did," he says, fishing his notebook out of his back pocket. He pauses, his eyes landing on one name scrawled in his chicken scratch handwriting. He sighs. "So, I think one of them is the guy who stabbed me. Couple nights ago."

She stares blankly at him before erupting, throwing her arms up into the air.

"I fucking *knew* you weren't telling the truth about Promenade de Gloire! Why didn't you say anything?!"

"It didn't seem relevant!" He grimaces. "I trypped, anyway: it's not like I'm walking around with a knife wound in my back."

"I would appreciate having *one* day where nobody tries to kill either of us."

"I'm working on it."

She stares at him, her jaw churning in frustration. Eventually she lets out a short, sharp sigh.

"Come on," she says, flicking through the notebook and scanning the addresses. "I'll drive you back to your apartment."

He follows her to the Sudumobil, wincing as he ducks down and parks himself in the passenger seat. He carefully pulls the seatbelt across his chest and locks it in place, exhaling as he sinks into the chair. Dupont inserts the key, fires up the ignition, and begins the drive back to the Waterfront. They go quietly, Sanskrit softly muttering the lyrics to some biographical track detailing the life of an obscure Revolutionary politician on the speakers. Eventually, in the lull between one song and the next, Dupont speaks.

"I can't believe Ergot is going to get away with it." She shakes her head, fingers tensing around the wheel.

"I mean," Garcia says as he glances over at her, "he *did* shoot himself in the head."

"Sure, and if there's Tryp in his system he immediately jumped to another reality. He can anticipate that the other Esther Dupont is on her way, turn around just in time, and put a bullet in her chest. He can escape. He can get away with subjecting people to human testing. Maybe he can even get away with killing Krishna Klein, assuming he's dead in that reality too."

"And you know what's worse?" she continues, her eyes flashing. "Most people *can't* do something like this. EnCorp, the CMM, high-end Union assholes like Ergot – we have the luxury of doing whatever we like and can just bounce out when it gets inconvenient.

Everyone else? They have to live with the consequences of their actions."

Garcia nods, staring out the window.

"You know, I remember being frustrated a lot back in the bad old days." He sighs. "Sure, it was scary knowing that crossing the wrong person would get you killed, but in everyday life the most immediate concern was knowing that there were people out there doing evil things and getting away with them. This was before Tryp, of course. Back then, if you wanted to get out of something you just had to be rich or have your hands in the right pockets."

"What are you saying?"

"I'm saying," he says, softly, "that I understand how you feel."

She falls silent again, the twinkling outro to one Sanskrit song folded into the intro of another. Garcia waits a moment before speaking.

"Are you okay?" he asks, timidly. "You just saw a person commit suicide. That's the kind of thing that leaves a mark."

"I don't know. I think between me getting shot yesterday, and Ergot shooting himself today…" She sighs. "I think I just have a lot to process."

Silence once more, just the Sudumobil's purring engine and the rolling bassline of Marko Sanskrit's *Dragonfly* filling the air. They pass through Place de Moteur and through the winding galleries of the Scaffolds back towards the Waterfront. Eventually, Dupont coughs politely.

"It's Klein's funeral in a couple days," she says, softly. "They're holding the service at the Shipyard. Cremation, I believe."

"I'll be there," Garcia replies, looking out onto the passing Scaffolds. "My uniform could do with airing out."

"I can pick you up if you like."

"That would be appreciated. Given my luck, a damn anvil will probably fall on my head if I were to walk."

"I don't know if it's your luck, Pluto," Dupont says, a faint smirk on her lips, eyes fixed on the road, "or if you just keep walking under falling anvils."

She begins to move her head slowly in time with the beat, the road through Place de Moteur stretching before her as the sun continues its slow trawl across the virgin sky.

"It's growing on me," she says, gesturing to the cassette player. Garcia lets out a short laugh before cringing at the pain.

"You don't have to be nice to me because I got shot, you know."
Dupont grins, eyes on the road.
"Thank fuck."

"The folklore of Annalise is not unique in its role as propaganda, spinning the universal experience of children and adults into the great, arcane world of the Political."

Cameron Bach, foreword to *Folk Tales of the Annalissian Archipelago*

THIRTEEN

It is close to noon when Garcia wakes the following day, the sun already hanging heavy in a sky striped with thin white clouds. He lies in bed for a moment, his arm taut and beset by a blunt aching, his dark eyes stinging in the light. He forces himself up, slowly and with great caution, before rising to his feet and staggering into the lounge where his pill bottle rests on the coffee table. He pops it open and swallows a single pill, feeling it mulch into a bitter paste on his tongue as he pours a glass of water and downs it. He stands, barefoot and shirtless in the kitchenette, hand resting on the counter as his coffee pot steadily hisses and fills with steaming black liquid.

Once he has drank his coffee and eaten a meagre breakfast of pastries and fruit confit, he begins the slow process of redressing his wound. The dull ache is replaced with a sharp, spiteful pain as his torn skin snags on the saffron cotton medallion and, biting down, he tugs it loose and replaces it with a clean bandage daubed with antiseptic. He finishes up, panting softly from the pain, before slipping on a loose fuschia short-sleeved shirt and a pair of sandals and carrying a basket filled with soiled clothes down to the laundry room. There, he finds Scud sitting on a bank of rumbling machines.

"Damn, sharper – you look like dogshit."

"You should see the other guy," Garcia replies, setting the basket down and stretching his arm back to loosen the muscles.

"You been fighting?"

"Nah, just got shot at," he says, stuffing his laundry into the open maw of the machine. "It's not so bad – I imagine my boss will see how badly I can take a bullet and put me on desk duty. I *like* desk duty."

Scud gives a weak smile. Garcia squints at him.

"You okay, Scud?"

"Sure, fine." He sighs, plucking a pouch of tobacco from his back pocket and proceeding to roll a cigarette. "Ration check hasn't come through so money's a little tight."

"Ah, yeah, there was a printer malfunction over at Precinct 3." Garcia kicks the washing machine door shut. "Look, I need to head to the store later – do you guys need me to pick anything up?"

"Shit, man, you don't have to do that."

"Hey, you and your mom would do the same for me." Garcia picks up his laundry basket and hoists it beneath his good arm. "Bread, milk, eggs?"

"Sure, that," Scud says as he breaks into a tired smile, "that would be great, thanks."

"Don't mention it, I'll drop it by later." Garcia turns and begins the slow process of climbing the stairs, pausing halfway for a momentary breather leaning against the guardrail, basket on his hip. He reaches his apartment and drops the empty basket on the floor, a dark sliver of crimson running down the back of his shirt. He gives himself ten minutes to dry off and regain his breath before heading out into the hall, a canvas bag slung over his shoulder. He stops at the phone and dials the number for the Tank, smiling when Gallardo picks up.

"Hey, Manny, can I ask a favour?"

There is a deep, long sigh before the cadet speaks.

"Sure, what is it?"

"Kid in my building says his ration check hasn't arrived yet – could you look into that for me? Should be addressed to Marcie Bautista, apartment 241."

"Sure, swing by later and I'll have it ready for you." There is the brief sound of pencil on paper. "How's the arm?"

"It's a little tender, but I'm doing okay." He feels the bandage tug slightly against his shirt and shifts uncomfortably. "How's everything at the Tank?"

"Busy," he says. "The Captain and Manansala are out investigating a call that came through this morning, so I'm on papers."

He thinks of the kid, swallowed up by a tidal wave of forms and disclosures, his writing hand a rictus claw as it works through sheaf after sheaf. Kids like Manuel Gallardo keep the municipal machine ticking over. Old hats like Pluto Garcia get shot at. The former is real Militia work. The latter, he thinks, is just a shitty habit.

"Keep up the good work, Manny," Garcia says, mustering what little authority he has into his voice. Gallardo smiles on the other side of the phone.

"You got it, Lieutenant."

The South Seychel dispensary is empty when Garcia arrives. The counter is staffed by a woman in her early sixties, her skin tanned a deep brown and her hair a bleached, pearly platinum. She does not look up from her book, a true crime paperback detailing some high-profile murder in the glitzy streets of San Ernesto. Garcia slinks into the dispensary and begins shopping, grateful to be out of the heat.

First the basics: eggs, milk, pasta, rice, and bread, doubling up where permissible. Then to the produce aisle, where wide rows of misted vegetables and fruits farmed in the Jardin Communautaire glint in the fluorescents. He selects a couple bell peppers, their skins taut and shiny, and wraps them in a paper bag alongside a handful of brown onions and a garlic bulb. A few Funam carrots are added to the mix for good measure, followed by a plastic tray of fleshy, raw chicken. He rests these neatly in his canvas bag, the weight tugging across his chest and onto his wound as he hoists it up onto his good shoulder. He brings the bag to the counter and produces his ration check. The attendant glances up from her book, irritated at having been pulled away from a particularly juicy stabbing, and scans her eyes over the card.

"I'd like a bottle of Black Tiger import too, if you don't mind." Garcia flashes her a smile, fishing ten dollars from his wallet and handing it over. The attendant cocks an eyebrow.

"Little old for a teenager's drink, aren't you?"

"Apparently not." He fires an affable grin at her, only for it to bounce off of her impenetrable unperturbedness. With a sigh, she reaches up to a high shelf behind her head and plucks down a bottle of dark liquor. She slides it over the counter and Garcia places it gently among the assorted groceries and tentatively lifts the bag, checking its weight before heading back out into an apocalyptic sun.

Given the weather and the reduced pressure of not having anywhere to be, he opts for a scenic route home. He cuts across Rue D'Ecoulement, narrowly dodging the speeding rush of rickshaws and the occasional trundling streetcar, heading down an alley towards the narrow strip of skinny trees and greenery that makes up the Denstone Memorial Gardens. All around, disused canneries that have been converted into public housing rise up to form a bulwark against the warm coastal winds that blow in from the Baratte, giving the small stretch of garden a sheltered, distant feel.

He follows a path flanked by two rows of miscellaneous wildflowers, the kinds that grow well in weather as varied as Morrissette's. By winter, the thick bushels of crocus and primrose will be bare down to their slender stalks, their leaves still and stoic against the steady snow. Now, however, the garden is a bright, warm splotch of lavender and yellow in the red and brown brick heart of the Waterfront. Feeling the heat beat down onto him, Garcia shifts the load on his shoulder and parks himself on a nearby bench overlooking the field.

He sits for a while, breathing slowly and feeling the low ache of his shoulder in the sun – heavy and nagging but not entirely unpleasant, a curious reminder of the previous day. Wincing, he reaches into his pocket and takes out the painkiller bottle, popping one tablet into his hands and dry-swallowing it. He relaxes as the pain begins to subside, noting with interest a slight trickle of sweat as it rolls down his back, his limbs growing heavy and still. He feels his eyes fall out of focus slightly, the park becoming a hazy blur of greens and purples and whites, dark shadows cutting sharply across the field, the sky a bleached denim canvas stretched overhead. He blinks and when he next opens his eyes the light has changed slightly, it's dimmer, less directed. Standing before him is a silhouette, lean and human, face obscured by drowsiness and form hidden beneath a red bomber jacket.

"Do you know the story," the voice asks in a strange, hoarse voice tinged with a Laccannesse drawl, "of Oszkár the Otter?"

"I..." Garcia blinks blearily, looking up at them. A coin-shaped sun shines down on them, drenching them both in pale golden light. "I don't, no."

"I don't remember it too clearly," the voice says, distant. "A friend told it to me, before he died."

"I'd like to hear it," Garcia says, his own voice sounding faraway through the lingering fog of painkiller-induced revery.

"Once, there was an otter who grew tired of eating fish," the voice begins, heavy and slow as a falling tombstone. "He wanted to make himself a home on the islands south of Morrissette. The first he went to was beautiful, but a great hog lived there and hoarded all the food for itself."

A single white cloud slides across the sun, a knife resting upon a dinner plate.

"The second island was inhabited by many animals, but was ruled by violent apes who only shared food out to animals with two legs like them, and so the otter fled to a third and final island, a paradise: *Île d'Abondance*, where animals of all shapes and sizes lived together."

The voice takes on a melancholy edge, a wistfulness, a sentiment that floats on the warm seaborne winds of Morrissette.

"However, on this island all the food grew atop the tallest trees, and the otter simply could not reach. Saddened, he returned to the sea to a meagre life of fish. Had he only stayed on *Île d'Abondance,* perhaps he would have seen the other animals working together to gather the fruit they needed."

Stiff-limbed and drained, Garcia gives a queer smile.

"You're quite the story-teller," he says. "Did you call me the other night?"

The figure goes silent. Their face, hazy and distant like something glimpsed in a dream, flickers into what may be a sad smile.

"I'm sorry about what happened to Dean," it says. "And I'm sorry about your arm. It was always going to happen."

"It's," Garcia replies, his eyes growing heavy again, "it's alright."

Somewhere far away, a seagull screeches into the blue sky. The figure wavers as Garcia's eyes begin to close, his head lolling downward as if pulled by a great weight.

"I'll see you tomorrow, Mr. Garcia," the shape says, before Pluto Garcia falls into a strange sleep.

He wakes up an hour later, the sun forming a halo around the buildings that flank the park. His mouth is dry and a granular feeling stretches from the base of his tongue up to the roof of his mouth, a strange fizz rattling at the back of his throat. He rubs his eyes and sits up, scanning the park around him. No figure, no strange shape clad in a red bomber jacket, no indistinct face smiling sadly down at him. Just a park, an afternoon sun, and a bag of groceries.

He forces himself unsteadily to his feet, staggering slightly as he hoists the bag back onto his shoulder. Thankfully the pain caused by his bullet wound has dimmed to a gentle tug, his current discomfort brought on instead by his dry throat and the thin layer of sweat that covers his whole body.

He makes his way back to South Seychel, checking over his shoulder as he staggers back to Block Vingt-Neuf. He assaults the stairs slowly, cursing the busted elevator with each huffed breath. By the time he reaches apartment 241, his face is damp and his lungs are all-but empty. He leans up against the wall, taking a moment to recuperate before knocking on.

Scud opens, dressed in a pair of jeans and a baggy sleeveless shirt bearing the logo of the L'Anormal band GRIM. He smirks.

"You good?"

"If I don't die from getting shot, those stairs are going to kill me." Garcia offers up the groceries. "Milk, bread, eggs, some veg, and a bottle of Black Tiger for you and FUCK IS ASS out there."

"Their name is Thierry," Scud says, taking the groceries with a wide grin. "Thank you so much for this, sharper."

"Don't mention it," Garcia replies. "You'll want to refrigerate that milk straight away, though – I kinda fell asleep in the sun."

Scud's smile falters slightly.

"You sure you're okay, man?"

"Sure, sure – just the pain pills is all." Garcia picks the now-lighter bag up and slings it over his good shoulder. "I've got a guy at the Tank looking into your ration check too, I'll let you know when it turns up."

"Thanks, sharper." Scud's expression remains concerned as he looks over the lieutenant – his shiny forehead, his ill-fitting shirt drenched with sweat, his left shoulder bound with gauze. "You get yourself home. Rest up, yeah?"

"Plenty of time to do that when I'm dead, kid."

"It might be sooner than you think," Scud says, seriously. "Thanks again, man."

"Like I said: you'd do it for me." He goes to turn before something stops him – words, spray-painted on the interior walls of his mind, black and stark against dull wallpaper. He turns.

"You know anything about this graffiti showing up across town? 'I see with many eyes' or something?"

"Oh, uh." Scud gives a vague shrug. "I dunno. It ain't one of ours."

"You're not in trouble, Scud, I've just noticed it around is all."

"I'm telling the truth, it just ain't our style." Scud scratches his nose awkwardly. "L'Anormal slogans are short, y'know? Like that mural over on Piston Central."

"The one with the skull that says 'Pig Fuck' underneath it?" Garcia smirks. "That was you?"

"Sure was," Scud announces proudly, flashing a gap-toothed grin. "We're headed back over there to top it up tomorrow night."

"Alright, just don't go spraying shit where it ain't wanted, okay? It's my guys at the CMM that have to clean it up."

"No promises, sharper." Scud sniffs, an impish smirk on his face. "You got the weekend off?"

"Maybe. Might ask someone from the Tank to bring my paperwork round."

"I get why you ended up in the Militia. Sounds exciting."

"It ain't for everyone." Garcia says with a grin. "I'll see you around, Scud."

Garcia turns and takes the stairs down to his apartment, unlocking the door and dumping the remaining groceries on the countertop. He heads into the bathroom, splashing his face with cool water and drying off with a towel. The fog of the pain pills has lifted, bringing with it a degree of clarity. He thinks of the figure in the park, the sonorous speaker flanked by indistinct wildflowers. He shudders, hanging the towel up and heading back into the front room. Out in the hall the phone begins to ring, rattling like a maraca against the wall. He heads out to answer it.

"Pluto," Captain Marchenko says, "we've found the car."

"Row how we row out there, out to sea,
For shoals of herring and bream;
Salt-shorn we return to shore every eve,
For want of our sweet Annalise!"

Common Annalissian sea shanty, Unknown
author.

FOURTEEN

The sun glints down on the warm waters of Le Lavage, a thick strip of shifting white on dark green waves. Small, silvery fish dart amidst the sand and seaweed, and further out rickety boats carry leathery men and their hauls. Further still, the rocky outcrops of the Annalissian archipelago crest whale-like from the distant sea. On the silt-laden beach, upturned and partially torched, is a CMM Sao San Valiant.

Marchenko stands with her hands on her hips, squinting down at the car from the dock. To her left, First Lieutenant Manansala lights a cigarette and brings it to his lips. To her right, Second Lieutenant Garcia wrinkles his brow.

"Called in an hour ago," Manansala announces. "Apparently it showed up overnight."

"And it's definitely ours?" Garcia asks, weakly.

"Yep. The plates weren't too badly burned so we were able to confirm it pretty quickly."

"Well shit," Garcia mutters, looking up the beach. Two deep furrows run through the sand before swerving suddenly, ending in a deep crater of silt and burnt plastic. Amongst the rubble, thin ribbons of bubbling, smouldering vinyl lie like dead serpents on the sand. Garcia points down. "Are those…"

"My tapes, yes," Manansala cuts him off.

"Ay. Sorry, Eddie."

"This is all kinds of messed up," Marchenko says, almost to herself. "You said whoever took the car shot at you, right?"

"Yes, ma'am. Jardin Communautaire, while I was working the Klein case with Auditor Dupont."

"It doesn't add up." She shakes her head down at the burnt shape on the sand. "Who would take pot-shots at Coalition members, steal their car, and go on a joy-ride, only to dump it on the beach like this?"

"It *is* a Vali," Manansala says between drags. "It's not like they could've sold it for much."

"That's not the point. Someone fired a weapon at a lieutenant of the CMM and a member of the Liberté Enforcement Corp. That kind of thing hasn't happened since the '70s."

"Dupont and I are operating on the assumption that the bullet wasn't meant for us," Garcia adds, reaching out as Manansala passes him a cigarette. "We think they mistook us for a suspect, fired, and got spooked when Dupont mentioned that she's with the Union."

"Not to sound conspiratorial," Eddie says, flicking his lighter open and passing the flame over the tip of Garcia's cigarette, "but could this be a warning? Set fire to the car, letting us know we should back off?"

"If that's the case," Marchenko says as she straightens her back, "they shouldn't have done it in my fucking district. Do you have any ideas as to who shot at you?"

"Only thing we know is that they were using a .44 Magnum, probably some kind of hunting pistol."

"I suppose that narrows things down." She turns to Manansala. "Who called this in?"

"Ah." Manansala takes the cigarette from his lips and flips open his notebook. "You remember the boat guy?"

"You've got to be fucking kidding me."

"No, ma'am." Eddie returns the notebook and takes a slow drag. "He's got some kind of neighbourhood watch going up this stretch of coast. Old-timer, doesn't seem to trust the Guild to handle things properly."

"What's his name?"

"Elijah Sinclair. Lives in a hut up the beach there." Eddie gestures with the glowing tip of his cigarette. Garcia shades his eyes.

"I'll go talk to him."

"Like hell you will," Marchenko says sternly. "You got shot yesterday."

"And the day before that I lost the car." Garcia turns to face her. "Besides, this guy has been actively pissing you off for almost a week now, right? Might go a little smoother if I take the lead on this one."

"Garcia, with all the best will in the world: the way your luck has been going, you're likely to trip on your damn shoelaces and be swept out to sea."

"I've made it fifty-seven years without dying, Captain."

"Pluto," she says, "everyone here knows that isn't true."

"Look," he replies, a pained expression on his face, "I get I've screwed up a lot lately. Let me try and make it right."

She stares at him, her eyes scanning his stooped frame, his lined face, his scruffy crop of greying hair. With a low, exhausted sigh, she shrugs.

"Fine, go talk to him." Her eyes scan the horizon, light bouncing off of the waves and dappling her face. "Good luck, Pluto."

The shack sits in the sand some two miles up the beach and about thirty yards off the promenade proper, a small structure crudely constructed out of timber planks painted white. A single window peers darkly out onto the sea, obscured by a thin net curtain, and set into the southernmost face is a faded periwinkle door bearing a scuffed brass 36. Garcia pads across the sand, the sea spray misting his face and dousing his clothes with the rich smell of brine, and raps gently on the door. The shack shudders with each knock, and from within there is the sound of pots being knocked over and glass clinking.

After a moment, the door opens to reveal a stooped man in his eighties, his face baked a ruddy pink from the sun and his scraggly beard stained a deep goldenrod around the lips. Leathery skin droops from his high, pronounced cheekbones, and his large ears jut out oddly from his thin hair, giving him the overall impression of a poorly upholstered wingback. He squints out at Garcia with deep set, murky green eyes.

"Wondered when you was coming," he sneers. Unlike the lyrical offshore dialect of Dupont or Garcia's own muddled immigrant lilt, he speaks in the sharp, clipped consonants of the Northern Annalissian Peninsula. "Come in, we've lots to talk about."

"Thank you very much," Garcia says, ducking as he enters. "Mr. Sinclair, I presume?"

"Aye," the old man grunts, kicking a small pile of ragged clothes to one side and gesturing to a seat obscured beneath it. The shack interior is as ruinous and unsteady as its exterior, the sun intruding through various small slits in the wood and lighting the room a dull amber dashed with bright yellow-white. Clothes hang to dry, stiffened by the salty air, and piles of worn and tattered books stand atop rickety crate tables. "You're CMM? Here about the boat, no doubt."

"Amongst other things." Garcia sits down, feeling the chair creak slightly under his weight. He angles himself so that, should it collapse beneath him, he won't fall onto his stinging bullet wound. "We understand you called in the car wreckage up the beach this morning."

"Aye, that was me. Walked up to the payphone on the Casa. It's about time one of you showed up."

"Apologies, we've been fairly busy. Did you try contacting the Guild? This *is* part of their district."

The old man lets out a hoarse barking laugh, shaking his head.

"The Guild? Bunch of old whores and minstrels. Folly. This needs real policemen, doing *real* police work."

"Well I'm sorry to disappoint, Mr. Sinclair, but the CMM aren't police."

"You can tell yourself this, sure, but I am old enough to remember before the Coalition, before the Revolution. You may have swapped out the red armbands for yellow stripes and clipboards, but the folk who trained you were trained by fascists and cops."

"Be that as it may," Garcia says, shifting in his seat, "we don't really go in for all that police work talk. We're here to help the community."

"Tell that to the smoking vehicle halfway up the beach." He flashes a devilish grin. "It looks *very* helpful."

"Did you see who was driving the car?"

"No, it happened early this morning while I was asleep. I was combing for salvage when I found the damn thing."

"Did you pick anything up from around the car?"

"Siphoned what gas hadn't been burnt off for my oil lamp. Had a poke 'round in the trunk and glove box, didn't find nothing but some shitty burnt up crime books."

"I see," Garcia says, hands twitching uncomfortably, reaching for a notebook that is currently located in Dupont's pocket. "Thank you, Mr. Sinclair, the CMM appreciates you calling this in."

"If you're looking to help folk," Sinclair growls moodily, "you should start by catching whoever stole my damn boat."

"Of course. This happened a few nights ago now, right?"

"Aye. Was performing my nightly ablutions when I heard the old motor going. By the time I got out to see what was occurring, bitch had already sailed it a mile out to sea."

"You saw the person who took your boat?"

"Sure did – I've got a little crank-lamp hooked up to the motor. You set that old girl rumbling and the whole thing lights up like a firework."

"What did they look like?"

"Gal, she was, skinny thing. About 170, 175 centimetres. Light brown hair, I think, tied in a ponytail." He leans forward conspiratorially. "Looked like she might be Wojtecci. Likely why she stole my boat."

Garcia ignores this, his face settling into a frown. He thinks back to the ID badge found at Melnyk's apartment, to the girl with mousy brown hair and a comfortable smile. He nods.

"Did you see which way she went?"

"Out into the archipelago, as far as I can tell. Thought I saw some light out on the sea the other morning, so she's got to still be out there sailing around."

In the ticking machinery of Pluto Garcia's brain, dulled by pain medication and sand-stripped by sea air, a theory begins to slot into place. A bullet is fired, bloodied clothes are secreted and sewn away and, on a dark night, a woman takes a boat out to sea. He smiles.

"Thank you so much for your help, Mr. Sinclair. I'll have a word with our colleagues over at the Icehouse and try to get out to the archipelago as soon as possible." He rises to his feet, ignoring the creaking of his knees. "You said there was a payphone nearby?"

"Casa's probably the closest one, aye."

"Excellent, thank you." He gives a polite nod, heading to the door. "You know, the CMM is always looking for volunteers. You'd make a good militiaman."

"Like I said, I'm old enough to remember what you *used* to be." The old man remains seated, his narrow limbs bunched like the legs of a spider in the cramped interior of the shack. "No, sir, I'm happy keeping this stretch of coast clean and safe. I'll leave the food deliveries and leg breaking to you."

Garcia parts with a brisk handshake and heads up off the beach and into Madame Syndicat. He walks jauntily, his pace swift as he cuts between cafés and boulangeries and into the tall, sandstone heart of the Casa. He finds the payphone Sinclair mentioned and slots in a dollar coin, taking up the handset and dialling the Liberté Branch number from memory. The phone rings and, after a second or two, a reedy voice cuts through the dial tone.

"Salut, Liberté Enforcement Corp."

"Salut," Garcia says, a smile on his lip. "Is Junior Auditor Esther Dupont there? It's Lieutenant Garcia from the CMM."

"Please hold," the voice says. There is a soft, dull tone followed by the sound of a phone line being reconnected. Then, a new voice.

"Pluto? Everything okay?"

"I have a theory," he says, proudly. "I have an idea as to where Melnyk is."

"What?" Her voice pitches slightly in excitement. "How?"

"My luck is on the turn, I guess. A woman matching Melnyk's description was seen stealing a boat on Le Lavage the same night Klein was murdered."

"Okay, well that's a start," she replies, her voice more measured now. "Do you know where she was headed?"

"Out into the archipelago. Old-timer over on the beach thinks she might still be out there, says he keeps seeing lights on the water."

There's a pause.

"There are over a thousand islands out there."

"I know." Garcia waves a hand vaguely, grinning. "But we can narrow it down. Go back to Melnyk's apartment, see if there's anything there that can point us to the right island."

"Alright, well... Just don't get your hopes up, okay? It's promising, but it's not *concrete*." Her voice wavers slightly. Garcia leans against the telephone and smirks.

"You sound unconvinced."

"I trust your judgement, I do," she says. "I just have this nagging feeling that Ergot's suicide has… Changed things somehow."

"How do you mean?"

"I don't know. I can't read Morrissette the way you can. I just… There's talk around Liberté that it was definitely Ergot. You've got to admit – dropping Tryp and immediately killing yourself isn't exactly innocent behaviour."

"But he had an alibi," Garcia says, limply. Dupont sighs.

"Hasn't stopped the Bureau before." Concern creeps into the edges of her voice. "Hey, are you sure you're okay to come to the funeral tomorrow? You're supposed to be resting."

"I find funerals *extremely* restful."

"Don't be smart, Pluto."

"Sorry," he says. "Yes, I'll be fine. I'll load up on painkillers, just in case."

"Alright. I have some paperwork that needs filing, but I'll pick you up at 10AM, okay?"

"Perfect, thank you. Take care, Esther."

"You too, Pluto."

"As each man is entitled to the city in which he lives, so too is he entitled to the earth in which he rests."

Administrator Du Beke, *The Book of Common Speech*

FIFTEEN

The sky is ice blue as Krishna Klein's coffin is carried to the churchyard of Our Lady of Revolution.

Mourners stand in neat rows, eyes low to the ground. The Council stand at the forefront of the crowd: Somsak Chang, Eden Khazi, Moreau Chaudhary, Roxanne Swan, black armbands over their customary Union red jumpsuits, dark glasses to block out the high, unforgiving sun. Behind them, Esther Dupont stands straight-backed and formal, her untied hair looking like a halo around her head. Then comes Agent Anne Dao in her neat grey bureaucratic suit, and right at the back stand Pluto Garcia and Cassandra Marchenko, dressed in black jackets with horizontal yellow stripes on the shoulder denoting rank – one for Garcia, three for Marchenko.

The proceedings are fairly traditional. The coffin is carried in by temple attendants to an old Laccannesse dirge that drones from a cassette deck. They set the coffin down and a eulogy is delivered by an Administrator, in this case a passage taken from the Book of Common Speech, while the distant sounds of industry – muffled by the high walls that surround the churchyard – rumble on. Somsak Chang, as Mediator of Proceedings, gives a speech about Klein's work, his keen mind, his effortless devotion to the people, all while narrowly talking around his erraticism, his unsteadiness, his uncertainty. He lowers his eyes and places a folded Union flag atop the coffin, and gives the close-fisted salute of the Revolutionaries as it is lowered into the ground. An attendant subtly pushes a button on the tape deck and the Laccannesse hymn *He Rests Upon a Stretch of Blue* starts to play, beginning with a long, sustained D note on a pump organ. The first few handfuls of dirt are gathered up from the ground by Chang, Khazi, Chaudhary, and Swan, and sprinkled onto the coffin as it descends finally into the earth. There are no tears, no great racking sobs. Just the quiet, conflicted relief of the Union.

Once the service is concluded the crowd disperses into huddled groups speaking in respectful, hushed tones. The remaining Council members go off to a secluded corner of the churchyard, Chang nodding politely to Garcia and Marchenko as he passes. Dao, solo and unassuming, mills around the congregation, a slight limp concealing the firearm perpetually held on her hip. Through the crowd, Esther Dupont sidles towards Garcia and Marchenko.

"How's the arm?"

"Tender. I'm cutting back on the pain pills, they keep knocking me out." Garcia gestures over to her. "Captain, this is Esther Dupont. Esther, Captain Marchenko."

"Pleasure to finally meet you, Auditor." Marchenko offers out a hand and Esther briskly shakes it. "The two of you have been doing some good work on this Klein case. Garcia mentioned that you trypped?"

"Yes, ma'am, two days ago. I'm doing much better, thank you."

"Neither of our jobs should be this dangerous, Comrade Dupont," Marchenko says, sternly, her eyes flitting over the crowd. "Morrissette no-doubt appreciates all the work you've done to keep it safe."

"Thank you, ma'am." Dupont flashes a prim, neat smile before turning to Garcia. "Lieutenant, may I have a word?"

"Absolutely."

The two secrete off to the northernmost corner of the churchyard, where a high wall blocks off view of the docks and their dark waters. Overhead a cool wind carries the smell of salt and the first reminders of the coming autumn from distant lands. The attendants quietly pack up the tape deck and the Administrator gathers his hand-typed notes, stuffing them into his worn but well-cared-for copy of the Book of Common Speech. Garcia gestures back to the final few members of the dispersing congregation.

"Quite the service."

"Hmm. Lot of people not speaking their mind."

"That's just funerals," Garcia says with a shrug. "Ideally a person's death would be marked solely by the good they did in life, but the sad fact is by the time one dies they've inevitably racked up a sizeable list of grievances against them."

"Human testing is more than a 'grievance', Pluto."

Garcia lets out a short, sharp laugh.

"I suppose that's fair."

He watches the attendants and Administrator return to Our Lady of Revolution, its stark concrete walls decorated with murals of Kamote the Martyr, bullet wound upon her left breast, stony face wet with tears for her fallen comrades.

"Wasn't expecting to see Dao here," he says eventually.

"Did you notice she was packing?"

"I did. Fairly standard for Bureau agents, as far as I'm aware."

"Is it standard for them to be wielding a Magnum .45?"

Garcia looks sharply at her.

"You're shitting me."

"Afraid not. Got a glimpse of it when she shook Comrade Khazi's hand on the way in."

"You think she's the one who shot you?"

"At this point? I have no idea." She stuffs her hands into the pockets of her jumpsuit, eyes turned skyward. "You remember what Ergot said about the Bureau? How they've infiltrated just about every part of Morrissette?"

"Sure. It's the most well-known secret in Annalise."

"I've been thinking," Dupont says quietly, carefully. "What if Melnyk was Bureau?"

Garcia goes quiet, watching her intently. She continues.

"Think about it: she was able to escape a crime scene, dispose of evidence, and disappear without a trace. She was intimately involved with one of the most important men in the Scaffolds, and was present at his death. *And* she has access to Tryp, despite working in a fairly safe profession."

"It makes sense." Garcia rubs his chin thoughtfully. "You think Melnyk was sent to spy on Klein?"

"Maybe. Could be that they'd gotten wind of his private project and wanted to find out more. When they realised that it would make their lives infinitely easier, they decided to take it."

"But how? Ergot was convinced that they'd managed to keep it a secret."

"Krishna Klein went on at least one drunken bender a year," Dupont says, looking at the hole where the coffin now lays. "For all we know, he told every single sex worker in Madame Syndicat."

"What about Bukowski? It's a little suspect that a guy on the list of testers attacks a CMM operative just before he's put on the case."

"I don't know, Pluto," she says. She is tired, exhausted even, her shoulders low and her head tilted slightly to one side. "Maybe he's with the Bureau too? Maybe he's just some poor bastard who got wrapped up in all this. I investigate suspicious shipments and you oversee food deliveries: we're *clearly* out of our depth on this one."

Garcia chews his lip, pride stinging like a bullet wound.

"So the Bureau sent an agent into Syndicat to infiltrate the Guild, knowing that she can pump Klein for information. Then what?"

"Well, look around you: both Ergot and Klein are dead, and their company is about to be formally seized by the Morrissette Coalition. Amongst said company's assets is the most powerful supercomputer the world has ever known. One that can predict the future."

"*Madre Kamote.*" Garcia's jaw drops slightly. "You think the Bureau killed him to get their hands on ARGUS?"

"It makes sense. Ergot said he suspected sabotage after that disc went missing. If the Bureau got hold of it they'd have concrete evidence that ARGUS exists. Then we come along, Ergot kills himself, and the Bureau have an opportunity to seize it." Dupont shrugs sullenly. "With Ergot out of the way, the only loose end is Maria Melnyk. Which is probably why she's being hunted by someone with a .45 magnum."

Garcia thinks back to the phone call in the Tank, the clipped tones of Agent Dao as she told him she had "pulled some strings". He curses himself silently.

"Where's ARGUS now?"

"Carted off to a warehouse in Shipyard somewhere." Dupont wrinkles her nose. "You remember when we first took on the case? You said that we're not meant to solve it. I think you were only half right. I think this is as far as we were meant to get."

"So what now?"

"My guess? I imagine we'll get back to our respective offices, receive a call from the Bureau or some other higher-ups, and be quietly removed from the case."

"*Politics*," Garcia snarls. "But we're so close. We have an idea of where Melnyk went, we can track her down and get a confession out of her."

"And go against the Bureau of Records?" She looks up at him, a look of incredulity on her face. "Pluto, that's what got people lined up and shot back in the old days."

"These aren't the old days, Esther. Morrissette has moved past that."

She stares at him, expression unwavering. He continues, pacing around her.

"Esther, I need you to know that even if they do take me off this case, I'm going to find Melnyk. Somebody needs to answer for all…" He gestures limply at the empty churchyard futilely, at the green grass and the denim blue sky, at the weeping figure of Our Lady of Revolution. "All this."

"Come on, Pluto," she says sadly. "I'll drive you back to the Tank."

She's right, of course. The call comes in an hour after Garcia arrives at Precinct 14. He is called into Marchenko's office and sat down, told that following the death of Comrade Dean Ergot, prime suspect in the assassination of Krishna Klein, investigations are to cease effective immediately. The case hasn't been closed, not formally, but for now "resources are to be moved elsewhere". He protests. She explains, simply and devoid of emotion, that the maintenance man has rescinded his corroboration, and has spoken directly to Bureau agents confirming that Ergot was not in the office the night Klein was killed. With Ergot dead, there is nothing to challenge this statement.

Marchenko's expression is grim, dour, her fingers laced in front of her, her eyes dark. She purses her lips as Garcia protests and, once he has stopped, gives him a sad smile. He quietly rises to his feet and walks up the narrow stairs to the roof, where he smokes two of Eddie Manansala's cigarettes in a row. When he comes back down, Manny Gallardo offers him a cup of coffee, black and hot, and he drinks it gratefully.

Once his hands have stopped trembling, he heads over to Gallardo's desk and makes a call to Liberté. After a moment, he is patched through to Esther.

"It happened."

"Yes," she says simply. "We did good work, Pluto."

"The person who killed Krishna Klein is still out there."

"Probably, yes." She sighs softly.

"It's fine," he says, not meaning it. "I have work to do here at the CMM, anyway. Wellness checks, deliveries."

A silence falls over them, accented by the gentle hum of the line and the distant background noise of Liberté. Garcia stares at the blank walls of the Tank, all imported pine and the residue of sticky tack, a hasty construct to mark the start of a hasty regime. Dupont, in Liberté, taps her pencil on the desk in front of her, while other Auditors go about the busywork of overseeing import and export.

"Regardless of whether or not he killed Krishna Klein, Dean Ergot was not innocent," she says, eventually.

"You're right. But it doesn't change the fact that a killer *is* out there and that we haven't caught them."

"Pluto, you work in domestic support and this is the most corporate crime I have ever come across. Why does it bother you so much that someone is going to get away with something?"

"I don't know," Garcia murmurs, the tightness in his arm beginning to break through the hazy fuzz of his painkillers. "Because it feels like we're going backwards?"

"In the case?"

"In Morrissette!" he exclaims. "There was a Revolution! Things were meant to be different, Esther!"

"Revolution can't fix everything," Dupont replies delicately. "The future doesn't give to just one singular push."

Garcia falls silent again, looking despairingly at the desk before him, at the heavy plastic case of the telephone and its curled eggshell wire, at the pens and pencils jammed awkwardly into a see-through cup, at Gallardo's handwritten notes reminding him to chase up food and medical supply deliveries. Good work, mundane, and organised at minimum capacity; underfunded yet vital.

"You're right," he says, quietly. "Thanks, Esther."

The call ends amicably enough, and Garcia goes about the rest of his day in the funk of the admonished. He works at organising a temporary rehousing following a burst water pipe on Rue

D'Ecoulement, calling in a Union maintenance team to assist in the repairs. With this out of the way, he checks the reports left on his desk by Manny: tucked into the delivery notes is an envelope addressed to Marcie Bautista, Apartment 241, Block Vingt-Neuf. With a smile, he pockets it.

In lieu of a lunch break, he takes to the roof and smokes another of Manansala's cigarettes before writing out a quick IOU promising the other half of his next beer import and leaving it on the first lieutenant's desk. By the time he has to clock off, he's smoked two more cigarettes and updated the IOU to include a Lupe Celentano tape.

The walk home is slow and warm, the streets already beginning to fill. He lets his feet navigate themselves along the winding path towards South Seychel: curve up the alleyway that runs alongside the Tank, turn left on Rue D'Ecoulement, follow the road for ten minutes into the Southern Packing District, dodging the occasional half-drunk sailor as they stumble down the sidewalk, before heading right onto Kamote East. Fork out four dollars and fifty cents for a box of noodles, two dumplings, and a bottle of soda at the food stall on the corner, pocket the change, follow the concrete steps onto Block Vingt-Neuf, and take the third left.

He heads up to the second floor, pushing the envelope through the mail slot. From inside he can hear the sounds of raucous punk music blasting through the walls, the customary pre-drinks ritual of the L'Anormal. He smiles to himself and heads to his apartment, depositing his stun gun and badge by the door. He sulkily finishes the last of his noodles, depositing the box in the trash and washing it down with the now lukewarm soda. He pops a pain pill – his final one of the day – and sits down hard on the couch, feeling an intrusive shape jab into his ass. He reaches into his back pocket and produces the notebook and, with a noted bitterness, flicks through the last few pages. Addresses, phone numbers, names, reminders, tallies, small details hidden and obscured behind large ones. The details of the testers stare dumbly up at him, Jonah Bukowski's name double-underlined. He sneers and flicks back a couple pages to the address of Maria Melnyk. Beneath that he sees in his barely legible writing the words "KEEP NADIA UPDATED".

He stares at the words for a moment, an indignance rising up inside him. He flicks the notebook closed, jams it back into his pocket, and heads back out into Morrissette.

"Let us be lazy in all things, for that which we work for is ours!"

Camille Kamote, *Battle Hymn of Annalise*

SIXTEEN

Evening arrives at the Scaffolds, and the Boiler bursts with life. Workers have gone home, replaced their sooty jumpsuits with collarless shirts and high-waisted pants, clean leather shoes and aviator shades, leering grins and hair pomade. The two bar staff work in tandem to pour drinks and crack the tops off bottles, counting dollar coins and bills and slipping them into the cash register to ensure that, by the unforgiving light of tomorrow morning, a new import order can be placed for Wojtecci vodka and San Ernesto mezcal.

Pluto Garcia makes his way across the dancefloor and up the stairs towards the mezzanine, orders himself a bottle of Kosmo, and scans his eyes over the crowd. A modern disco revival hit plays on the thumping speakers, the pulsing bassline rattling through the metal guardrail he leans on. It samples an old Petrovic Sisters hit and, to his slight amusement, he finds his head bobbing in time. He takes a pull on his bottle and wipes his lips on the back of his hand, spotting a dark-haired woman chatting to a young man in a brown leather jacket, short-legged grey pants, and red socks pulled up past the calf. Garcia begins to push through the crowd, meekly apologising as he goes, feeling the biting pain of his arm each time someone jostles clumsily into it.

She spots him before he has finished making his way over, her eyes wide and unblinking as they fix on his. She leans into the man in the leather jacket, places a tender hand on his arm, and says something with an apologetic smile. He bows his head and hurries up, returning to the bar with drink in hand. She, in turn, rises to her feet, dressed in figure-hugging black pants and a suit jacket with exaggerated shoulder pads.

"You just lost me a john," she says, her face unemotive. Garcia winces.

"My apologies, Nadia. How've you been?"

"Worried, mostly." She stares at him. "You said you were going to get in touch."

"Until now we've not had much to get in touch about." He points up to the ceiling, yelling over the pounding bass. "Is there somewhere quieter we can talk?"

"There's a terrace," she says, gesturing with her head. "Come on."

She leads him through the floor, smiling coquettishly to johns and fellow Guildmembers alike with effortless, practised grace. They climb some metal stairs off to the other side of the dancefloor, cutting through a narrow hallway and to a large door painted tar black. When they come to the terrace, she produces a packet of cigarettes from her breast pocket and flicks one out before offering the packet to Garcia. He gratefully takes one and she lights them both before turning and leaning out over the guardrail.

"She hated Morrissette," she says, quietly. "Maria, I mean. She was from a little commune up in Montetrieste. She hated how distant everything felt in the city, how everything felt like it's part of a *system*."

Garcia joins her, looking down into the crowded streets and alleyways that link the factories and warehouses of Piston Central. People flow like blood through the city's veins, drunken and giddy as they pass from bar to food cart to the sprawl of Charbon and out into the Warrens.

"Now me? I was raised here. Mom was a dockworker on the Waterfront, dad was with the Guild." There's a strange look on her face, ill-lit by the glow of Morrissette, shadows cutting deep lines across her cheeks and on either side of her eyes. "This is the only life I've ever known, and I *love* it. I love the Guild, I love my job. This city isn't perfect, sure, but it tries *so* hard."

She turns to face him but almost seems to look past him, her eyes fixed on the dim orange-black sky.

"Did you know there are some places where people don't have homes? Where they have to pay for the medicine that keeps them alive? Morrissette may not be some perfect little community in the mountains, but fuck... It's got to be better than *that*."

She turns away once more, white cigarette smoke curling up from her lips.

"I have a lot of respect for the CMM, for the Union. Hell, even the Bureau. You all do good work. You bypass that mean, cruel part of us that says we can only take and never give." That strange look returns to her face as she takes another slow drag on her cigarette, a distant and dark expression approaching a sickly smile.

"That's what I'd say to her if she were here right now: just because it's part of a system, doesn't make it inhuman."

She shakes herself loose from the thought that was carrying her flotsam-like out into the night.

"Where's your friend?" she mutters, cigarette still held firmly between her lips.

"Back at Liberté. We're technically no longer working the case."

Nadia freezes, cigarette halfway between her mouth and the guardrail she leans against.

"What's going on, Lieutenant?"

"Our main suspect, Comrade Dean Ergot, committed suicide. With that, we're out of leads." He gives a grim smirk. "Personally, I think there are too many loose ends to tie up, so I'm out here. Still working it."

Nadia's voice wavers slightly.

"Have they found Maria?"

"Not yet." He takes a drag of the cigarette before looking over at her. "We have reason to think she's in trouble."

"I've already told you everything I know."

"No, I don't think you have. And that's okay – you have no reason to trust me, or my partner. We *could* be Bureau, right?" He turns to look at her, his expression piercing and sympathetic and fixed. A gumshoe stare. "Anyone could be Bureau."

She shifts uneasily, looking out over the flickering lights of the Scaffolds.

"So it's true, then," she says finally.

"You knew?"

"I'd worked it out. There's a saying amongst us escorts: if you don't know at least one Bureau spy, you're it."

"Do you think she'd been with the Bureau for long?"

"Couple years, maybe." She gives a sad shrug. "Probably around the time she started seeing Krishna on the reg."

"Did you tell anyone about your suspicions?"

"Fuck no." She shakes her head, a queasy smile on her lips. "The Guild is built on discretion, Lieutenant. We have each other's backs."

"She may have killed someone, Nadia."

"Don't be fucking stupid," she sneers. "She *liked* him. They were *friends*."

"He was found with a bullet in his head."

"We don't carry guns around with us. It scares off the johns."

"We found a dress covered in blood at her apartment," he says, his tone soft and insistent.

"She didn't kill him."

"How do you know?"

"She didn't kill him."

"*How do you know?*"

"Because she fucking told me, alright?!" She spins sharply to face him, venom in her dark eyes. She snarls, closing in on him. "She called me the night he died, told me she was in trouble."

She falls silent, the keenness dropping from her features. Garcia continues.

"What else did she say?"

"She didn't say anything, just that she was going away for a while."

"Where did she say she was going?"

"Fuck if I know." She waves erratically, the glowing tip of the cigarette drawing glowing shapes in the air. "Some Laccannesse name, I didn't recognise it. *Ile d'Abondance* or something."

Blue moonlight washes over him and Garcia finds himself back in his apartment, drowsy with pain pills, telephone handset in his hand. A dreamy voice tells him a story, a story of an otter with blue-black fur who leaves *Ile d'Abondance* for a sorry life at sea. He blinks and looks up to see the bemused face of Nadia, cigarette held limply between her fingers.

"You alright? You've gone grey."

"Just," he stammers, finishing the cigarette before stubbing it out on the guardrail and flicking the butt over the side. "Just remembered something, is all. I think I know where Maria is." He backs away, pushing the door open and the feeling the music wash out into the warm night air, echoing over the rooftops and bouncing amid the spires of Piston Central. "If I find her I'll let you know, I promise."

She stares silently at him. Eventually, she gives a sharp nod. "You fucking better."

Pluto Garcia rushes through the streets of the Scaffolds as fast as his legs can carry him, feeling the sharp tug of his bandage against the still sticky wound on his arm. Chemin vers L'Industrie is alive, filled with music and stumbling drunks who hold one another up as they slur through cheap insults and cheaper liquor. A billboard lights up the night sky, displaying a sea of grinning workers surrounded by a joyful tangerine wash, above which the words "REJOICE IN ALL THINGS, BOTH IN WORK AND IN PLAY" are written in huge black letters.

Garcia cuts down an alleyway to avoid another wave of swarming crowds, the residual glow of Piston Central lighting his way. He reaches into his pocket and feels a couple loose dollars jangling just beyond his fingertips, and scans his memories desperately for the nearest payphone. He recalls a visit to Piston Central years ago, a trip with Eddie and Marchenko not long after he'd been made second lieutenant, and how halfway through the night he'd drunkenly called his mom to tell her about the promotion. He pieces together a hazy patchwork of memories. Charbon, on the border of Place de Moteur. There's a payphone there.

He makes an immediate beeline towards it, feeling muscle memory taking over. His mind races as he dips into another alleyway, the change clinking in his pocket, the acute pinching his arm drawing his focus only when he moves too sharply. He thinks about Klein, sitting in a room surrounded by the slumbering mind of the infant ARGUS, scribbling in his notebooks. He thinks about Klein, his skull vacated by a 9mm bullet, lying prone on the floor of room 312. He thinks about an otter cresting the waves. He turns another corner, then another, closing in on the intersection of Charbon and St. Vincent.

The payphone is affixed to a heavy aluminium pole on the sidewalk outside a hardware store. Garcia reaches into his pocket and produces a single dollar coin, slotting it into the machine and beginning to dial.

"Hello?" Esther says, blearily.

"Sorry, you were sleeping."

"Dozing," she yawns. "What's up, Pluto?"

"I know where Maria Melnyk is," he says, a grin creeping across his lips. "I think she went to Pietnera Island."

"What makes you say that?"

"I just spoke to Nadia."

"Pluto, we're not working this case anymore!"

"It was a wellness check!" He grins, leaning against the pole. "Nadia told me that she spoke to Melnyk before she fled. Apparently, she said that she was going to a place called *Ile d'Abondance* to lay low."

"The island from Oszkár the Otter?" She sounds puzzled, trying to keep up with Garcia as he giddily rambles. "So what? Why do you think she's on Pietnera?"

"That's the name Klein wrote in his storybook, right? The one that, according to Klein, was used as a reference point for one of the islands in Oszkár the Otter."

"Why..." Puzzlement gives way to exasperation. "Why would she go there?"

"There's something we're still missing, I think. Nadia said Klein and Melnyk liked each other, that they were friends."

"You think that he told her about Pietnera?"

"Ergot said he told *everyone*. Liked to show off about it, liked to have his ego stroked. Seems like the kind of thing he'd mention to a regular escort."

"Okay, well... Do you have a plan on how to get out there and check?"

"The CMM have a boat over at the Icehouse. It's not great, but it'll do."

She falls silent for a moment. The faraway sounds of Piston Central drift over the tops of buildings and into the strip malls and commercial blocks of Charbon. Nearby, the soft echo of footsteps down an alley.

"This is dangerous, you know," she says, eventually.

"What is?"

"All of it. Going against the Bureau. Tracking down a murder suspect without back up. We're putting our careers and lives at risk."

"Maybe," Garcia replies. "I don't know. Even if I get kicked from the CMM, even if I get shot in the head and tryp, it'll be worth it to remind the Bureau that they don't run Morrissette."

Silence, again. No more footsteps, now, and even the sounds of Piston Central seem dampened. Clouds roll in overhead, bunched up in the dark sky and trundling inland.

"Okay," Dupont says. "I'll meet you at the dock in the morning."

"Thank you, Esther. Sincerely."

"If you get shot, I'm kicking your body into the sea."

"Perfect. Saves the Tank from having to apply for a state funeral." A rhythmic robotic *ding* rings out in his ear. "Okay, I'm running out of time. I'll see you tomorrow, Esther."

"Goodbye, Pluto."

She hangs up and Garcia returns the handset to the holder, a bittersweet smile on his face. Somewhere, out towards the dark waters of the Shipyard, a lonely horn marks the end of the night shift. Garcia thinks of Maria Melnyk, freckled face lit by a fuel-powered lamp, sitting on a distant beach as the night wind carries the smell of salt up from the water.

He is so deep in thought that he does not notice the shape watching him from the far end of a nearby alley: a lean shape, skinny and darklit against the industrial shine of the Scaffolds; a shape dressed in blue jeans and a red bomber jacket, face obscured beneath a hood. A voice snaps him from his revelry, a slow, heavy voice tinged with a Laccannesse drawl.

"Mr. Garcia?"

"WITH MANY EYES I SEE."

Nanti Bukowski

SEVENTEEN

In the intestinal darkness of Piston Central, between the thoroughfare of Chemin vers L'Industrie and the open courtyards of Charbon, Pluto Garcia finds himself paralysed.

The memory of a blade slices up from the base of his spine, severing a suite of veins and leaving him cold and heavy. The sun glints golden off the sea as he bleeds out on the Waterfront, as he stands under amber streetlight. He swallows down and tries to suppress the memory as his heart pounds against his ribcage, moving so hard as to almost break free. Throughout his body his vascular system begins the hurried process of prioritising movement over function.

"Jonah?" he says, his voice raspy as his mouth dries up. "Jonah Bukowski?"

The shape in the alley looms before him, a malformed and blocky form given a spectral, inhuman vagueness by the dark shadows that surround it. Bit by bit a numbness creeps into Garcia's fingertips, his nerves falling silent as his focus shifts away from his periphery and onto the silhouette that stands before him. Unthinkingly he begins a mental checklist: right pocket heavy with jangling change that his brain uselessly calculates at eight dollars and thirty-eight cents; stun gun is back at the apartment, lying on his coffee table next to his badge and a pile of unread crime novels; in his left pocket, the near-weightless aluminium cube of his pillbox presses eagerly against his thigh, containing four pills of Repodimethyltryptamine.

"Have you been following me?" he asks, planning a route back out through the winding alleys and out into the densely-populated Chemin vers L'Industrie. If he moves *now,* a small prey-like and internal part of him screams, he might just be able to disappear into the crowd.

"Nanti," comes that voice, hoarse and harsh. "My name's Nanti."

"Sorry. Nanti." Garcia swallows down the urge to run, ignoring the phantom stab wound that has followed him across ProbMat and whose breath glances hungrily off his back. "You called me the other night, didn't you? At my apartment?"

There is no movement save for the hammering of Pluto Garcia's heart and the imperceptible clenching of his muscles. He tries again, louder.

"Why are you following me, Nanti?"

"I haven't been following you." The voice rings out into the dim street. "I've been waiting."

"Have I done something to hurt you?"

"Not yet," the voice replies. "Not me."

Garcia steps back a little, his eyes narrowing. There, in the indistinct glow of the Scaffolds, he can just make out some features: an unruly fringe swept low over dark, heavy-lidded eyes, a clean-cut jawline, a faint stubbly moustache on a curled upper lip.

"What do you mean?"

"You haven't hurt me," Nanti says, a curious confidence creeping into his voice, "but you're going to hurt my friend."

Garcia scans the alleyway. There's enough space on his right to maybe dart past him, *maybe* get out into Charbon before he catches up and pulls the knife and–

"Who am I going to hurt, Nanti?" He watches closely, scanning the face for any change in expression, any chance of attack. "Do you mean Maria?"

Nothing.

"I know about your work with Ergot and Klein," Garcia calls out to him. His eyes nervously dart across the hardware store windows, across the neighbouring dispensaries and outlets and offices, hoping to see any sign of life. No luck. It's the weekend, and Charbon is empty. "I know about your work on ARGUS."

There is an imperceptible shifting, a movement in the shadows.

"I," Garcia stammers, feeling his heart heavy in his chest. Somewhere in a deep, primordial part of his brain, he feels a creeping coldness, the coldness of death. "We can help you. We can try and get you to a hospital, get you the support you need."

Somewhere, in an adjacent reality, the terror sitting like a lead weight on Pluto Garcia's chest tips him over the edge and his heart clenches like a fist. His mouth tastes sharp and coppery, and a numbness grips him as his blood refuses to travel the breadth of his body. He falls to the floor and dies, a limp mass crumpled in the street. That does not happen here.

"It's okay, Nanti. You're not in trouble."

"I attacked you," the man named Nanti Bukowski says, quietly, a trembling in his voice.

"I know." Garcia raises an open hand. "It's okay."

"I thought it would help." Nanti shifts uneasily in the shadows. "I thought if you weren't around, maybe she'd get away. That's what he wanted."

"Who are you talking about?" Garcia asks. "Do you mean Klein? Krishna Klein?"

In an adjacent reality, Nanti Bukowski panics at the sound of the dead man's name. He dives forward, crying out, the knife clenched in his slender hand accidentally flying forward and stabbing Pluto Garcia in the thigh, severing his femoral artery. Garcia stumbles to the floor and dies, ice-cold and bloodless, in the arms of a scared young man. That does not happen here.

"We were friends. He taught me things." In the darkness there is the hint of a sad smile. "He showed me how to use ARGUS."

Garcia steps tentatively towards the alley, movements so slow as to be barely noticeable. From the alley, Nanti continues.

"He didn't want you to find her. He didn't want that, but ARGUS… ARGUS knew that you were going to. Ninety-seven-point-nine-eight percent chance across seventeen-thousand-four-hundred-and-ninety-two potential realities."

"So you wanted me dead. To take me out of the equation."

Silence, for a moment.

"I'm sorry," He says, eventually. "It's just, with you gone, her chance of escaping increased from forty-two-point-three-three percent up to fifty-six-point-zero-three percent. Then I would need to stop the Bureau agent somehow. I thought about cutting the brakes on your car, but that would increase the chance of you dying before they had a chance to steal it by seventy-six-point-nine-nine percent."

"Did ARGUS tell you all this?" In the low light, Garcia sees a flash of teeth.

"ARGUS told me everything." Nanti says. "It told me about Comrade Ergot shooting himself in the head to evade capture – seventy-two-point-eight-zero percent. It told me about a sudden storm causing a breach at Estuary West, leading to twenty-eight thousand dollars in property damage – thirty-one-point-two-two percent. It told me about an explosion at the Laurent Oil Rig killing one hundred and twelve people – thirteen-point-zero-two percent."

Garcia exhales sharply.

"Did it tell you about Krishna dying?"

Silence, again, leaden and ponderous in the air.

"Ninety-nine-point-zero-eight percent," he says, sadly. "Sometimes the bullet just paralyses him."

"I'm sorry, Nanti." Garcia takes a step forward. "Really, I am."

"If you're sorry, you'll leave her alone."

"I can't do that. I'm sorry, but we need to talk to Maria. We need to find out exactly what happened to Krishna."

"He didn't want that." Nanti's fingers clench and twitch, his voice rising in pitch. "He wanted you to leave her alone."

"Nanti, if we don't figure out what happened to him, some very powerful people are going to become even more powerful. They'll be able to arrest citizens before they've committed any crimes, and I know how that ends. It ends just like it did last time, and the time before."

"I won't let you arrest her." Nanti steps from the shadows and his face shines faintly in the light of the streetlamp. "She did nothing wrong."

"Nanti, please. Just come with me, okay? We can help you."

"No!"

In an adjacent reality, the furious Nanti Bukowski lashes out with his blade, catching Pluto Garcia's open hand. The cut goes deep, slicing through two tendons and partially cleaving through a third. He clutches his shattered hand and screams, and Nanti, panicking, flees into the night. After several weeks of treatment, Pluto Garcia dies of blood poisoning caused by an infection in the wound. That does not happen here.

In an adjacent reality, Pluto Garcia's next step is too quick and Nanti, startled, bolts backward. Garcia reaches out to grab him but it's too late – his head hits the concrete with a sickening thump and his skull cracks open, killing him instantly. That does not happen here.

In an adjacent reality, Pluto Garcia steps forward in the exact moment a Union truck, bearing a late delivery caused by an abnormal rainstorm earlier in the day, screeches around a corner. The driver pumps the brakes but the tires can't get enough purchase on the wet streets, and eleven-thousand kilograms of steel and aluminium crash into the militiaman before he can leap out of the way. That does not happen here.

Across infinite realities, across immeasurable timelines, across the roiling sea of probability and beneath the uncaring eyes of ProbMat, Pluto Garcia dies. Again and again and again, stabbed and crushed and beaten and shot and strangled, pushed from atop buildings and cast into the dark sea and left for dead on the sidewalk without cessation or end.

That does not happen here.

Here, Nanti Bukowski lunges forward and grabs Pluto Garcia by the collar, throwing him back. Garcia brings his knee up to crash into Nanti's stomach, winding him and causing him to drop the knife. Nanti lunges forward, teeth clenched and arm reeled all the way back before cracking down on Garcia's nose. Rivets of blood explode from his face and splatter across the sidewalk, and somewhere in the deep recesses of his skull he feels something crunch. He reaches up and attempts to push the kid off, his left foot finding purchase on Nanti's stomach and extending hard. Nanti cries out in pain as he flies backwards and clatters to the asphalt. Garcia tries to push himself up, blood streaming darkly from his nose and the torn flesh of his arm screaming through his pain medication. Nanti is quicker, and by the time Garcia has risen to his feet Nanti has brought a foot up to kick him square in the jaw. He falls back in a crumpled heap and Nanti descends upon him, his hands around Garcia's throat.

Up the road, there is the sound of footsteps and leering voices. Garcia and Nanti both glance over to see four L'Anormal kids clad in makeshift punk get-up, layers of oilskin and tarpaulin salvaged from Place de Moteur or the Waterfront patched with denim and leather. One kicks a bottle and sends it shattering on a nearby lamppost while the others scream with laughter. Then one – standing at the end with a high-pointed quiff of red hair, stops in his tracks.

"Sharper?"

The kid named Scud looks from the broken, battered Garcia to the shape looming over him. His eyes widen and he bolts forward.

"Ay, get the fuck off him!" He runs towards them and the others follow, yelling encouragement as Scud grabs Nanti and yanks him back. He strikes him hard across the face with the back of his hand, sending Nanti spinning to the ground. The other L'Anormal fall upon him, striking and kicking. Garcia spits out a thick wad of bloody mucus and cries out.

"That's enough!" He staggers unsteadily to his feet, one eye all-but swollen shut. "Don't hurt him, just – for Kamote's sake, don't hurt him."

Scud reaches out and holds Garcia's shoulders.

"Fuck, you alright, man?"

Garcia pats his right pocket with trembling hands, before reaching in and producing a couple dollar coins. He hands them to Scud and points shakily to the payphone.

"Just," he stutters, the adrenaline flooding from his system, his heart lurching sickly in his chest, blood dribbling down his chin. "Just, ah, call Dubois General. Get – get them to send an ambulance. The kid, he needs help."

"Fuck that, sharper, look at you!" Scud says, all but holding Garcia upright. "Just sit down, yeah?"

"Scud, please – call the hospital."

From the floor Nanti Bukowski struggles and screams beneath the three L'Anormal pinning him down. His face is pressed against the floor and he kicks desperately, his cheeks wet with tears. Scud heads to the payphone and dials four-one-one as Garcia slides slowly to the ground, pain washing over him. He comes to a leaden stop on the edge of the sidewalk, his lungs screaming and his nose clicking grotesquely with each breath.

Ten minutes later the ambulance arrives, and a sedative is applied to the screaming Nanti. As he begins to go limp, so too does Pluto Garcia, fear and pain giving way to deep, lingering exhaustion.

The lights at Dubois General are bright and glaring, a phosphorous white that leaves those lit by it looking strange and pale.

Garcia sits in the waiting room, lukewarm coffee held in his hands, his leg bouncing on the ball of his foot. His nose has been stuffed with cotton and fixed in place with two adhesive strips, and he has been administered a painkiller similar to the one he was taking for his arm. His sandy face has begun to blossom into thick blooms of purple and black, blood coalescing beneath the skin and puffing one eye shut. His breathing is slow and laboured, each inhalation marked by a thin, reedy whistle. All around him doctors and nurses go about their business, carrying clipboards and pill bottles and strange, arcane tools for measuring blood pressure or temperature. On a chair opposite him, a woman cradles a bloodied hand wrapped in a thick wad of bandages. To his right, an elderly man with a cast on his leg reads a newspaper written in Wojtecci. He sips his coffee and stares at the clean tile floors, his eyelids heavy and stinging.

"Pluto?" a voice says from the entrance. He looks up to see Esther Dupont, an expression of worry on her face. She is dressed in her civilian clothes – faded jeans and a simple white t-shirt tucked in at the front, a grey-black jacket thrown on over the top. She rushes forward and almost goes to hug him before stopping herself. "Are you alright?"

"Fine, fine. A nurse checked me over: my right cheek is pretty busted and my nose is fucked, but I don't have a concussion." He rises to his feet, wincing as the pain rattles through him, and heads to a secluded area of the waiting room. He gestures down a corridor with a nod. "Bukowski is in there."

"What happened?

"He'd been using ARGUS to follow me, I think," Garcia says with a shrug. "He wanted to talk to me but... I don't know. He got agitated, lost his cool. Next thing I know, he's kicking the piss out of me and that Scud kid from my apartment is trying to stop him."

She stares at him in disbelief.

"Your luck is turning around, Pluto Garcia."

Garcia laughs before immediately grimacing in agony. Esther places a hand on his shoulder – performing some quick mental calculus to work out which one he was shot in a few days prior to avoid causing any more pain – and scans his battered face.

"You okay?"

"I don't know. I think he was trying to tell me something about Klein and Melnyk but…" Garcia shrugs, sadly. "That machine really fucked him up, Esther."

"Well, he's safe now at least." Dupont crosses her arms over her chest. "Did he say anything about the case?"

"I think he attacked me to help Melnyk escape. He'd used ARGUS to work out the probability of us finding her and panicked."

"Why would he help her like that? Do they know each other?"

"No. I think he thought he was helping Klein. They were friends." He looks back down at the floor, his vision blurred. "I don't think Melnyk killed Klein. I've got a theory as to what happened, and I think I know how to prove it, but you're not going to like it."

"Pluto, you need to rest."

"I'm fine, Esther."

"No, you're not," she says firmly. "You could have died."

"But I didn't." He looks up at her with one bloodshot eye. "There are so many realities across ProbMat where I died, but in this one I didn't. There are realities where I didn't even make it past the Waterfront, where I didn't even get out of Karnassas. Where I died before you and I even met. Literally countless lives lost in small, stupid ways. And yet here I am. Alive. Don't you think that means I *should* keep going?"

She looks at him. His face has begun to swell in odd angles, misshaping his face into a lumpy, discoloured mass. Vivid, angry, purple blotches accentuate the shadows beneath his eyes and deepen the wrinkles by his eyes and lips. His upper lip is stained a deep, lingering fuschia, and his nose is splayed and heavy in the centre of his face.

"You're like a baby," she says, eventually. "Whenever I leave you on your own, you stick your finger into the power outlet or get your hands on bleach somehow and drink the whole bottle. I don't think you're self-destructive, I just think you're so… Fucking careless."

If he is crestfallen beneath all that blood and bruised tissue, it doesn't show. His knobbly, uneven face remains immobile, unblinking.

"You just dive in, fearless, as if nothing can hurt you, as if Tryp is a safety net that stops you from crashing into the consequences of your actions. It's noble, sure, but it's so fucking dangerous – for you and for everyone around you. Sometimes, you *should* feel afraid."

She's on a roll now, her hands flailing and gesticulating angrily.

"Don't you think it's weird that you've died three times already?" she continues. "You work for the CMM. Your job is *admin*. And yet you're constantly being swept downstream or stabbed in the back or shot in the arm or beaten half to death in the Scaffolds. Is the world really this violent? Or is it just violent around cops?"

"I'm not a cop, Esther–" he begins but is cut off.

"You act like one," she says with a finality that would put pause in the heart of God. He gives her a blank, malformed stare, his vision bleary and his breathing laboured. She, in turn, is stony, impassive, stern. He lets out a sad sigh.

"You're right. Tryp makes me complacent." He reaches up and scratches his cheek. "But it's not like I don't feel fear. Being cornered by Bukowski just now: that was the most afraid I've ever been. Not just that I might die, but that he might hurt you. That he might not get the help he needs. That one day he flips out on the wrong guy and is left to bleed out on the Waterfront."

He looks to the ground, a soft expression of shame beneath his blackened, bloated features.

"Like I said: you're probably not going to like what I have planned. But I'm going to do it anyway, and I would appreciate your company."

Around them, the sounds of the hospital go on. The distant dull beeping of machines, the soft *ping* of an elevator door opening, the muffled speech of doctors and nurses discussing medications and prognoses and what they plan on doing once the night shift is over. Someone opens the zip on a bag and produces a foil-wrapped sandwich, sneakily taking a bite while the receptionist isn't looking. Another sneezes into a handkerchief with *JD* neatly embroidered on the top right corner before crumpling it into a ball, stuffing it into their pocket, and spritzing their hands with sanitizer. The sounds of the hospital go on.

"Okay," Dupont says, quietly. "What's the plan?"

Nanti Bukowski is only barely awake when Garcia and Dupont visit him. He is dressed in a eggshell-white gown, his left cheek shiny and bruised and smattered with small cuts from where it was held against the ground. He looks at them dreamily as they enter.

"I'm sorry," he says, his lip trembling as he speaks.

"I know," Garcia says quietly, sitting down. "It's okay."

"I think ARGUS has been messing with me."

"I think so too," Dupont says, standing by his bed. "Did you work on ARGUS for long?"

"Two years. Every day."

"You must've come to understand the system pretty well by that point, right?"

"Hard to say. It's not like using a computer: It's like talking to something, something that has its own ideas." He gives a limp shrug. "ARGUS doesn't always do what you think it will. Half the time it does what it *wants* to do."

"When we spoke to Comrade Ergot," Dupont says, softly, "he says that someone had sabotaged the machine. Stole a storage disc. That was you, wasn't it?"

Nanti stares at the hospital sheets spread out before him, the creases darkened into black canyons across its white expanse by the bright lights of the hospital.

"It's okay, you're not in trouble," Garcia says. "You did it to keep her safe, right? If ARGUS was working at full capacity, someone could have used it to find out exactly what happened."

Dupont places a hand on the edge of the bed, her skin stark against the crisp white sheets.

"Nanti, we need to find that disc. You understand that, right?"

The silence is punctuated only by Garcia's whistling nostrils and the occasional *ping* of some unknown machine. Nanti's face crumples.

"I made a promise to Krishna."

"And it was unfair of him to do that to you. It was unfair of him to involve you in all this." Garcia offers up a sympathetic smile but Nanti does not look at it, staring instead at the featureless duck egg blue wall opposite him.

"Pass me my jeans, please," he says, finally. Dupont rises to her feet and heads to a chair over which Nanti's clothes have been neatly folded. She takes up the jeans and brings them over to him, and he fumbles around in the pockets before producing a small, plastic square. In the centre, a small spherical saucer glints pleasingly in the light, and at the top a small metal pully conceals a strip of nine copper nodes. He hands it to Garcia.

"I meant to give it to you tonight," he says, "but I panicked."

"It's okay. I wasn't as sensitive as I could have been. I'm sorry, Nanti."

Nanti goes quiet, chewing on his busted lower lip.

"The nurse said I'm going to be here for a while."

"It's for the best," Dupont says. "They can help you here."

"I saw *so* much, using ARGUS. More than I could have ever imagined. It felt like looking at the world with new eyes – billions of them, like stars in the sky. Sometimes it was beautiful but most of the time, it was terrifying."

"So the graffiti was you?" Garcia asks. Nanti lets out a soft snort, something almost approaching a laugh.

"Krishna said I needed a hobby. Creative outlet. He had his computers, I had spray."

"It's good work." Garcia chuckles. "Catchier than the "PIG FUCK" mural on Swordtail."

Nanti laughs at this before looking back at his hands.

"I really am sorry, you know. I've been lashing out. It's just, with Krishna gone I feel lost."

"He was your friend. It's understandable to miss him." Garcia shakes his head sadly. "And like you said: you've not been thinking so clearly."

"This place will help with that," Dupont adds. "You'll get the help you need."

"Thank you," Nanti replies, looking back up at the wall. A clock ticks softly, marking the passage of each second as they march rigidly into the future. 3:07AM. "What are you going to do now?"

"I have to make a couple calls, and then…" Dupont shrugs, glancing over at Garcia who, in turn, is staring at the floor. "We'll work it out from there."

"Please be careful," Nanti says, looking at both of them. Through the bruised skin and broken cheekbones, Garcia smiles.

"We will."

"The central theological concern surrounding ProbMat is not the existence of God, but her persistence."

Tomasz St. Michael, *God Is Dead? Musings on Repodimethyltryptamine and its Effects on Modern Religion*

EIGHTEEN

It is 4:37AM, and Pluto Garcia is sitting in a dull red Sudumobil outside an unmarked warehouse in the Shipyard District.

He can feel his pulse clenching in his cheeks, his eyes stinging in the low light. He winces as his head falls back to sit uncomfortably on the headrest, the vertebrae in his neck clicking softly as he moves. He closes his eyes and feels the weight of exhaustion settling over him, pooling in his hands and feet and rendering them leaden and useless. He begins to drift off, each exhalation pushing him deeper and deeper into the darkness behind his eyelids.

Dupont opens the door and sits down in the driver's seat, jolting him awake. His head shoots up and his ribs burn as he adjusts in his seat.

"Any luck?" he asks.

"If I get caught I'm so fired," Dupont says, staring straight ahead, hands tight on the steering wheel. "They're keeping it in Halle-Sullivan 096. Two blocks away."

"Who'd you call, in the end?"

"My old mentor, on Laurent. Turns out his husband works in logistics, was able to track it down on his home computer." She looks over at him. "He wasn't happy about being called at 4AM."

"Thank you, Esther. Sincerely, I appreciate it."

"I know."

They drive in silence, streetlight passing over them in waves, a diluted wash of yellowy-grey already beginning to spread on the eastern horizon. The streets are empty, the city's revellers having already retired to their beds to sleep off the worst of the booze. Out on the water, the city-sized sprawl of Laurent looms against the sky, its lights blinking off periodically as shift workers shut down for the night.

The Halle-Sullivan warehouse block stretches across much of Lower Shipyard. A maze of squat buildings zig-zags its way to the shore, inside which all manner of imports and exports are prepared: processed wood from the Rampart mountains, great sheets of aluminium for construction, row after row of computer processors and microchips, storage containers holding great car engines that coil like the giblets of a slaughtered bird. At the gate a night watchman reads a travel magazine beneath a flickering fluorescent light, his feet propped up on the desk in front of him and a long-cooled cup of coffee by his side.

"Salut," Dupont says as they pull up. "We're here with the Union. I'm Auditor Dupont, this is my partner from the CMM, Lieutenant Garcia. We're here to investigate some unlawful cargo at warehouse 096."

The night watchman glances up from his magazine and recoils.

"Fuck me, what happened to you?"

"It's been a long night," Garcia says, nodding to the closed gate. "Mind if we go through?"

"I'll need to see some ID," the watchman says, kicking his feet down and placing his magazine to one side. Dupont offers up her Union papers and he scans them before handing them back. "Sure, you're good to go."

He pushes a couple buttons on the console in front of him and the gate unsteadily shunts open, swinging back to reveal an open driveway leading into the heart of the warehouse block. He then reaches into a filing cabinet drawer, flicks through a couple files before producing an envelope labelled "096". It jingles as he hands it over.

"Thank you," Dupont says as they drive on. They go quiet, scanning the numbers stencilled onto the warehouse doors as they pass, before eventually coming to warehouse 096. It is near-identical to the warehouses that surround it, a squat redbrick building similar to the old pre-Revolution canneries out on the Waterfront. Dupont reaches into the envelope and produces a small key affixed to a simple keychain and, unlocking the padlock, rolls the shutter up to reveal it: a cyclopean bulwark of machines sitting in dull silence, their impossible tangle of wires leading to a single umbilical cable attached to a cumbersome headset. ARGUS.

"This is the one," she says, turning back to Garcia. "Help me with the generator."

She cracks the trunk of the car and they both reach in, grabbing either side of the gasoline generator pilfered half an hour ago from Krishna Klein's apartment. Garcia grits his teeth and groans as his bruised ribs and torn arm scream in protest, having to catch most of the generator's weight on his hip to stop himself from dropping it. They carry it into the warehouse and set it down, panting from exertion, before closing the shutters behind them.

The generator is easy enough to hook up to the machine's console. Dupont, flashlight held between her teeth, configures the wires and cables in accordance to a stack of notes also taken from Klein's apartment, pausing occasionally to decipher his impenetrable handwriting. She inserts the last cable and flicks a switch, and one by one the consoles stir into wakedness, a distorted digital chorus rising in the air, their lights blinking red, then orange, then a constellation of dull blues, whites, and greens. The warehouse fills with a sickly glow, casting dark shadows that creep across the concrete floor and settle at Garcia's feet.

"Are you sure about this?" Dupont asks, holding the storage disc in her hand.

"Not especially," Garcia replies, his eyes fixed on the headset in the centre of the room, suspended like a paper wasp trapped in a spider's web. "But I think it'll work."

She walks the perimeter of the room, the light cast from the consoles just barely bright enough for her to check Klein's notes without her flashlight. After a moment or two of cross-referencing and trial-and-error, she eventually finds the slot from which the disc was stolen. She inserts it, feeling it give ever so slightly against her hand before being sucked into the belly of the machine. A vibration ripples through the room, a strange warmth beginning to rise around them. She turns to face Garcia.

"Alright," she says. "Should be ready for you."

Garcia nods and approaches the headset. He takes it in his hands and slides it up so that it hovers just above him before stepping forward and bringing it down to rest over his shoulders, his head entirely swallowed by darkness. It is a tight fit against his face, and his bruised cheek and busted nose ache dully as he blindly reaches up to find the one switch located on the headset's exterior. He finds it and, with a push, the world shifts.

A dull black glow fills the breadth of his vision, a pulsing electric sable shade passing over him, followed by a sudden, sharp magenta glitch. There is a thrumming vibration within his skull, a psychic piss-shiver that rattles through him and prickles his skin. His fingers clench involuntarily as he feels the throbbing sync with his heartbeat, losing track of where his body ends and the machine begins. Then, in the darkness, as if floating in the night sky some hundred feet before him, phosphorescent green text.

`//welcome//`

He stares at the text blankly, hands reaching for a keyboard with which to respond. A hum scuttles through his brain and the text shifts.

`//manual input not required :: subcranial input operational//`

He blinks. The text remains, hovering in the air before him, impassive and uncaring as the face of God. Somewhere, his heart pounds in his chest as he thinks a single word.

Hello?

`//welcome//`

He wants to grin, to feel the corners of his lips twitch upwards in wonderment, but he cannot feel his face. There is no bodily feedback, no tactile response, not even the pain of shattered cartilage and burst blood vessels. There is only text, thought, and darkness.

Are you ARGUS?

`//input not recognised//`

He feels weightless, endless, suspended in the void.

Where am I?

`//GetLocationData :: morrissette, annalise, population 3,206,987//`

I can't feel my body. I can't feel anything.

`//input not recognised//`

Garcia stares eyeless up at the text. If he had hands, he thinks, he could reach out and grab it, feel its weight in his palm, feel the jagged edges of its glowing green boundaries.

What are you?
`//GetVersionHistory :: ARGUS v1.1//`
The conscious mind of Pluto Garcia floats atop a sea of black water, the waves cresting around him, enveloping him, drowning him. He struggles, feeling the distant fluttering of a bird's wings before realising that it's his heartbeat, elevated and panicked. He breathes without lungs and forces his focus.

I have questions for you.
`//input query//`
I want to know what happened to Krishna Klein.
`//searching//`
The seas are no longer calm. He is buffeted, barraged by a towering monsoon of information. Green dots and lines fill his vision, exploding from the depths of the dark horizon and blinding him, swallowing him, the brightness of every star in every galaxy burning into his skull at once. He goes to jolt backwards, to turn his head and look away, but he has no head to turn, no body to move. Instead he can only stare, watch as unbidden knowledge from every corner of probability beats down upon him, flooding over him like the waters of the surging Pallias, like a wrench to the base of the skull, like a knife to the back, like a bullet to the arm. He screams and the data fills his mouth, stuffing down his throat and expanding his lungs until they are ready to burst like fireworks in his chest, shattering his ribs outwards and spraying shards of bone and fire across the blackened void.

He fights against the waters, the screaming statistics coursing through him, into him, over him, each second forcing him to spiral deeper into the disorienting heart of an agonising sun. There, in the negative space between the blinding green labyrinth before him, peering from the screeching unlit eternities, he sees the magenta eyes of ProbMat leering hungrily at him, come to claim him as they always would, to snatch the heart from his chest and the eyes from his skull and to leave him, blind and undying forever and ever.

The maws of fate close in around him and finally, sensation returns. Bodies, countless bodies, slipping on ice and cracking skulls and burnt to death and crushed by machines and withering in the night and sinking to the ocean floor and devoured and stabbed and shot and infected and eaten. Accidents and intents and fate, cruel fate, swim into him without cessation, looping around and around with its tail in its mouth until, yes, finally.

A body, a new body, taller and wider and bulkier than his, prone upon a springy fabric, warm flesh pressed against warm flesh, salt, wet, tears. A hand that isn't his holds something heavy, hard, cold, a sharp angle of plastic, a cool curve of metal pressed against the index finger. Then a feeling, metallic and icy, pressed to the temple, more salt, more wet, more tears. The index finger pulls sharply and it all shifts, it all stops, one final time.

The screen goes dark, returning to a backlit black glow that stretches until the end of time, bearing a message, singular and apocalyptic against the dark sky.

`//search complete//`

He is pulled from the darkness, gasping and flailing as if yanked from the sea. He breathes in great greedy gasps of air, his one working eye wide and staring. A warehouse, lit blue and white and red by blinking LEDs. Wires, snaking and coiling things that run from every available surface into the hefty arachnoid shape above his head. Hands, soft, small, pressed on his lower arm: Dupont. He looks at her, the stinging pain of his face crashing into him full-force like a streetcar, and wheezes two words.

"I know."

"The trappings of the Republic's Fascist past are seldom felt in the city of Morrissette these days, though the indomitable, neo-classical architecture of the Bureau of Records – which once housed the Nationalist Party's secret police – nonetheless acts as quite a startling reminder."

Eleanor Gordillo, *The Annalise Architectural Digest*

NINETEEN

The sky is a subtle orange-grey as the sun peers over the eastern horizon. It shines through the lumbering figure of Laurent, casting deep shadows across the water in which small, quick, silvery fish flit about. White clouds streak across the sky, bisected by the occasional contrail and flocks of migratory birds, their silhouettes marking the steady decline from summer into winter.

It takes them an hour to get from the Shipyard through to the Icehouse. A skeleton crew of CMM members man the building, many dressed in thick cardigans to protect against the chill pulsing from the air conditioners. Garcia flashes his badge as he enters.

"Sorry to be a pain in the ass, but we need to borrow the boat."

The receptionist, a small woman with arched eyebrows and a pinched look, glances up at his face before looking down to the ID in his hand.

"Everything okay, Lieutenant Garcia?" she asks, her eyes flitting to Dupont briefly.

"I'm fine. I was attacked over in the Scaffolds."

"I see," the receptionist peers closely at him. "Do you know how to sail a boat, Lieutenant?"

"I do," Dupont says, inching forward. Garcia attempts a smile, his cheeks creaking with exertion as he does so. The receptionist eyes them both.

"You know I'll have to file your names in case anything… Happens, right?"

"Absolutely. Second Lieutenant Pluto Garcia, Precinct 14; Junior Auditor Esther Dupont, Liberté EnCorp Branch." He flashes another smile, this one somehow even less naturalistic. "Is that everything?"

She scribbles their names down onto a scrap of paper, followed by the word "Boat", followed by something that Garcia cannot see and that she underlines several times. Then she reaches into a drawer, produces a key with a small plastic "GREETINGS FROM SAN ERNESTO" keyring, and slides it over the desk.

"It's yours for twenty-four hours," she says. "Bring it back when you're done."

They leave, feeling the trickling warmth of the sun glance over them, their blood beginning its steady return to their extremities. Garcia flicks the keys over to Dupont, who pockets them.

"She thought you were kidnapping me," he says with a grin.

"If she only knew," Dupont muses, following him to the back of the precinct and towards the docks. The boat is a small thing, just barely big enough to fit four people comfortably, with a guardrail at the bow and a cramped box cockpit in which the skipper may pilot the vessel. Across its starboard side is a faded CMM logo, worn away by years of exposure to salt and sun, and at its stern flies a tattered Annalissian flag: black and red dissected diagonally, atop which sits a crossed rifle and wrench, the symbols of the Violet Revolution. Dupont steps off the jetty and onto the boat, offering up a hand that Garcia gratefully takes as he joins her.

The process of starting the boat's engine is as uncertain and unsteady as the vessel itself: Dupont inserts the key into the slot and attempts to turn it, feeling it rattle awkwardly in her grip once, twice, before grinding in a clockwise semicircle and forcing the boat into a juddering half-life. She gives the cockpit a brief glance over, checking various tanks and measures and displays before turning to Garcia.

"Ready?"

He sets himself down on the narrow lip at the stern of the boat, his hands resting either side of him.

"Ready."

She pushes a few buttons and the engine begins to rumble, slowly pushing the boat away from the jetty and out into the Baratte. The wind blows close to the water's surface, kicking up thin jets of white frothing sea spray and whipping them back into Garcia's face in a gentle mist. The smell of salt fills his nostrils and he hungrily breathes it in, grateful to be away from the dark warehouses and humming machines of the Shipyard. Dupont steers the ship, keenly navigating around the hidden subaquatic ridges and reefs that rise up mountainous in the water, evidence of the city that once stood here. Garcia looks down and watches as shoals of yellowtail flutter in the water around them, the rising sun glinting silverly off of their scales. Further out, sitting atop the frothy waves, a romp of otters interrupt their play to watch the ship pass with dark, curious eyes.

The growl of the engine makes talk impossible, so they are contented to sit in silence, the distant falsetto of hunting seabirds echoing down upon them, the sloshing and splashing of the water against the hull of the boat enveloping them. Some way off they spot a small fishing tug bobbing amongst the waves, captained by a tall, lean woman in a tarpaulin slicker, her skin a deep, tanned brown. Garcia attempts a wave, but either she does not see it, or chooses not to respond.

Eventually the Analissian archipelago rears into view, a sprawling outcrop of small, dark islands sparsely covered in thin greenish grass and veritable mounds of bird shit. The islands are uniform only in their relative emptiness: great, bizarre spires of layered black rock that climb finger-like into the sky; flat, boulder-like plateaus that sit just above the water's surface; steep hillocks that rise uneasily from the sea before ending with an abrupt deadfall. Every now and then they'll pass one with a single crooked tree clinging hopelessly to the bare stone, or a handful of mad-eyed goats chewing cud in the wild winds, and Garcia will break out in an incredulous smile. The air is raw and salty and rich, harsh as the seagulls that soar above it, clear as the waters below. Eventually, they come to it: Pietnera Island.

It is considerably bigger than its siblings, a jagged shape that could well mark the spinal ridges of some huge underwater beast, some grand cetacean dragon that, upon being disturbed, will shake loose the grass and shrubs that cling to its surface and descend once more into the dark depths. The wind ripples through tall fronds of yellowing marram grass, causing them to shudder and shiver as the boat approaches. By the time they reach the island they have spotted the boat pilfered from the Lavage on the south-eastern shore, a skiff of glossed wood painted the deep blue-green of a peacock's tail. They steadily bring the ship in next to it, the engine slowing to a soft purr as they pull into the rocky shoreline. Amidst the rushing wind and the sloshing waves, Pluto Garcia hears a faint click.

"Don't move," comes a voice from behind him, soft and unwavering. He raises his hands and glances over to Dupont, who does the same.

"We just want to talk, Maria," he announces over the wind and water. He begins to slowly turn.

"I said don't fucking move." Not an exclamation. A statement, sharp and imperative. No threat, no uncertainty. Garcia stays put, arms over his head, hands splayed open.

"I'm sorry about what happened to Krishna," he says, a little quieter this time. The breeze rustles through the bent grass, carrying the smell of the sea inland, whispering as it passes.

"You're Bureau?"

"No. I'm Pluto Garcia of the CMM. This is Esther Dupont of the Union." He shrugs. "Like I said, we're here to talk."

The silence holds for a moment, before giving way to the rustle of fabric.

"Alright. Turn around. Slowly."

Garcia and Dupont both turn, arms still raised above their heads, to see a young woman. She is thin, with narrow hips and low shoulders obscured beneath an oilskin coat slightly too big for her. Her mousy hair is pulled back into a ponytail that quivers in the wind behind her head, and the freckles that cover her nose and cheeks have darkened into a ruddy russet from constant exposure to the sun. Her expression is stern, unflinching, and held in both hands is a Moricco 9mm, barrel pointing at the sandy floor.

"You want to talk?" she asks over the wind. "Talk."

"I know about what happened," Garcia replies, a sad smile on his beaten and battered face. "I'm sorry."

"Yeah, well," she says, scanning the two of them for weapons before holstering hers on her hip, "sorry isn't going to stop the Bureau from shooting me in the head. Come ashore. It's cold."

Garcia and Dupont lower their hands and begin the awkward process of trudging through the cool waters of the outer Baratte and onto Pietnera island. They leave the engine running, tying the boat to an ancient and weathered post that juts a metre and a half from the sand before following Maria up the steep banks of the island and to a small tarpaulin tent at the top of a hill.

"You knew we were coming," Dupont says, puffing as she climbs.

"Saw you about half an hour ago. You get a good view from up here; it's why Krishna suggested it, I think."

"You were close with him, right?"

She doesn't say anything, cresting the hill and looking west to the blank, featureless stretch of sea ahead. Somewhere out there, on the other side of the horizon, lies the sprawling quantum anomaly of Wojtek, the home of her ancestors, a cold and quiet place muffled by snow, sitting in the heart of a frigid inland sea; further still is Lacan and its erstwhile colonies, with their fine foods and ancient empires, great monuments to the god-kings of the past; a reminder of what once was, and shall never be again. She sighs.

"Don't suppose either of you smoke?"

Garcia pats his pockets and shrugs.

"Sorry. I usually bum them off my colleague."

"That's a shitty thing to do," she says, not turning back to look at him. "Nadia smokes Vanguard, these cigarettes from Wojtek. I'd fucking *kill* for a Vanguard right now."

"You'll have to ask her for one next time you see her," Garcia says. Dupont scans the campsite: a fishing pole rests against the side of the tent, a couple spools of spare line lying in the grass beside it; a couple foil disposable barbecues are stacked up beside a smouldering campfire built up out of sticks and twigs; spent blister packs of Repodimethyltryptamine lie discarded in a deep, heavy cast iron pot in lieu of a trash can. Maria scoffs and turns to face them both.

"Cute. So what did you come here to say?"

Garcia sits on a nearby rock.

"What happened on the night Krishna Klein killed himself?"

Garcia expects her to blanche, to step back wide-eyed and mournful, to raise a trembling hand to her lips and sadly gasp. She doesn't. There is no discernible expression on her face, no glimpse of sorrow or pain. That was burnt out of her a while ago, now. Instead she stands, sharp chin held slightly up, eyes cast out over the horizon.

"He was pretty high. Taken a whole bunch of shit. He was in one of his *moods*." Her wide eyes seem to glow, deep and sunlit, the colour of the forest floor. "He got like that sometimes. Depressive, irritable, impossible to please. He could be difficult."

"We heard," Dupont says. Maria gives a sick smile.

"You spoke to Dean, then?" She crosses her arms over her chest. "He wasn't always like that, and usually he didn't get that bad. He'd nail a couple drinks, snort a little coke, lighten up. This was different."

"Had he been like that before?" Dupont asks, standing by the tent.

"Yeah, but I'd never seen it. He told me about it afterwards. He'd, ah–" There is a brief crack in her voice. "He told me that before we met, he'd drop a tablet of Tryp and see if he could go through with it. Drink himself to death. Shoot himself in the head. Succeeded more than once."

"Cry for help?"

"No, no. Nothing so dramatic. He was a scientist." She exhales. "He was doing experiments. Trial runs."

"Did he ever tell you *why* he ended up in these moods?" Garcia asks.

"Sure. He said it's because the world didn't meet his standards. That no matter how many times he'd trypped, no matter how many realities he'd come across, the world was never *quite* right. There was always something wrong, something missing: small, most of the time, but… Gnawing."

"So that night," she continues, facing the sun as it slowly crests upwards, "he figured he'd bail. He didn't want to be alone, I guess, and I'd already stayed with him every night in the hotel that week. Bringing him meals, keeping him company."

"Were you ever intimate?" Dupont asks.

"Yes, but I'm an escort. It was more about conversation." She lets out a laugh, delightful like the fluttering of a bird's wings. "*Fuck* that man could talk."

"What did you talk about?"

"A lot of things. Politics, technology, culture, art. You found this place, so you've already heard his pet theory about that damned book."

"He sounded like a brilliant man." Garcia nods. She laughs again.

"He'd certainly tell you that, yes." Overhead a seagull spirals on a rising thermal, yellow eyes fixed on the sandy grass below. "He'd ask me about my life, my family. About Montetrieste, living in the commune. We'd talk about Morrissette, and how it… How it hadn't quite worked for either of us."

"When did you start working for the Bureau?" Dupont asks. The nostalgia drops from Maria's expression.

"Two years ago, I think," she says. "I was thinking of moving. Getting out to San Ernesto or Kumari, somewhere where the winters don't get so cold. But plane tickets are expensive on a Communist's budget, and I could never quite save up enough. I guess they got wind, because eventually they contacted me. Steady paycheck, triple what I was getting from the Guild, and the promise of a new passport when my work was done."

"And what was your work?"

"It was easy enough. Krishna was never a particularly discrete man: I just had to listen and report back to the Bureau about anything of note. At the time I didn't realise they meant ARGUS, but I figured that out pretty quickly."

"Did Krishna tell you about ARGUS himself?"

"He couldn't shut up about it." She puffs out her chest and puts on a faint Laccannesse drawl, her full lips curled upwards. "'The machine of the future!' he called it. I always hated the cursed fucking thing, but he loved it. Sincerely and with all his heart, he loved it."

"Why did you hate it?" Dupont asks, and Maria's eyes flash over to Garcia.

"Because I know what it does. It shows you more than any person has any right to see. And because I know what the Bureau wants it for." Her gaze wanders back over to the horizon.

"When did you get the order to kill Krishna?" Garcia asks, hands clamped between his knees.

"Three months ago. I wasn't going to go through with it – I was getting ready to run, to get my ass over to the nearest airport and get the fuck out of Annalise. Then Krishna had one of his benders and…" She gestures sadly. "Here we are."

"Did he know?"

"I'm sure he worked it out. He *was* a genius, after all." She drums her fingernails on her arm, a pleasing scratchy sound rising from the oilskin. "That's probably why he told me about this place.

He knew I wanted to escape, and he knew that the Bureau would be following me."

"So he helped you escape, before shooting himself in the head," Dupont says, slowly. "You were, what, lying on the bed together? Cleaned up after him, changed out of your bloody clothes, and moved his body to the front door to make it look like an execution."

"The bullet in the wall was my idea," she says, smiling and not meaning it for a second. "I hoped that if the Bureau thought I'd killed him, they'd go easy on me."

"And then what? You got back to your apartment, stuffed your nightdress into your mattress, and bolted?"

"That's the long and short of it, yeah." She purses her lips. "Had I stayed, the Bureau would've treated me like a loose end, as I figured they always would. Shoot me in the back of the head, dump me in the sea. So I ran. Grabbed everything worth carrying, made my way to the Lavage, stole a boat, and came out here on Krishna's recommendation."

"Obviously I can't live out here forever," she continues with a sigh. "I can't fish for shit, and I used the last of my Tryp two days ago. The plan was to wait it out, take the boat back to the mainland, then try to smuggle myself past the northern border and out into Annalise."

"And then we showed up," Garcia finishes. She nods.

"Yeah. Good work, by the way."

"We had help. Nanti gave us a missing ARGUS disc and we used that to track you down."

"Oh shit, Jonah." She gasps, looking down at Garcia. "How's he doing?"

"Not great," Garcia says, pointing at his face. "He did this."

"Fuck, I'm sorry," she says, sincerely. "What happened?"

"He thought he was doing right by Krishna by helping you escape."

"No shit." A flash of anger runs over her fair features. "*Fuck.* Krishna was *such* an asshole sometimes. That is exactly the kind of shit he'd pull. He *knew* how much Jonah worshipped him."

"Why was Krishna so set on helping you escape?" Dupont chimes in. Maria seethes and throws her hands up in the air.

"Fucked if I know," she says. "Probably some bullshit attempt at legacy. He always said I was the only one that knew the 'real' him.

Guess he thought I'd go out there and spread his story like a fucking evangelist."

"Do you think he could have loved you?" Garcia asks. She spins and points at him.

"Don't be cute, militiaman."

"I mean it," he says. "I don't think he was a good man, but I don't think he was irredeemable. I think he tried his best to make a better world than the one he was part of. When that's your goal, it's easy to lose sight of one's ethics."

She stares at him, blankly, her chest rising and falling slowly. Her nostrils flare ever so slightly.

"So what now?"

"Now?" Dupont replies with a small shrug. "I'm not sure. By rights, we should take you back to the mainland. There you'll be subject to questioning by the Enforcement Corp and judged before a trial of your peers. Then, depending on the verdict, you'll either be free to go or be subject to imprisonment or exile."

Maria's pilot light eyes are fixed firmly on Dupont's, unblinking and intense. Garcia coughs into his fist.

"But," he interjects, "we know you didn't do it. According to ARGUS, there is a seven-point-zero-zero-three-eight-one percent chance that you murdered Krishna Klein. Whereas, if we bring you back to the mainland, there's an eighty-six-point-nine-two percent chance that an agent of the Bureau of Records assassinates you before you go to trial."

She stares at them both.

"So?"

"So, what my colleague is saying," Dupont continues, "is that we need a third option. One that doesn't involve you getting murdered or starving to death on this island."

"One of my jobs with the CMM is overseeing immigration. Usually it's people coming into Morrissette, *but...*" Garcia smiles. "I could probably forge some papers taking you out instead."

"I have access to a Union Sudumobil, and I have family up in Montetrieste," Dupont says, going to stand over by Garcia. "If you like, I can try and get you past the checkpoint."

Maria's lip quivers briefly before she steels herself. She goes quiet, her face lit a soft gold, her hair whipped back by the wind. Eventually, she uncrosses her arms.

"Thank you," she says, simply.

"Don't mention it." Garcia rises to his feet and dusts his hands off on his knees. Maria shakes her head.

"No, really, thank you. You could both lose your jobs for this."

"You can ask Comrade Dupont: I'm not an especially cautious person when it comes to things like that." He attempts a cheerful grin and rests a hand on Maria's shoulder. "Get your things together. I'll head back to the precinct and start work on getting those papers together. We'll be back here tonight."

There's the briefest hint of wetness to her eyes as she nods. Wordlessly, she pulls away from Garcia and looks over the camp, over the discarded tins and smouldering ashes of the fire, over the makeshift tent held up by two simple extendable poles. She nods.

"Okay, thank you." There is a momentary flicker, an uncertainty on her features. "Wait – do you… Do you guys have any Tryp? Like I said, I ran out and… Well, if the Bureau does find me…"

"Say no more," Garcia says, reaching into his pocket and producing the aluminium pillbox. He hands it over. "Take these. There's four in there, that should easily see you out of the city."

She takes it in her hand, feeling its lightness push down on her palm. She slips it into the pocket of her oilskin and nods.

"Alright," she says, a smile on her lips. "I'll see you tonight."

"Death is not the end, sir,
No sir, not the end of the line,
Just remember what I say to you;
It hurts, sweet darlin',
It hurts every time."

Marco Sanskrit, *The Trypper's Elegy*
ProbMat Reality 7406.21

TWENTY

The sun is almost halfway across the sky as Esther Dupont and Pluto Garcia make their way back to the mainland. The light glances off the water, causing Dupont to squint and shade her dark eyes. Garcia, his own eyes closed, sits with his back against the stern, listening to the roar of the engine and the screeching of seagulls. Every now and then another vessel will cruise past, its engine harmonising with theirs, and he'll open his one good eye and watch it go by, the fishermen on board chattering amongst themselves as they shake off the morning's hangover. Eventually, he sleeps.

He doesn't dream. There is no magenta beast that waits for him in space beyond this world, no dark water filled with voyeuristic eyes. There is only blackness, the sinking blackness of restless, exhausted sleep.

Dupont pulls the ship in at a quay just off of Promenade de Gloire, turning the engine off and setting herself by his side. She lets him sleep, his heavy limbs twitching gently in primal reflex, and watches as morning fills the Promenade with dog-walkers, street vendors, and the unlucky souls covering the weekend shifts at the various tackle shops and canneries on the Waterfront. Eventually, she sees fit to stir him awake.

"Hey," she says.

"Hey," he replies, sitting upright with a wince. "How long was I out?"

"Only a couple hours," she says. "How do you feel?"

"Like a new man." He grins and she, unable to stop herself, grins as well. She shakes her head and looks back up at the Promenade for a while. She looks over at him eventually, scanning his face.

"Are you sure you're okay?"

"I don't know," Garcia says, his eye focused on the street ahead. "Do you think we're doing the right thing? Letting her go?"

"Well it's this, or she's assassinated by the government, and we both know your stance on that."

He smirks, wiping his mouth on the back of his hand. The smirk falters.

"ARGUS could be wrong, you know. I mean, seven-point-zero-zero-three-eight-one percent isn't *zero* percent, right?"

"No, you're right. Maybe the calculations were off, maybe we didn't insert the disc right, maybe you misinterpreted the data." She shrugs. "I don't know, Pluto. I think based solely on what we *do* know, this is the best we're going to get."

"That sounds dangerously reckless for you."

"Shut up," she says, nudging his shoulder with her elbow. "Look, I'm better at numbers than I am with people. I'm not entirely sure that letting her go is the right thing to do, but I am *mostly* sure that she's innocent."

"Okay," he says. "Thank you, Esther."

"Hmm," she says. The sound of surf washes over them, a steady pulse that sways their sun-faded vessel. Dupont sighs, her chest sinking slowly, before turning her head imperceptibly.

"Pluto..." she begins, reticent. "What did you see? In ARGUS?"

"Nothing," he says, staring straight ahead. A short exhalation escapes Dupont's nose in lieu of a laugh.

"You're right," she says. "You *are* a shitty liar."

He doesn't reply, not right away. For a moment the birds speak for him, chattering their ghastly auguries into the salt-strewn air.

"It's difficult to explain," he says eventually. "I don't know if I *saw* anything. It was hints. Impressions." He chews his lip and picks at the skin of left thumb with his right pointer finger. "I felt the weight of a pistol in my hand. I felt the metal against my temple, followed by the faintest second of searing heat. I felt that wave of silence, the kind you get when you hit ProbMat. I felt…" He pauses, breathes. "I felt those eyes. Those purple fucking eyes."

Dupont remains quiet. A narrow ridge of white skin begins to crest on Garcia's thumb and he flexes his fingers, feeling the knuckles creak.

"He was sad, I realised. Devastatingly so," he continues, breathing slowly, "and proud. He wanted so much from the world. He thought people were so much better than they were, and whenever they proved him wrong he felt betrayed. That's why he did it."

Silence again. Stiff joints click as he adjusts himself, shifting his stiff back against the inner hull. He smiles. It is a sickly thing.

"I felt this weight, too. The weight of expectation, too heavy for one man to lift on his own. A weight that can't be lifted by computer blueprints, by fairy tales, by crime novels, by pretty women. All the times he pushed forward, all the terrible things he allowed himself to do – he did them to get out from under that weight." The smile drops, leaden and dead. "The weight of those damn eyes."

He says nothing now, his body slack and heavy against Dupont's shoulder. His dark eyes with their deep, drooping bags and heavy lashes fix upon a single scant cloud as it meanders across the sky. He sighs.

"Truth is, I think those eyes have always been there. Watching me. Watching Klein. ARGUS just let me see them."

Dupont hesitates for a moment, before putting an arm around his shoulders. He does not move, and she does not move either – they sit, awkward in their embrace, half-entwined and unsteady in affection. Eventually, Garcia checks his wristwatch and groans.

"We should head out. I need to get those papers together for Maria."

"We have time," Dupont replies softly, simply. Garcia feels a wave of weariness wash over him, the warmth of the sun lighting upon his aching face, his stinging cheeks, the bruised skin on his hands and knuckles. He closes his eyes, and Morrissette goes on. Across the Waterfront people wake blearily in their homes, sheets crumpled around them as they rise to their kitchens and pour coffee and toast bagels. In Madame Syndicat, citizens embrace the morning sun with the languid, pleasurable slowness of basking cats, seated outside of teahouses and dispensaries, smiling warm smiles. In the Scaffolds, factories whir and shift and pulse and shudder, machines churning under the skilled, strong hands of men and women to whom this labour belongs. And in the centre, in the dark heart of the city, the Archive stands firm, unbuckling, unbent.

It is 10:37 in Morrissette, and Pluto Garcia falls asleep.

ABOUT THE AUTHOR

LP Mills is an author, game designer, journalist, and beard owner. He currently lives in front of a computer screen in Nottingham, UK, where he feverishly tells stories in an attempt to ignore his day-to-day responsibilities. His dog, Jack Daniels, has yet to compliment him on his writing.

To learn more about our authors and our current projects visit: www.mirrorworldpublishing.com, follow @MirrorWorldPub or like us at www.facebook.com/mirrorworldpublishing

Keep reading for a sneak peek at our upcoming new release:

The Pheeworker's Oath

By Adam Gaylord

"Survivors." I pointed across the debris-strewn clearing to a tangle of timber and metal where phee, the natural power that flowed over my world, the Great Egg, swirled the faintest semi-transparent blue-green. It was a subtle difference from the strands around it. Only an experienced healer, such as myself, would have noticed.

Hassan whistled and a half-dozen humans converged on the pile.

"Careful." I stepped between two females to crouch down and peer under a timber bearing deep claw marks, extending my tail for balance. While I couldn't see the humans trapped within, I could tell by the flickering of the phee that flowed through the pile that their situation was dire. "Move slowly. They're badly injured."

Hassan's people shifted the debris as gently as they could manage. Like most dwellings in the various human settlements, the structure had been cobbled together with parts of their downed spacecraft, held together with what they call adobe—bricks of dried red mud mixed with straw. This home had been small and took little time to dig through. With a grunt, the largest male tossed aside a hunk of what had been their ship's outer hull, exposing a tangle of human bodies.

I crawled forward to kneel by the motionless forms.

Hassan crouched beside me, his brows pinched. "They're alive?"

Humans can't see phee. Hassan had once told me their home planet, that most planets, don't have anything like phee. I think it is more likely humans can't see phee and are therefore unaware of it. The thought of a phee-less world, so cold and dead, made my tail tingle. Regardless, Hassan couldn't see how the flowing strands of semi-transparent color and light, as delicate as frost on a leaf, failed to interact with the humans atop the pile, an adult male and a female, both with dark brown skin and black hair, presumably mates.

"Help me move them," I instructed.

Together we rolled the bodies aside, exposing two adolescent females, both unconscious. I rested my hand against the back of the oldest, the deep brown smoothness of her skin contrasting with my light blue scales. Closing my eyes, I stretched out my consciousness, coaxing a thin tendril of turquoise phee from the flow around us. With a subtle hand gesture, I willed the tendril into the small of her back, traveling with it through the alien anatomy that had grown so familiar to me. I kept the phee insubstantial to pass through bone and tissue rather than to manipulate or cut. From her tailbone, I guided the strand around the curve of her pelvis before traveling back up through the spine, minute changes in how the phee interacted with the girl's body setting my path.

"Broken hip, broken vertebra," I listed the girl's injuries. I could bind the broken bones, and at her age she would heal quickly. The general anatomy of a human was curiously similar to that of an Atipok, each species composed of mostly the same organs and bones of similar shape and placement. Similar but noticeably different, like a drawing by an artist who'd been told about an animal without ever actually seeing it.

"Ruptured spleen," I continued. That would be a bit trickier but might be survivable if addressed quickly. "Broken ribs." I winced. "Punctured collapsed lung, massive internal bleeding." I leaned back, withdrawing the phee and my hand. A moment of fatigue washed over me. Manipulating phee in such a precise fashion was always draining. "I'm sorry. I can't save her."

Hassan touched my arm and I opened my eyes. "Takey, are you sure? Can you try?"

I managed to suppress a hiss of anger. Although he was human, I considered Hassan a friend. A craftsman of some sort before their arrival, many humans now looked to him for leadership. He also embraced phee as useful, even if he didn't understand it or shrink from its use in fear like so many other humans. But friend or no, I didn't appreciate having my judgment as a healer questioned.

"I'm sorry," he added quickly. "I didn't mean anything by it. I'm just frustrated. This—" His gesture took in the whole of the wreckage that had been a community only the previous day. Two men were lining up bodies next to their mechanical wagon. Like the other attacks, I suspected some remains would never be found, having been dragged away or completely consumed. His eyes settle on a row of claw marks gouged deep into the soil. "This can't keep happening."

Chatraka, the huge apex predators of the southern grasslands, rarely strayed this far north. In their native range, attacks were rare, and only upon lone travelers. This was the third attack on a human settlement in as many lunars. Something had changed.

Of course, since the humans had crashed into our planet, much had changed.

I exhaled, my anger dissipating, and moved on to the younger female. She lay on her side, apparently unharmed, shielded from violence by her familial cocoon. I rested my hand on her shoulder and harnessed another tendril of phee, willing it into the center of her limp form.

The phee tendril blunted and bent like a piece of straw thrust against the side of a wagon.

I flinched.

"What's wrong?" Hassan asked.

"Just a moment." Again, I tried to coax power into the girl, this time more subtly, much as I would for one of my own kind. Medical pheework is invasive by its very nature. Insinuating phee into another without permission is an attack and a grievous crime amongst Atipok, second only to forcibly coercing a pheeworker's ability. As a healer, I'm allowed such intimate contact, but only with great care. Over the solars, I'd grown used to rougher treatment with my human patients given that they couldn't sense phee one way or the other.

On an Atipok, one of the easiest entry points is the tip of the tail. I figured the vestigial human tailbone might be an equivalent. I closed my eyes and traveled with the strand, attempting to gently needle it into the base of the girl's spine. Just as before, the strand deflected, not upon her skin, but upon a thin layer of elemental power that lay just atop, like a coating of liquid armor.

My scales rippled in surprise. My eyes swept the forest surrounding the clearing, the light blue needles of the pines swaying in the light breeze, but found no sign of outside manipulation. My mind raced as I tried to come up with some kind of explanation, but I quickly conceded there was but one.

I leaned back. "Fascinating," I murmured, as much to myself as Hassan.

"What? What's wrong?" Concern creased Hassan's broad face. Like all his kind, he was rather ugly, but in a kindly sort of way. He had brown skin, although much lighter than the girl's, with short cropped black fur circling his face.

"Who is this girl?" I asked.

"I think her name is Molly. Her parents are, were, Sam and Monica."

"How old is she?"

"I don't know, twelve or thirteen. Why?"

I glanced at the other humans standing around us, watching the scene. Several eyed me with suspicion, a common reaction to pheework among humans. A couple looked downright hostile. Hassan caught on and dismissed them to look for salvageable provisions. Then he turned back to me. "Okay, what's going on?"

"This girl is the first known human pheeworker."

"What? Are you su—" He hesitated. "I mean, how is that possible?"

"I   don't   know."

"Well, is she okay?"

"She's encased in phee."

I felt around her head, checking for lumps, unsure of whether her shield would contain a fracture. I tried and failed to lift an eyelid and had similar luck opening her mouth. With care, I was able to roll her gently onto her back, but my fingers were met with physical resistance when I attempted to feel her abdomen. All I could do was lower my head to her chest, counting her heartbeats and listening to her breath.

I sat up. "She seems fine, but I can't be sure."

"You can't see into her?"

"No. She's blocking me." I didn't revel in admitting a human child's pheework was giving me trouble, but thankfully Hassan didn't react. "I think I can get around it, but I might damage her without help."

"Help?"

I nodded. "I see no physical reason for her to be unconscious. I suspect she's trapped within her own shield. Barriers like the one she is using are mostly instinctual. If I simply muscle my way through it, I might seriously damage her unconscious mind. I need support from other healers."

Hassan stroked his chin fur. "When can you get someone here?"

"Not for some time, I'm afraid. Atalan starts in three days. All Atipok are called to Salitat." The annual sacred gathering held in our great stone capital city was not to be missed. "I leave tomorrow. Once Atalan starts, none will leave until it ends."

"Crap. How long will Atalan last?"

"Many days. It's impossible to know for sure."

"Can she wait until it's done?"

I looked the girl over, then shook my head. "Setting aside the very real chance of death by dehydration, she's more than just physically trapped. She's trapped within her own mind. Unless her parents were secretly pheeworkers, which I doubt, then she's had no training. She needs a guide to coax her out of her own head or she might destroy herself." Small bumps arose on the girl's naked skin. I pulled a blanket from the nearby debris and draped it over her. The poor thing was just a nestling. I couldn't help but feel bad for her, which might explain why I didn't take the time to consider the implication of my next words. "There is another option. I can take her to Salitat and get her the help she needs."

Hassan's thick eyebrows arched skyward. "I didn't think humans were allowed in Salitat."

"They're not," I conceded, equally surprised by my offer. "It will be a risk." That was an understatement. Anti-human sentiment had been increasing. To bring a human to Atalan could easily be construed as treason. I would be putting us both in danger. "But I don't think she has any other options."

Hassan sighed, massaging his temples with one large, calloused hand. "Very well, I'll pull together a few men and we'll-"

I help up a hand. "No one else. Only the girl."

"But I can't let her go alone," Hassan protested.

"She won't be alone."

"You know what I mean. I can't just let you take her."

"Then she will stay, and she will die." I didn't like being so blunt with Hassan. He was a caring man and a good leader, but the situation was grim. I shouldn't have made the offer in the first place and there were no other options.

I could see conflict play on the human's features. He looked around, like he was searching for another way. "Crap," he said finally. "Gimme a minute." He stomped off in the direction of his people.

I watched him, mulling over another consideration I hadn't shared. In the thirteen solars since their crash landing, other than some initial hostilities and the Battle of the Red Plain, humans and Atipok had managed a tenuous peace. We mostly kept to our own, them in their adobe villages, us in our stone cities. But there were a few individuals, such as myself, who worked to bridge the gap. I felt it was my duty as a healer to help them. I'd taken an oath to do so. And over time I'd developed a certain respect, even a fondness for their ways. But my time with them had also revealed their tendency toward violence. They loved their weapons. I rarely saw an adult human who wasn't carrying a plasma pistol or rifle. Even now, Hassan carried one of each, a pistol on his hip and a rifle across his back. Such things were unknown to us before their arrival and while they were no match for skilled pheework, humans still managed to kill each other on a regular basis. I sometimes wondered how readily they would abandon their makeshift towns in favor of our great stone cities if not held at bay by their fear of phee. If this girl represented a new trend, if humans gained the ability to pheework, it would completely change the balance of power between our species.

I had to present this girl to the queen.

Hassan returned looking no less frustrated. "I asked around and nobody seems to know if she has any other family. Her group's been on their own for the last couple years, really sticking to themselves. She's all alone now." He looked down at the girl. "My guys think I should decide but..."

"You think it should go before the council," I finished for him.

"Unfortunately, yes."

To call the human's system of organization and decision making an actual government was a bit too generous. Every group seemed to have their own leader or leaders, Hassan among them. And, like Hassan, some actually followed the general rules set out by the charter of their spaceship, which he explained to me at one point. Of course, other leaders had their own ideas. The general disorganization was something I didn't understand but Hassan assured me had to do with the human desire for freedom and independence. To me, it just looked like chaos.

There were times, though, when a decision had to be made and that decision abided by all humans. This fell to their council, a group of as many of the various leaders as they could gather. I had limited experience with the council but to say they were wary of Atipok, and with anything involving phee, was optimistic. Some were downright hostile.

I glanced at Dulkat and Galt, the twin suns, then over at Aesop, my old dolk, grazing on a nearby patch of sweetgrass. Hassan said he looked like an oblong haystack with legs, his long black fur sun-stained yellow after too many solars pulling my wagon. I'd named the herdbeast after the author of my favorite human fable, the tortoise's slow and steady approach mirroring both my own philosophy as well as my dolk's usual pace of travel.

"It's mid-morning. I need to leave tomorrow before first light, with or without the girl."

"I'll send a runner ahead." Hassan signaled a nearby female. "We'll be lucky to make a quorum, but we'll have to make do."

I wasn't sure what that meant but I nodded anyway. "Hassan, I don't know what you told your people, but I suggest...discretion on the matter of the girl's phee abilities."

"I can't lie to the council," he said simply.

"Then don't. Tell them the truth. Tell them that I am a healer who needs help to treat a serious ailment. Tell them without that help, she will die. Leave it at that."

He cocked his head. "You don't think we humans can handle the idea of a human pheeworker?"

My eyes flicked briefly to the pistol on his hip. "Do you?"

He returned my gaze for a long moment, then turned to instruct his runner.

This book is coming soon!

Follow our blog, newsletter, Facebook Page or website for updates.

We are an independent publishing house based in Windsor, Ontario. We publish quality paperbacks and ebooks that feature other worlds, times and versions of reality. Our novels are for all ages and are creative, unique, imaginative and engaging.

We pride ourselves on our originality and 'outside the box' thinking, while taking a good look at the question, 'what if?' Our stories are never ordinary, the dialogue and action engaging, the characters believable, and there will always be some element of romance, adventure, science or magic. We are dedicated to bring our readers novels that will not only entertain them, but also teach them something about the world they live in by showing them one that mirrors it. We hope you'll consider picking up a novel from our collection today so you can see for yourself what we're all about.

You'll find a wide variety of our wonderful titles in our online bookstore and you can also purchase or review them through most major retailers worldwide. To learn more about our authors and our current projects visit: www.mirrorworldpublishing.com or follow @MirrorWorldPub or like us at www.facebook.com/mirrorworldpublishing